# Blazing Deception

## DeQuindra Renea

# ACKNOWLEDGEMENTS

This journey has been so long, and honestly is one I never thought I would complete. I am so thankful to everyone who has supported me and been patient as I stumbled through this project. It was a hard journey, but one that I plan on making again and again. I never dreamed that people would really want to read what I wrote and get to know the characters I created, and for that I have no one to thank but God. Thank You so much for giving me the ability to see things vividly and tell them in a way that others can see it too. The love that I have for writing is because of the talent You gave me and for that I am eternally thankful. Thank You for everything You bless me with daily, things I may forget to say thank You for every day. For today and the rest of my life, thank You.

To my beautiful daughter Nylah Lyons: Mommy loves you so much more than you will ever know. I always say God was showing off when he made you and He absolutely was! You are so precious, beautiful, smart, sweet, loving... the list goes on and on. You have the ability to put a smile on my face no matter the mood I'm in and EVERYTHING I do is for you. I hope you are proud to have me as your mother like I am proud to have you as my daughter.

My mother Belinda Palmer: You are the best mother in the whole world, hands down, there is nobody better than you. You always support me, have my back, get excited with me, and brag about me to whoever will listen. I never have to question whether you are proud of me. Thank you for being just as happy when I told you I wanted to be a writer and not a singer. But you know I will still sing for you anytime! I love you and I can never thank you enough. Thank you to my wonderful stepfather Charles Palmer for always loving me like one of your own. I know my father is so thankful for the man you are and the way you take care of me and love me. And you know I love you back!

Corey Lyons: I love you so much and thank you so much for always supporting me, loving me and encouraging me. You always listen to my ideas and make sure I make the right choices. No matter what you have my back and you love me. I love you so much and I appreciate you for your love and support.

To all of my brothers and sisters: Shonte' Johnson, Janelle Palmer, Veronica Walker, Antonio Martinez, Tony Walker Jr., and Chris Palmer. I love all of you so much! Each one of you are special to me in different ways. Thank you for your support and love (even though you really don't have a choice!).

Thank you to my grandmother Sarah Toney for always telling me I can do and be anything. My Grandma Daisy and all my supportive aunts Cheryl Johnson, Nicolette Garth, Toniette Saunders, Shirley Smith, and Crystal Palmer.

Mel Toney: I love you so much. You been there through everything. Thank you for your support in everything I ever did. You took care of me just like you told my Daddy you would.

Chris and Keisha Gates: Love you all so much! Thank you for everything you did in taking care of me and the support!

Chandra Walker-Smith: Thank you a million times for your support, ideas, enthusiasm and love. You are so special and wonderful and I am so glad I have you in my life.

Tia Walker: Love you baby. Thank you for naming my character!

Antwan Johnson: You believed in me as soon as you heard about me writing a book. Thanks for the excitement, support and love. I love you!

Valerie Reese: Thank you for everything you do for me! I appreciate you more than you know and I love you very much! Thank you to the Reese family for everything you do for me and taking extremely good care of Nylah. I love you all and thank you for treating me like family.

Thank you to Vick Lyons, Leontine Tipton, Kyle Laustriat, Raylander (Quiet Storm) Thomas, Sharonda Cager, Alida Wilson, Damika Empson (Sissy), Antoinette Prevo, Brandy and Brianna Walker, Karla Lawrence, Kayla Welch-Lawrence, Destiny Avant, Cynthia Hatcher, Cora Blu, Caron Darkins, Elaine Dorsey and Tiffany Davis for the support.

I wish I could name each and every one of my family members individually, but since that would be a whole other book, I would like to send my thanks and everlasting love to the Johnson, Walker, Palmer, Gray, Tipton, Empson and Dorsey families.

Thank you to my excellent pastor and wonderful church family for loving me, teaching me and raising me. I always know where home is.

Dangerous Lee: Love you cousin! So glad we met and you told me the first steps I to starting my writing career, even though I talked about it forever before I actually did it. Thank you for the support and love!

To my beautiful, supportive best friends Whitney Boose, Ashley Tipton, Qwanese Evans, Cierra Banks, Deborah Empson and Mozezetta Stewart: I love you ladies with all of my heart! Each one of you have been there for me and definitely got me through this project. I appreciate everything you do.

To my girls, Symone Person, Brittani Morgan and Martina Motley: You have been reading my stories since they were on spiral notebooks, gave me my first deadlines, and called every week so I could read them to you over the phone (Symone). I will never forget about that support and I thank you and love you for it now.

Thank you to my Walmart 1928 family including, but definitely not limited to: Shuntel Walker, Tyshida Cooper-Williams, Cheryl Chrzan, Patrice Wright-Fowlkes, Lisa Gould, Cynthia Ellison-Walls, Marsha Gilbert, French Jones, Delicia Skinner, Liana Williams, Lashonda Burns, Kareene Bell, Deramis Green, Jessica Gonder, Nakia Watkins, and Freddie Boyd. You all are my family, I love you. I would have never finished without you asking me about it every day.

Natasha Avant: Thank you for giving me my first writing assignement in 6th grade. It is where I discovered my talent as a writer. Thank you for everything else you did in between!

Einn Bryant: Thanks for the support! I finally stopped trippin'!

Jade Young: Love you very much! Thank you for your support and love. I will never forget when you prayed with me that day. You will never know how much that blessed me.

Carrie Mattern: I love you and thank you so very much for everything. I would have never completed this journey without you. You have made such a huge impact in my life in so many ways. Schools need more teachers like you, and the world needs more people like you.

Dan Waltz: Thank you for making my book cover look incredible! You took one email and made a whole cover. You are an incredible artist and great man. I appreciate you very much.

Danielle Green: Meeting you was a gift from God. Thank you for answering all of my questions and supporting me. You are an incredible person and the world is not ready for what you have planned!

Mya Adkisson: Thank you for your support and advice. I love all of our talks at your boutique and I look forward to more great times with you!

Brandon "B-Ray" Jamison, Dwon Scott and Jeff "Napkin Hunter": Thank you for inviting me to my very first podcast and supporting me before we even met. Also thank you for my nickname "Miss Million Words."

Thank you to my high school English teachers Katherine Hamadeh and Judy Hillis for whipping my writing skills into shape. I appreciate it now, no matter how much I complained then.

Special thanks to Stacy Brackins and Moments to Remember Photography for taking my beautiful pictures and for the support!

Thank you to the Facebook groups The Writers Block and Support Michigan Authors for being there at all hours to answer my questions and for the support.

To one of my favorite author Daaimah S. Poole for

writing great books and keeping me entertained since middle school. You were the only author that answered my email so many years ago when I was just a teenager dreaming in my bedroom. You will never know what a tremendous difference that small email made in my life. I will never forget it and thank you so much for taking the time out to reply to me.

Special thanks to my Granny, Nana, and Paw Paw's in heaven, that couldn't be here but made me the person I am today.

Last but certainly not least, my father Tony R. Walker Sr. How I wish you were here to celebrate this accomplishment with me. I know you would be so proud. I love you so much for making me feel so special and loving me so genuinely. Every little girl deserves a Daddy like you and I'm glad I got to have you for 14 years. I love you, I thank you and I miss you every day.

If there is anybody I forgot please blame my head and not my heart. I truly appreciate every person who liked my page and statuses on Facebook, left comments and inquired about my book. You gave me the motivation to finish, and I am thankful for that.

With all my love,

*DeQuindra Renea*

# PROLOGUE

*I tried to hold my breath as I stumbled down the long hallway. The smoke stung my lungs and the fire crept up on me as if the devil himself was chasing me down. I didn't have much time. The hairs on my back started to burn. The fire was right behind me. I opened my mouth to call out for anybody; there had to be somebody that wanted to save me from this turmoil. Somebody had to care that I was going to be burned alive. As I opened my mouth to scream, I began to choke. I tried to take a breath, but my lungs were attacked by more smoke.*

*I fell to the floor and knew that was it; I was going to die. I couldn't stop choking. All I could see was smoke. I tried to scream as the fire began to tear through my skin and flesh. I thought of all the bad I had done and hoped that everything I had learned was true... I hoped there was a heaven... I hoped I wouldn't spend the rest of my life being burned alive like I was right now...*

I jumped out of my sleep, hot and out of breath. I didn't know where I was. I looked around for any sign of a fire or smoke, but there was nothing. With tears streaming from my eyes I held my neck trying to suck in enough air to breathe. I was drenched in sweat and my pink silk nightgown was stuck to my light brown skin.

"Kari! What the hell is going on?"

My husband Marvin sat up in bed next to me and turned on

the nightstand light. After seeing I was only having another dream, he rolled his eyes and turned the light back off.

"Go in the guestroom if you're going to be doing all that tonight. I have work in the morning."

He turned over and pulled the covers up to his neck. After catching my breath, I crawled out of bed and went into the master bathroom. Too afraid to move, I sat on the toilet in the dark. Those nightmares brought back horrible childhood memories that my therapist always said I had, "repressed long ago." They haunted me to my soul and as I sat there, my heart continued to beat out of my chest. Emotionally, I knew I would be on edge all day.

Looking into the mirror, my golden brown skin was covered in a layer of sweat. My silk scarf had fallen off my head during my slumber and my brown hair that hung past my shoulders was wild all over my head. My brown round eyes were starting to form bags underneath. There was no way I would be able to go back to sleep. Making sure my hair was neatly tucked away under my scarf, I peeled off my clothes and ran myself a bubble bath in my spacious Jacuzzi tub. Turning on the jets, I sunk into the luke-warm water and closed my eyes. Trying to relax was a lost cause, because I could still feel the Devil breathing down my neck, the fire close enough to burn me to a crisp. My skin crawled and I scrubbed myself with a sponge to try and make it stop.

It had been months since I'd had a nightmare about the fire and it seemed each time I dreamed, the fire got closer. I would continue living my life running from the fire, and that alone was enough to make me never want to sleep again.


The blinking lights from the Christmas tree reflected off the walls as I descended the stairs. Countless gifts crowded underneath for our friends and loved ones. The small bulbs on the tree were my only source of light as I reached my kitchen in the dark. After pouring myself a cold cup of orange juice, I sat at the kitchen table without bothering to turn on the light. The Christmas lights were enough light at the moment for my somber mood. I needed to talk to my brother, Kevin. He was the only person that understood what I was going through. He too had survived the fire and continued to have nightmares for years. My psychiatrist said I would probably have to endure them for the rest of my life, but talking to Kevin would help.

I sat at the table nursing my cup of juice. Desperate for someone to talk to, I took my cell phone out of my purse and started to dial my brother's number. After a second thought, I went back into my phonebook and began to scroll through the numbers. Stopping at the J's I stared at his name long enough to convince myself it was a bad idea to call him.

I continued to scroll through my phonebook, but it was 3:22 in the morning and I knew nobody else would be awake. Holding my breath, I went back to Jonathon's number and hit the call button. The phone rang three times before he picked up.

"Hello?"

"You sleep?"

"No. What you doin' up?"

"I can't sleep."

"Why can't you sleep, it's three in the morning."

"I just can't. What are you doing if you're not sleeping?"

"I'm watching TV, bored. What are you doing?"

"Sitting at the table drinking OJ."

"So you aint gonna tell me why you're up?"

"Why does there have to be a reason for me to be up?"

"Because you're usually asleep."

I smiled and took another drink.

"Do you miss me? Is that why you're up?" he asked in his low sexy voice. I was sure he could hear me blushing through the phone.

"I can't sleep," I repeated.

"And that's why you called?"

Smiling like a fool, I couldn't remember the last time Marvin had even attempted to make me smile. Jonathon could do it without even trying.

"I can tell something is wrong with you Kari. Why won't you tell me?"

"Because I'm not ready."

"Not ready for what? What could you possibly not be ready for?"

"Jonathon-"

"You trust me right? You know I got you right?"

"Yeah."

"So you aint never gotta be scared to tell me nothing."

"I'm not scared, I'm just not ready."

"So when will you be ready to tell me?"

"The sooner you stop bothering me about it the sooner I'll be ready to tell you."

"You wanna come over and see me?"

"I can't. I can't get out tonight."

"Its three in the morning, I know Marvin is sleep. You can't sneak over here for a few hours?"

"Not tonight."

"I miss you. You know that right?"

"I miss you too."

"So come over and give me a kiss."

I smiled again, feeling like a teenage girl being asked to sneak out the house.

"I can't."

Jonathon liked a challenge. I could tell he was smiling on the other end, but I hope he knew I was serious about not coming over this late.

"I'm gonna come see you soon, I promise."

"You better. What you doin' today?"

"I don't know. I might go to the gym later. I need to work out."

"I'm offering you a work out right now."

I laughed.

"You tryna get us both in trouble."

"It's worth it."

Jonathon and I stayed on the phone for almost an hour. He continued to make me laugh and pretty soon I didn't feel as badly as I did before. The sun was starting to come up and I knew Marvin would be waking up for work soon.

"I gotta get off the phone. I'm about to start cooking breakfast."

"You know you could have come over here and talked to me, right?"

"I do know that, you only told me about twenty five times since we've been on the phone. Now I gotta go, have a good day."

"You too baby."

Pushing the end button, I stared at the phone in my hands. I knew it was wrong and I didn't mean for it to happen, but now after a year, I was in too deep to go back. I was falling in love with my husband's close friend and I didn't know how to stop it.

# CHAPTER 1

Stepping out of the bathroom, I checked the clock next to our bed. It was six-thirty and we were running late to dinner at Marvin's parents' house. I knew my husband would be upset. He hated tardiness, especially when he was meeting his father.

I went back into the bathroom and continued straightening my hair. Marvin walked in a couple of minutes later dressed in a black and gray Armani collared shirt. His shoes weren't on yet, but I was sure he would wear his black Stacy Adams. His black hair was freshly cut in a low fade and he came in with a stunned look on his handsome face. He had dark chocolate skin and dark eyes. His teeth were white and perfect thanks to years of braces. He resembled the actor Morris Chestnut, but it was not only his good looks, but his sweetness, charm, and romantic nature that attracted me to him at the tender age of fifteen.

His scowl showed that he was pissed I wasn't dressed yet, so I started explaining before he had a chance to say anything.

"I'm almost ready. All I gotta do is put on my clothes. They're already ironed."

"It's six thirty. You knew all day we were going to my family's house for dinner tonight."

"I know Marvin, time got away from me."

"Hurry up."

Marvin left the room without saying anything else. I rolled my eyes in the mirror and finished my hair and didn't let Marvin's attitude bother me too much. I knew I had nearly cut the usual two hour process of straightening my hair in half for the sake of being on time. My hair appointment wasn't for another couple of days so my thick, long mane had to be manually tamed to look presentable for dinner.

Once my hair was done I slipped on my purple and black knee high dress with black heels. After spraying White Rose perfume, I made my way downstairs where Marvin was waiting in the living room.

"You look good," he said after giving me a once over. It was more of a critique than a compliment. I grabbed my Coach purse and we headed to his car.

Marvin was quiet the whole ride. His jazz music was playing softly, but I could tell he didn't hear it. He was deep in thought. I watched him as he drove through the streets preparing for what should have been a relaxed family dinner, however nothing with Marvin's family was relaxed. They were a strained family and barely talked, so I knew this dinner had a specific reason. Marvin did, too.

The jazz music coming from the speakers was the only sound until we reached Marvin's parents' house. They lived in a two story, four bedroom brick home in the heart of Fenton which was almost forty five minutes from where we lived. I got out of the car and Marvin grabbed my hand. It was the first sign of affection he'd shown me all day, but I knew it was only a front for his family. All they cared about were appearances and since none of them thought our marriage would last from the very beginning, Marvin thought it was important to prove to them we were the perfect couple, even though we were far from it.

Before Marvin could ring the doorbell, his mother, Paulette, opened the door with a huge smile plastered on her face.

"Marvin! Kari! We were starting to get worried."

She gave us both kisses on the cheek and led us into the warm house and out of the cool spring air. As soon as I walked in, I was hit with the aroma of food. I didn't know what was on the menu, but it smelled delicious. Paulette was talented with cuisine. Marvin didn't like to visit his family, but when we did, the food was excellent.

Marvin and I followed his mother into the dining room where

his father and half- sister Christina were waiting. Christina was his father's daughter. She had light brown skin and long, silky black hair. Her mother was Mexican and Christina was the product of one of his father's too many affairs. She was quiet today, but usually very much opinionated and arrogant like their father. She was wearing a money green business suit, looking as if she was going to a meeting instead of a family dinner. She stayed at the table and didn't acknowledge us, but Marvin's father, Malcolm, stood up scowling.

"Well it's about time you showed up. I thought I was going to have to put my food in the microwave. What time did I tell you to be here?"

"Six-thirty."

"And you didn't make it until after seven," Malcolm said, shaking his head.

"I'm sorry Dad, I had to make a couple stops-"

"So you come late and still hold dinner up?" Malcolm asked stopping Marvin mid- sentence. Marvin was clearly embarrassed and immediately I felt bad for making us late.

"Kari, how are you?" Malcolm asked giving me a kiss on the cheek. He was tall, towering over my 5'3" frame. Marvin clearly had his genes. He had on a tailored blue pinstripe suit and blue dress shoes. He didn't hug Marvin, and just looked at him.

"Let me talk to you for a minute son."

"Yes sir."

Marvin followed his father out of the dining room and Paulette, Christina, and I were left in an awkward silence.

I sat at the table across from Christina and she forced a smile. I didn't return the favor.

"The roast is still in the oven anyway," Paulette said, trying to lighten the mood.

"It might be dry by now Paulette, they are over a half an hour late," Christina said as if I wasn't sitting directly across from her.

"I'm sorry, it really is my fault. I lost track of time."

"Don't worry about it Kari. Things do happen sometimes." Paulette said.

We sat at the table in silence until Malcolm and Marvin came back. I could tell by the look on my husband's face that whatever his father had said to him wasn't nice. He sat next to me at the table without making eye contact. I tried to hold his hand under the table, but he pulled away.

"Paulette bring the food out, everyone's here now," Malcolm ordered sitting at the head of the table and putting his napkin in his lap, "And get Marvin and Kari some wine."

"I can help Paulette," I said getting up and following her into the kitchen. I hated the way Malcolm ordered Paulette around without ever helping.

After pouring Marvin and I both a glass of champagne, I helped Paulette carry out dinner which consisted of pot roast, macaroni and cheese, greens, and corn on the cob. We were saving the apple pie and ice cream for dessert. After Marvin led us in grace, we all fixed our plates and started eating. The only person who talked during dinner was Malcolm. He barely ate as he talked about the changes that were being made to Fairmount Inc. He could never have a moment of leisure without talking about the company. There was no typical conversation between the strained family members. I had spent half of my life in foster care and I'd never seen a family so distant. They never just talked or spent time with each other. It was all business.

I was enjoying the taste of my meal, yet counting down the minutes until it was time to go. I never felt comfortable around his family, but I always visited to support him.

"I have an announcement to make," Malcolm's voice boomed loudly getting everyone's attention and nearly stopping my heart.

"I called everyone over here for a reason."

He cleared his throat and took a drink of water.

"As I've explained earlier there are some things going on and some decisions being made about Fairmount Inc., and I want you all to hear it from me and not at the office."

Some years ago, Marvin's father created an accounting program that makes it easier for small businesses to run, operate, and manage finances. Each program was tweaked upon order to specifically fit the purchasing business. Now, they were trying to expand and sell the program to major corporations, as well as other countries.

Malcolm took a moment before going on.

"I've had a couple of personal meetings and basically I've come to the conclusion that it is time for me to take a step back from the business and retire."

I looked around the table and the only person that looked

surprised was Marvin. I knew this was really an announcement for him.

"As you know in order for me to retire someone else has to step up and take care of business if we want the company to go global. With that being said, Marvin, it's time I relinquish my control over certain details. It won't be easy. Are you up for the challenge?"

"Yes sir," Marvin said, but we both knew that was really his only option.

"Then you know what I expect of you. Be punctual and professional, well dressed and on time. Don't disappoint."

"I won't."

I looked over at Marvin, but his expression was not one of joy. I didn't really understand what was going on. I knew Marvin's father was hard on him, but taking over the business should have meant he wouldn't have to deal with him as much. I thought that news alone would put a smile on his face.


Marvin was quiet through dessert and cocktails. When we got into the car to go home, I could tell Marvin was still in a bad mood. As soon as we got on the expressway, I picked his brain.

"Did your father tell you he was going to retire?"

Marvin shook his head.

"So you didn't know he was considering you to run the company?"

"I figured he would. He would never let a woman do it so I knew he wouldn't choose Christina."

"So you aren't happy about running the business?"

"I won't be running it, he will."

"But he's retiring."

"That retirement doesn't mean anything. He only wants to use me as his puppet. I won't be making any of the decisions."

"So why is he even retiring?"

"I don't know, to appease my mother maybe. Either way he is never going to give that company up. The retirement is just a show."

"Well maybe things will change with him working less. And the extra income will give us the stability to start a family."

Marvin shook his head again.

"The last thing I'm thinking about right now is starting a family."

That shocked me. We had been married for seven years and having children was the last thing on his mind? When the hell would it be the first?

"Marvin, I'm almost 26 years old. I don't have time to wait."

"Kari women in their forties and fifties have babies all the time."

"Well I aint those women! We don't know how long I have and I want to have children!"

"Well right now all I'm thinking about is this business and how my father is going to be breathing down my damn neck every damn day. Excuse me if I don't feel like arguing with you about yet another burden being thrown at me."

"A burden? Having a child is a burden for you?"

"Right now, yes. I just had my father's business, his pride and joy, placed in my lap. Now I've got to take care of his precious baby. Can you give me time to process that?"

Marvin was extremely irritated and I knew I should end the conversation before it got any worse. He was thrown the biggest curveball ever. But at the same time I had to think about what was important to me. It had been seven years, and sooner or later Marvin was going to have to give me what I wanted, too.

# CHAPTER 2

Early Saturday morning I awoke to a bunch of yelling. I couldn't make out the voices, but they were obviously excited about their discussion. I went into the bathroom. After showering and brushing my teeth, I put on my favorite pair of jeans and a sweatshirt. I walked right into the heated debate that had Marvin and his friends Jonathon, Carl, and Patrick yelling at the top of their lungs.

"I'm just sayin', yo old ass can't beat me man!" Jonathon said, jumping up off of the couch. "I played point guard for four years at Northern on Varsity."

"Some old school basketball will win over that street ball any day. And I'm only five years older than you so that doesn't exactly put me in the old man category just yet."

"Well old or not, I can beat you."

"You would never be able to beat me Jonathon. Remember I played high school basketball as well as some college basketball. I got another three years basketball experience on you," Marvin said.

"But you more outta shape than me. All that experience don't mean nothin' if you can't make it up and down the court."

"Yeah, you played slow today Marvin. It took you all day to make it up the court and pass the ball," Carl said.

"I'm too busy to work out like I want to. That doesn't mean I can't beat you on that court."

"So is ya'll gonna keep talking about it or is it gonna be some action?" How bout a game?" Patrick said, raising the stakes.

"We just ran two games!" Marvin complained, obviously tired. "We don't need a rematch, everybody saw how I made that shot over him."

"You got one lucky shot and all of a sudden you a NBA star," Jonathon said laughing. I laughed too, sipping my coffee. Marvin could be cocky, maybe Jonathon would beat him one good time and bring him down to earth a bit.

I was glad Marvin was finding time to play basketball with his friends. It was nice to see him having a good time and not sitting around worried about work and his father. Ever since he had announced his retirement, Marvin had been overly stressed. He was being watched closely by his father who scrutinized everything.

Glancing through the newspaper, I was trying my best to ignore the raucous the men were making. Marvin and Jonathon had agreed on a date for the game, but now everybody else was arguing about the time. Carl had a prior engagement and Patrick had to work and would miss out on watching the competition.

"We don't need no audience no way. All we need is somebody to take score so Marvin don't be tryna cheat," Jonathon said.

"I don't need to cheat, winners don't do that. My wife can take score. You just make sure you're this loud when you have to tell everybody how badly I beat you."

"Alright man, enough talk. You just start exercising and be ready to get this ass whoopin."

# CHAPTER 3

"I just don't understand why we can't talk about it," I said quietly, sitting on the bed watching Marvin get dressed for work.

"There is nothing to talk about Kari. I told you when we were ready we would have kids, but there is too much going on right now for all that."

"Too much going on for who Marvin? I'm the one who sits here all day long by myself. Not much is going on in my life."

Marvin did have a demanding job, however, that was the reason there was two parents. Marvin wouldn't let me get a job or go to school because he was raised that women belonged at home taking care of the home, so we should be having children.

"So you want to be with the kids all day long while I'm working all kinds of crazy hours and can never be home?"

"You do work a lot Marvin, but you do get plenty of vacation and sick days. If you planned right, there would be plenty of time for you to be home."

Marvin put on a red and black tie. He was wearing a black Dior suit today. He looked good in the color black. He was dark and black complimented his smooth chocolate skin.

"So what, you want me to let you go back to school?"

"I want you to get me pregnant."

Marvin took a deep breath and shook his head. I could tell he was getting frustrated.

"This conversation is getting us nowhere Kari," he said stepping into his black Stacy Adams' and leaving the bedroom.

That was his way of ending the conversation, walking away and ignoring me. Balancing tears, I sat there shaking my head slowly. This was one battle I was sure I was going to lose. Marvin had a tendency to only care about himself. Other people's desires and dreams didn't matter if they interfered with his.

Lying in bed until he left for work, I was starting to think he was never going to let me have kids. I wasn't getting any younger and I didn't know if he realized there came a certain point when women could no longer have children. He was acting as if we had all the time in the world!

I heard the front door slam and used that as my cue to turn off Good Morning America and go make breakfast. I wasn't going to let Marvin ruin my day. I was in a good mood. The sun was peeking through my window. It was as if Mother Nature herself was kissing me on the face. I loved waking up to the bright morning sun; it lifted my spirits.

Quickly I made myself a bacon and egg sandwich and sat at the table to eat. The house was lonely. When Marvin was gone I had nothing to keep me occupied. I just sat around the house and watched TV or cleaned. Sometimes I went shopping, to the movies, or to the gym. Mostly I was just wasting time until Marvin got home from work so I could have someone to talk to. Going out to meet people made me uncomfortable. I didn't have many friends.

I sat there long after my food was gone in silence. Waiting for Marvin to give me a baby was getting old. There had to be something out there for me.

"Hello, hey Kari. What's wrong?" Marvin answered when my call was transferred.

"Nothing, I just wanted to see what you were doing for lunch. I was thinking I would come and take you out somewhere."

"Yeah well that won't be necessary. I already ate," he snapped.

"What's your problem?" I asked.

"I'm working right now Kari, we can talk when I get home."

He hung up and I sat there with the phone in my hand confused. I swear my husband had an attitude problem.

I put the cordless phone back on the base and got up to get in the shower. It looked like I would be going to lunch by myself.

After taking a hot shower I threw on a pair of jeans and a purple button up and headed outside. Fall had always been my favorite time of year. I loved the colors and the leaves on the ground. It always reminded me of when we would jump into them as kids. My heart ached at the memory.

I got into my car and drove to a nearby *Applebee's*. Although I loved to cook it was nice to get out of the house a couple times a week. I went in and sat at the bar. Tara, the bartender, came and sat a drink napkin in front of me. She was skinny with long blonde hair

"Hey Kari, you having your usual drink?"

"Yeah, that'll be fine," I said. She handed me a menu and I skimmed over it unsure if I wanted to eat anything. She came back with the cold Sangria and placed it in front of me.

"So how have you been girl?" she asked, starting a drink for another order.

"I been fine, you know the usual with me, what about you."

"I'm trying to make it, I am. These bastards here aren't tipping anything," she whispered so no one would hear what she was saying.

"I know that sucks. How are the kids?"

"Well I think my son is going to eat me out of a house and home, and my daughter has already gained a bad attitude at the tender age of two."

"I heard about those terrible twos."

"Yes, she is a terror."

We both laughed. Tara continued to work while I looked over the menu. After placing an order with her for a Caesar salad and the Bourbon Street Chicken and Shrimp, I sipped my wine and scrolled through my Facebook page on my phone. When my food was ready, Tara came and sat it in front of me. We chatted when we could between her making drinks and serving other customers. It was slow since it was early afternoon.

I finished my meal and paid, leaving Tara a hefty tip for the excellent service and listening ear.

The tall, brown-skinned host held the door open for me as I made my way out. Just as I was going out the door, Marvin's friend Jonathon came bursting through. Marvin and Jonathon had been friends since before we met. Jonathon was a web designer and Marvin had hired him to do some work for Fairmount Inc. Previously Jonathon had worked for a design company, now he was freelancing and trying to start his own business.

"Hey Kari, what you doin' here? You aint got nothin' cookin' at home?" he asked, referring to my superb cooking skills.

"Not today. I took the easy way out."

He laughed showing a set of his beautiful white teeth. Jonathon was tall with light brown skin and silky, curly black hair. His eyes were a sexy light green. He was wearing a gray, long sleeved button up and a pair of black slacks. It was weird to see him out of his street clothes, but I liked the dressy look on him.

"If I could cook like you, I would never eat out," he said opening the door for an older couple.

"You would get tired of cooking. You don't think so, but you would. When someone else cooks for me, I always enjoy it."

"I feel you," he said looking me up and down the way he always did when he saw me. I didn't know if he meant for me to see it or it was just a male thing.

"You look nice, you on your lunch break?"

"Nah, I just came back from a meeting with some potential clients. They're thinking about letting me design the web page for their business. It'll be my first job under Bradshaw Innovative Designs."

"Really? That's great! Well I'll keep my fingers crossed."

"Yeah, do that for me," he said licking his lips. The way he did it, the way he looked at me and licked his lips, immediately, made me horny. I could feel the embarrassment written all over my face. I gave him a smile and headed into the cool air.

"Well I'll have to tell Marvin I ran into you."

His demeanor changed slightly at the mention of my husband.

"Yeah, tell him I said what's up. And get ready for that ass whoopin."

I laughed.

"I will. Have a good lunch."

"Thank you."

As I headed out to my car, I thought about Jonathon. He was so successful. It showed that despite his upbringing in Flint, he managed to overcome the odds.

On the way home I got a call from my brother Kevin. He was

checking on me like he did almost every other day. We caught up for a few minutes, and then he let me go to get to a meeting. I pulled into my house at almost four in the afternoon. It had been nice to get out for awhile, but now it was back home, back to the boredom, right where I started.

I spent the whole evening trying to forget the feeling I got between my legs when I saw Jonathon, but it was impossible. I hadn't had that feeling in so long. It was an itch that needed to be scratched. My battery operated boyfriend wasn't going to cut it. I needed the real thing.

When Marvin got home I was on fire. He didn't even get through the door and I was all over him. I took his briefcase out of his hand and led him into the living room.

"What's going on Kari?" He asked like he didn't feel like being bothered. I pushed him on the couch and climbed on top of him.

"Kari what's gotten into you?"

I covered my lips with his to shut him the hell up. This was one of those moments when words weren't needed and he was fucking up the mood and making that good feeling start to fade. He needed to cooperate and let me be in control for once.

I slid my tongue into Marvin's mouth and our tongues began to dance. His body responded through his suit pants. My pussy dripped. I needed him inside of me. My hands found the buttons on his shirt and after I finally got them undone, I slipped it off. He wasn't talking anymore. He lay back on the couch relaxing and staring at me with his sexy brown eyes.

Standing up, slowly, I took off all my clothes and stood naked before him. He licked his lips. He wanted it. He wanted me and I liked the way that felt. It had been too long.

Marvin lifted his hips to allow me to pull off his slacks and underwear. His dick was standing at attention. My hot juices traveled down my leg, while I climbed on top of him and sat on it slowly at first.

As he filled my insides, I moaned. I could feel his dick deep inside me as I bounced up and down. Sensations ran through my body; I felt the orgasm building.

Marvin grabbed my nipples and pinched them gently and I

moaned loudly. In slow motion I grinded on him allowing him to feel how tight and juicy I was. He pulled me into him and kissed me as I continued grinding. My eyes were closed. I could feel my orgasm getting closer. My body shook in anticipation. I didn't care about our argument. I didn't give a damn about anything at that moment. All I cared about was getting my orgasm. Every time his dick hit that spot, I could feel it. The spot that made my pussy juices squirt. I was fucking him.

All of a sudden I thought of Jonathon. The way he looked, all sexy and professional. The way he talked to me, the way he licked his lips. I imagined myself fucking him. For only ten seconds I imagined I was fucking Jonathon, that it was his tongue licking my neck and hard nipples; I was riding Jonathon's dick and that was enough to send me over the edge.

I cried aloud as I felt the beautiful feeling that made my whole body shake and go limp. Instantly, all the stress left my body. Marvin held my hips and thrust his hips upwards, pounding his dick into my dripping pussy. His mouth was shut, his lips pulled tight into his mouth. He was about to cum. He was pumping in and out of me, trying to join me in ecstasy. His body was moving fast and he was concentrating hard. He groaned and I could feel his dick jerking inside of me. He stroked my insides a few more times before his body went limp. He was in orgasm land, that faraway place where you think of nothing but how good your body feels.

I lay there on his chest with my eyes closed. My body felt so relaxed, I didn't want to move. He didn't want to move either. We lay there in silence both enjoying the feeling our orgasms had given us until we fell into a deep sleep. One of the few slumbers I had without interruption.


Marvin was in a way better mood the next morning. He gave me a kiss on the lips before he got up to shower for work. He sung Marvin Gaye in the shower and came downstairs with a huge smile on his face.

"You sure are happy this morning," I said as we sat together at the table. Apparently our romp on the couch had given me a temporary laziness so I didn't cook breakfast. Instead Marvin made himself a bagel with his cup of coffee. I sat there wearing nothing but a purple silk robe.

"I wonder why," he said with a smirk on his face like he had a secret I didn't know. "What happened? I thought you were mad at me."

I shrugged my shoulders.

"Forget about it. We had a disagreement, it happens with married couples."

Marvin smiled and took a sip of his coffee. He was looking through the newspaper.

"I'm glad you got over it. It wasn't that big of a deal anyway."

I ignored his comment and enjoyed the moment. There was no use in arguing about the same thing again. His mind wasn't changing about a baby so I had no choice but to sit and wait until it did.

"Are you working late today?" I asked switching the subject.

"Depends on if I have something to come home to like I did last night."

"You may."

Marvin gave me a sexy smile. I liked seeing him like this. It didn't happen often.

"You tease me."

I smiled. He was acting like he wanted me again and I felt like I did when we first started dating.

Marvin gave me a long kiss before he left for work.

"I'll see you when I get home."

"I'll be here waiting," I said putting his hand on my bare pussy. He gave me that smile again.

"You better."


I had no clue what had gotten into me, but all of a sudden, I wanted sex constantly. It was like it was when we'd first gotten married. Marvin and I were getting it in every day. I needed it. We had sex in the morning before he went to work and again before bed. It didn't matter if we were in the shower, bed, or kitchen… whenever I felt the urge, we fucked.

We were laying on the bathroom floor after yet another one of our sexual trysts. I was sitting with my back against the bathtub and Marvin was lying on the floor, his head between my legs using my thigh as a pillow. He had just made me cum with his mouth. I had that silly, 'I just had an orgasm,' smirk on my face. My juices were stuck on his mustache.

"You know you're going to make me late for work right?" he asked, looking up at me.

"You're making yourself late."

"No you're making me late with all of this sex you keep giving me."

"You haven't been turnin' it down."

"Well because I'm not a damn fool. But all of this unexpected."

"All of what?"

"All of this sex. I mean, you barely touch me for months, then all of a sudden I walk through the door and you're all over me."

"And this is a problem?"

"No, it's just... I don't know. I'm thinking too much into it."

"Marvin I'm your wife. After months of you not touching me, I got horny. You came home and I fucked you."

"You know when I met you, you didn't curse this much."

"I know, I cussed more."

Marvin shook his head. I didn't care if he was angry. I was so tired of him correcting me like he was my fucking English teacher.

Abruptly, Marvin got up and started washing his face. I didn't understand what the hell had just happened. How could a moment so sweet turn sour so fast?

"I don't understand you Kari. I mean one day you're happy, the next day you hate me, the next day you're all over me when I walk through the door, then you're in a good mood, then you stay in bed all day and want me to cover up all the mirrors in the house! You're up and down all the time! I don't ever know what to expect when I wake up in the morning."

"Are you implying that I'm unstable?" I asked being sarcastically proper.

"I'm not saying that Kari, of course you're stable. Don't overreact." I could see him looking at me through the mirror.

"You act like you're an emotional wreck," he said.

"Marvin you stand here and act like we haven't been married for seven years and you don't know that I lost everything in a fire! So when your parents burn to death, you come and you talk to me about being an emotional wreck!"

22

I left out of the bathroom and slammed the door so hard the framed mirror fell off its hinge. Marvin was completely out of line. Things were going good this morning. Why couldn't he just let it be?

I waited until Marvin came out of the bathroom to go in and take my shower. The hot water pelting my back soothed me. Marvin's words hurt. Emotional wreck? I felt like a psychiatric patient, always under his watch.

When I got out of the shower, I wrapped the towel around my body. My hair was pulled up into a bun at the top of my head so it wouldn't get wet. Marvin was in the bedroom dressed for work, wearing a white dress shirt, a black wool blazer, and a pair of slacks. He looked incredibly handsome; he always did when he went to work.

I put on some lotion and started getting dressed. Marvin was putting on his shoes, clearly taking his time. I could tell he wanted to say something to clear the air, but I really didn't want to hear it.

"I have a meeting at eleven. I should be done by twelve-thirty. Can I take you to lunch?"

"It's okay Marvin. Enjoy your day."

Marvin stood there for a minute trying to find a way to apologize without actually apologizing. Marvin didn't believe in apologies, at least when he was the one doing the apologizing. Marvin was invincible and anyone who wanted to be in his world had to understand that. I did. Completely.

Marvin finally left for work and I was alone once again in our house. Since I had nowhere to go or any errands to run, I started cleaning.

My house phone rang as I was carrying all of our dirty laundry downstairs to wash. I ran over to pick it up.

"Hello?"

"Why aint you answerin' your cell phone?" Kevin asked.

"Because I'm cleaning. I don't have my cell phone with me at all times."

"What you doin' today? We should go to the movies or something."

"Kevin you are not slick. I know Marvin called and told you to check on me. I'm fine."

"Why would Marvin call me?" Kevin asked unconvincingly.

"I'm going to hang up on you if you keep tryna lie to me."

"Okay Kari, but he's just worried."

"I don't even know why he's worried. I was in a great mood until he pissed me off. He had no reason to call you. He knows why I'm mad. So is he gonna call you later and see what you find out?"

"Possibly."

I held the phone on my ear with my shoulder and carried the laundry downstairs.

"If I say I'm fine that's what I mean. I don't know why you and Marvin feel it's so important to keep tabs on me."

"If you didn't shut everybody out, we wouldn't have to Kari," he reminded me yet again. "When is the last time you went to see your therapist?"

"I really wish you wouldn't do that Kevin, especially since I told you I'm fine three times since we been on the phone!" I yelled, annoyed.

"Okay Kari, I'm sorry. Can I come by later?"

I rolled my eyes, hoping he felt my irritation through the receiver.

"Yeah Kevin, if it'll make you feel better to come and look in my face and make sure I'm okay, you do that."

I didn't wait for a response from him before I hung up the phone. I was so tired of feeling like a toddler running around a pool. I was a grown woman! I didn't need anybody checking up on me!

Kevin wasn't the only person who decided to drop by for a visit that night. Marvin had come home with Damon, his cousin and colleague. A little while later Carl, Jonathon, and Patrick came by. It wasn't unlikely for people to drop by our house and visit, and it was a good thing I had made a big pan of lasagna so no one would go home hungry.

"So what all do you put in your lasagna?" Carl asked putting another heaping forkful in his mouth.

"You can put whatever you like in yours. I put hamburger, Italian sausage, pepperoni, green peppers, onions, cottage cheese, and of course, shredded cheese.

"What kind?"

"Whatever you like."

"So just layer everything?"

"Yup."

"I don't think mine is going to be this good."

"It will."

Marvin called my name from the living room.

"Get one of those cheesy breadsticks too, I think they're still warm," I said over my shoulder as I went to the other room to see what Marvin wanted. He was sitting in the living room talking to my brother and the rest of his friends.

"Kari can you please tell everybody I can cook."

I closed my mouth and eyes at the same time as if I was trying to avoid a repercussion for lying. Everybody in the room burst out laughing.

"Wait a minute! Wait a minute!" Marvin yelled over everybody. "She didn't answer."

"She didn't have to. Her face said it all," Jonathon said.

Marvin gave me a fake angry look.

"Kari knows I know how to cook."

"Fried bologna sandwiches," I finished. I couldn't hold in my laughter and everybody else joined in.

"See, I'm about to put everybody out. You too, Kari."

"That's okay little one, you can come live with me," Kevin said smiling.

"Marvin is not putting me out, he'll starve to death," I said patting his stomach. "Ya'll leave him alone."

"We just sayin' Kari, every time ya'll throw a party Marvin never cooks, but he always talkin' about how good he is at it," Jonathon said.

"If you never see him cook that shows you right there," Carl said coming into the living room to join the debate.

"I said I could barbeque, I never said I could cook."

"Don't change the story now that we caught you in a lie," Patrick said.

I went back into the kitchen to make myself another plate. One serving hadn't been enough for me lately.

"So can I get the secret recipe?" Jonathon asked coming into the kitchen. He was talking about the food, but he was looking at me like food was the last thing on his mind.

"It's just Italian sausage, green peppers, onions-

"Well I haven't had any yet, I can't wait to taste it," he said licking his lips. My panties instantly got wet and automatically I felt the guilt set in my gut. My husband was in the next room and that was supposed to be the man making me feel this way, not Jonathon. Not his friend.

"I hope you like it," I said picking up my plate to leave the room.

"I'm sure I will."

I went back into the living room and sat next to Marvin. He was talking to Damon about some company business. I ate my food quietly, tuning out the numerous conversations that were going on, but I could feel Jonathon's eyes on me from the kitchen doorway. The TV was on Sports Center and although I didn't have the least bit interest in it, I kept my eyes fixed on the screen to ignore the feeling I had between my legs.

That night I lay between our bedroom sheets naked and waiting for Marvin. My hot juices were already flowing. I was so damn ready. Marvin had no idea what was waiting for him.

When he came into the room, he looked tired. It had been a long day for him. He sat on the edge of the bed and took his shoes off. I got from under the covers and crawled over to him. I pulled off his blazer and threw it on the floor. I climbed on top of him to unbutton his shirt.

"I see you were waiting for me."

I bit my lip and nodded my head. After slipping off his shirt and pulling off his pants Marvin sat there naked with me, skin to skin. I could feel his hard dick pushing on my opening and it was driving me wild! I pushed him back on the bed and kissed him, my tongue exploring his mouth. His dick jumped causing a delightful feeling that traveled through my body.

Marvin flipped me over onto my back and began kissing my neck. He pushed his dick into my moist opening. Closing his eyes in pleasure, he began taking long strokes in and out of me. I moaned as my juices flowed. I could tell Marvin liked it too by the way he was moaning softly in my ear.

When Marvin licked my neck, my body trembled under his. His stroke got quicker closing in on his climax.

As I wrapped my legs around Marvin, my mind flashed back

to my encounter with Jonathon in the kitchen.

"Well I haven't had none yet, I can't wait to taste." The subject was lasagna, but the way he'd looked at me, the way he said it...food couldn't have been what he was talking about. He had to be talking about me.

Marvin thrust inside of me where I could feel every inch of him. My legs started to shake. I imagined Jonathon's lips all over me, kissing me and licking me in places reserved only for my husband. The thought of him with his mouth on my sweet spot made my pussy muscles clench around Marvin's dick. My juices gushed and ran down his shaft. I bit down on my lip and moaned in Marvin's ear. Marvin's orgasm followed mine as he rapidly pumped in and out of me.

I lay there underneath his weight. My body felt so good and my pussy throbbed, but I couldn't ignore the sinking feeling in my heart. Even when I was having sex with my husband, I couldn't get Jonathon off my mind. He made me feel things without touching me that I didn't feel even when Marvin did touch me.

I didn't know what was going on with me. I'd never fantasized about a man other than my husband, especially not his friend. Being around Jonathon would lead to nothing but trouble and I had to stay away from him.

DeQuindra Renea

# CHAPTER 4

"It's really not that bad Manuel," I lied, staring into my bathroom mirror. I had a handful of my brown hair that I had just pulled out of a ponytail; it hung wildly down my back. I'd inherited the thick mane from my grandfather who was Indian. I'd also gotten my smooth copper skin from him as well.

"Not bad? Kari, it's been three weeks already and you're canceling again."

I pictured Manuel with his cell phone to his ear, rolling his eyes.

"Yes, but I'll be there next week, I promise. I just haven't been out much lately."

"I don't care Kari. You know I don't like missed appointments. Now you have to get triple conditioned when you come in. Have you been moisturizing your scalp?"

"Yes Manuel," I sighed.

"Then I'll see you next Wednesday and I better not see one sign of breakage."

"You won't."

I ended the call and put the rest of my hair back into a ponytail.

After taking a dose of medicine, I lay on the couch to watch TV and try to get my energy back. I was supposed to meet my friend Jamie for lunch and not only that, my dishes and dirty laundry had piled up. For the past few weeks I hadn't felt like doing anything but lounging around. I couldn't wait for this lazy spell to pass.

After watching a couple of talk shows and every court show available, I knew there was no way I was going to make lunch with Jamie. I just didn't feel up to it. I picked up the phone to call her.

"Hello?" she sang.

"Hey Jamie, what you doin'?"

"At home about to get up and dressed. Is *Red Robin* okay?"

"Jamie can we got to lunch another day? I'm not feeling good."

"Okay that's fine," she sighed. I could hear her disappointment over the phone. "Do you need me to bring you anything?"

"I don't need anything I can think of."

"Okay."

"You can come over if you want. I'm not doing anything but watching TV and I'm not contagious. I haven't been throwing up or anything."

"Okay, I'll come over. I don't have anything to do until the kids get out of school."

"Okay well I'll be waiting on you."

"I'll be there in twenty."

"So how many single friends does Marvin have?" Jamie asked. She was sitting on my couch wearing jeans and a Flushing High School hoodie. Her long, wavy blonde hair was pulled back into a ponytail showing off her petite face and beautiful green eyes. She was short, like me, maybe 5'4". She had an incredible body. Nice perky breasts and full hips. I always told her she could be a model if she wasn't so short.

Jamie had recently separated from her husband and they were talking about a divorce.

"I don't know. A couple."

"So why haven't you introduced me?"

"You should come over more, they float in and out of here pretty often, whenever I cook."

"Are they ugly?"

"No, I mean some are better looking than others, of

course."

"Well don't try to set me up with anybody ugly."

"I wouldn't do that to you."

She gave me an 'I don't believe you' look then picked up Essence off of the table.

"What kind of men do you like anyway?"

"I don't know, good looking ones."

We laughed.

"Nice. I don't like mean guys. And a man that likes to go out, and not sit in the house all day like a hermit."

"Anything else?"

"Trust me, I could go on and on but I want to keep my options open."

"That might be a good idea."

"So do any of his friends sound like they qualify?"

"I don't know. Give me some time, I'll find somebody for you."

When Marvin came home from work I was taking a nap on the couch. I still didn't feel better and after Jamie left, I'd taken another chug of Pepto Bismol. I didn't have much of an appetite and I hadn't eaten anything all day.

Marvin came over to where I was lying on the couch and nudged me.

"Did you cook anything?"

I shook my head and closed my eyes again. I was exhausted and the last thing I was thinking about was cooking anything. I wasn't even hungry.

"And you didn't clean up either?"

"No."

"This house is a mess."

"Marvin, I'm tired and I don't feel good."

"You had all damn day to lie around and recuperate. It's almost eight. You need to get up and cook and clean. I been working all day, I'll be damned if I have to come home to a dirty house and no food on the table. Your job is to keep up our home."

"Marvin, I cook every day. I just told you I don't feel good tonight. I will do all that tomorrow."

Marvin grabbed my arm and pulled me up off the couch and out of my seat. I was so pissed off, I was near tears.

"Make me something to eat and clean this house. That's your job. I can't just not go to work every time I don't feel good. Sometimes you have to suck it up. Today is your day, suck it up."

"I don't fucking feel good."

"Then take your lazy ass upstairs and go to bed. You are so mutherfucking worthless. I work all damn day long and when I come home hungry I can't even get a home cooked meal. What the fuck is the point of being married and having a wife? My mother would have never done this to my father."

"Then you should have married her."

Marvin pushed me and I flew across the room falling into the loveseat. He looked like he wanted to smack the hell out of me.

"Take your disrespectful ass upstairs Kari. You're never too sick to run your mouth."

As much as I wanted to, I didn't say anything back to Marvin. I was not in the mood to argue. As soon as I thought things were better, he was back to his old ways. I didn't know if it was because he was having all of these extra meetings with his father in attendance or what the deal was.

Days passed and I still wasn't feeling normal. I had to force myself to clean and do the daily housekeeping. I knew something wasn't right since I was barely eating and my emotions were all over the place. Instead of going to the doctor, I spent weeks trying to pinpoint when I'd started feeling this way and what might be the source of my illness. Finally, I went to the drugstore and bought a home pregnancy test.

# CHAPTER 5

It had been almost a week since I found out I was pregnant and I still hadn't told Marvin. I was so excited, but I had to wait until he was in better spirits. He had been working extra hours and was still stressed. I didn't feel it was a good time to drop such tremendous news. Luckily, I didn't have morning sickness and wasn't far along enough to start showing, so he didn't suspect anything.

It was Friday and since Marvin had the weekend off, I felt it was a perfect time to tell him. This meant he would have couple of days to digest the news before work on Monday. I knew he wasn't crazy about having kids, but now that it was actually happening, I knew he would be pleased.

That night I cooked his favorite dinner: lobster tail, asparagus, mashed potatoes and apple pie for dessert. His plate was nice and hot when he walked through the door, just the way he liked. He put his briefcase down and took off his suit jacket.

"Hey Marvin."

"Hey Kari."

He came over and gave me a kiss and sat down at the table where his plate was awaiting him. We said grace and began eating our dinner. Marvin didn't say anything which was always a good sign when he was eating. I let him enjoy his meal in silence before I started.

"How was work today?"

"Fine."

"You got any plans this weekend? You off so I know you excited."

"Please use proper English Kari, I hate when you talk like you live in the ghetto."

I ignored his insult and continued to try to make small talk.

"You playin' basketball with Jonathon, Carl, and Fred tomorrow?"

"Yes Kari, I am playing basketball tomorrow. I usually do on Saturdays."

"Did you have a bad day or something?"

"No. Why do you ask that?"

"Because you're snappin' at me for tryin' to make small talk with you," I said suddenly becoming more interested in my dinner than sharing my news. Our news.

"Trying to make small talk Kari, damn I hate it when you talk like that."

I sat there quietly. Marvin had officially ruined dinner and the mood. I no longer wanted to tell him about the baby, but I had to.

There was a long silence as I tried to figure out how to tell him. At this point I wasn't so sure about his reaction, but I was hopeful.

"Marvin, I took a home pregnancy test about a week ago..."

He looked at me and waited for me to go on.

"... and I'm pregnant," I said, a small smile creeping on my face that I couldn't help.

Marvin didn't say anything. I couldn't tell what he was thinking. His facial expression was blank.

"You took the test a week ago?"

I nodded.

"And you decided to wait until now to tell me what the hell was going on?"

"I was trying to wait until work slowed down and you were in a better mood-"

"Well when you do stupid stuff like this it's hard for me to get in a good mood."

"I thought you would be happy, so I wanted to surprise you."

"Yes and this is the perfect time. Have you forgotten that I'm hosting the annual company dinner here in a couple weeks?"

Oh shit, I had forgotten.

"How are you supposed to do the cooking for the party when you're all sick and fat and pregnant?"

"Marvin the company dinner is really not my concern, I don't work there. We can hire a catering company to do it."

"Yeah I guess we could always waste money and do that," he said sarcastically. "You want to sit here and talk about how the company dinner is not your concern, but that company is one that my father built from the ground up. The same company that pays us all the money that you want to blow on caterers."

"I'm just saying it might not be best if I cook for the party because of the baby, so we can just hire someone this one time to do it."

"No we won't just hire someone else to do it. You will make an appointment to get an abortion and be ready to cook for the dinner."

My mouth dropped.

"You want me to get an abortion?" I whispered, choking at the thought.

"It's not the time for babies right now Kari. We had this talk already but obviously you didn't comprehend what was going on."

"What are you trying to say?"

"That you and your Flint Community School education obviously didn't comprehend the conversation you and I had in which we agreed we were not ready for kids right now."

"We agreed? That's what happened?"

Marvin took a deep breath and closed his eyes, a clear indication to me that he was pissed.

"So you want to really sit here and play these games with me Kari?"

"What games am I playin' wit you Marvin? I want to have a baby."

"Well I don't," he said bluntly. "And especially not by a woman who can't even speak English properly."

"I'm not getting an abortion."

"You will do what the hell I tell you to do and you can start by shutting your fucking mouth."

I slammed my fork down on my plate and busted up from the table. Tears started stinging my eyes, and I wanted to leave the table before Marvin could see them develop.

I went upstairs to the bedroom and lay on the bed. I couldn't believe what Marvin wanted to make me do. How could he ask me to abort our child? What was the point of marriage and building a life together if I couldn't fulfill my dreams? He wouldn't let me work or go back to school, but he didn't want me to have any kids either. What was the point?

My pillow was drenched with tears and I could feel my face start to puff up from all the crying. I had already started to pick out baby names. Cynthia, Samantha, Marvin Jr., all of my dreams of having a little baby calling me Mommy didn't feel real anymore. It was as if Marvin had sucked the life from me.

I put my hand on my stomach. It was just a little pudge, but I could feel it. This was my baby. How would I let him make me stop this life already blooming inside me?

Marvin opened the bedroom door flooding light into the dim room. The sun was going down.

"I'll make you an appointment tomorrow. I know you won't be up to it. I'll take the day off of work so I can take you and make sure you're okay."

Marvin didn't wait for a response from me before he closed the door and left me alone in the room. The sunset was beautiful, but there was nothing worth smiling about at this moment. Marvin was making me do something that was painful and irreversible. Once I had the abortion, that was it, and he knew it. How could someone that claimed to care about me want me to do something he knew was wrong?

I stayed in the bedroom for the rest of the night. I lay in that bed for hours trying to figure out what to do, but I knew Marvin would never change his mind. I had to accept the fact that as long as I was married to Marvin, he would never let me have kids unless it was his plan.

The appointment came quickly. I had tried countless times to talk to Marvin, but he wouldn't listen. He had his mind made up, and that was all that mattered. I was silent in the car on the drive there. My heart was heavy and I wiped my tears before they had a chance to run down my face. Marvin looked at me out the corner of his eye, but pretended not to notice I was crying. He was showing no remorse.

We sat in the waiting room for what seemed like hours until my name was called. When they did, Marvin got up with me, but I pushed him away.

"I can handle this myself."

"I'm going back with you Kari."

"I don't need you goin' back there with me holding my hand through this to make this look like we agreed. We didn't. I can do this myself."

"Kari, I don't think you should-"

"Well I don't think I should get this abortion but you don't give a fuck about that," I argued.

Marvin looked embarrassed; he looked around the waiting room to make sure nobody had heard me. I walked away before he had a chance to stop me and followed the nurse to the back. I was so scared that my legs were shaking and I could barely get into the gown when they ordered me to change. The procedure took about thirty minutes and they made me lie there for another thirty before I was free to leave. I got dressed and walked slowly out into the waiting room where Marvin was waiting. He stood up and tried to grab my hand, but I walked past him. I didn't need his help, and I wasn't going to allow him to feel good about being a doting, kind husband.

Silently I sat in the car and looked out of the window the whole ride home. Tears wouldn't stop falling. All of the dreams I had about being pregnant and being a mother were washed away with one appointment. I would never forgive Marvin for doing that to me.

When we got home I went straight upstairs to the bedroom and locked the door. I didn't want to be in Marvin's presence. I hated him with everything I had left inside of me. Every time I thought about him I got sick to my stomach. I had made a huge mistake in marrying him. He would never be the same person he'd been when I met him, that man was officially gone in my eyes. And I didn't know if my marriage with this "new" Marvin Fairmount would last.

DeQuindra Renea

# CHAPTER 6

Marvin's company dinner came quicker than I wanted. I hadn't spoken to him much at all since the abortion, but a week before the party he came into the bedroom while I was combing my hair. He wasn't dressed for work yet, so he had on his blue robe and black pajama pants. His beard was lined up perfectly. I could smell the coffee on his breath as he leaned in, grasping my hand.

"Look, I know you've been through a lot with this whole abortion thing, but it's my company dinner this week so I'm going to need you to swallow all that up."

I couldn't believe what the fuck he was saying to me! Was this muthafucka really trying to tell me to put the fact that he'd made me have an abortion aside for his stupid little company dinner? I bit my lip to keep from cussing him out.

"It's important that I impress some potential clients that'll be showing up. So please be on your best behavior and talk like you've got some sense."

I just stared at him, trying not to pull away. He had absolutely no remorse for the things he was saying. All he cared about was his image and what people at his company would think. If they only knew the truth about our life at home.

Marvin left me standing in the bathroom alone. I looked at myself in the mirror. I waited for the tears to fall, but none would come. I was used to Marvin hurting me. It was a part of my life. Being married to him was wonderful financially. I never wanted for anything. But that also meant putting up with his constant verbal abuse and putting my game face on no matter the situation. I was expected to uphold the trophy wife image, and as long as I played my part, I was paid handsomely. Being married to Marvin was no longer about love, it was a business arrangement, but when would I get paid?

I finished combing my hair and got ready to run countless errands not only for myself, but for the party. I hadn't left the house since the abortion, but Jamie was forcing me to meet her for lunch at 4. And besides, if I didn't do things around the house, they would never get done.

"Are you kidding me?" Jamie asked with her mouth wide open. I'd just explained to her why I'd been MIA for the past couple of weeks.

"I wish I was, but he took me last week."

"He took you?"

I nodded my head.

"He wanted to make sure I actually went through with it, not because he gave a damn about me."

"Why would he do that?"

"I honestly think he's afraid of his image at work."

"What does that have to do with you guys having kids?" she asked confused.

"Because if we have children and he's still working a lot of hours, he's afraid they'll start talking about how he never has time for his children. Image is very important to Marvin. He doesn't really care if he's a good father as long as everybody else thinks he is."

Jamie shook her head in disgust. I could tell she was beginning to see Marvin in a whole new light. At first, she thought he was the perfect husband just like everybody else, but when I started really talking to her she quickly learned the truth.

"How has he been treating you since the abortion?"

"We haven't really talked. This morning he came into the bathroom when I was getting dressed and told me to suck it up because his company dinner is coming up this weekend."

"You don't have to put up with that Kari. That's abuse! Did the people at the clinic know he was making you do it?"

"I doubt it."

"You really don't have to deal with that. He really needs to reevaluate his life. Once he thinks you're really leaving he'll change his ways."

"Marvin knows I aint goin' nowhere. I do still love him which I know is crazy. He didn't used to be like this. He really did used to be the perfect husband."

"But those days are gone now Kari. He's changed. Are you really going to live the rest of your life like this?"

"I don't know."

We continued our meal in silence. Relationships were complicated, and no matter how hard it got, it wasn't easy to just walk away, especially when you'd been with someone for so long. I was glad Jamie let the situation go, and not sit and lecture me for fifteen minutes about how stupid I was and how I deserved better. After we ate and paid our bills, we walked out to our cars.

"So what's the big deal about this dinner he's having anyway?"

"'It's like an annual dinner they have for potential clients. So they have to pretty much kiss ass for an entire night."

"Sounds fun."

"Oh it's loads of fun. And of course I will be running around playing hostess all night with a huge smile plastered on my face like I'm the happiest woman in the world."

"Well Travis gets the kids that weekend and I can come over and help if you want me to."

"Yes I do want you to," I said giving her a huge hug. "Thank you so much. I owe you big time."

"You don't have to thank me. Trust me, I'm only coming to steal some of your recipes, not to actually help."

I hit her playfully and she gave me a big hug once we reached our cars.

"I love you Kari, and I'm here for you anytime."

"I know. Thank you, Jamie. I love you too."

We got in the car and blew each other kisses as we drove away. I was glad she'd dragged me out. I felt a little better. Now it was time to put my game face on and get ready for the stupid dinner.

"Kari, come out here and take a picture with me and my

parents," Marvin ordered sticking his head into the kitchen. Jamie came over and took the wine bottle from me and continued pouring drinks. I threw my apron on one of the dining room chairs once again revealing my red evening gown and black heels. I looked stunning, and everybody at the party told me so. Unfortunately I didn't feel how I looked, so I was trying to hide out in the kitchen, but Marvin was making that impossible. Every five seconds he wanted me to come out and meet someone, or take a picture, or do something for him and a client. I was tired and my cheeks hurt from the fake smile I had plastered on my face. I only had a few more hours though, and then I could go upstairs and drown myself in my sorrow, and perhaps a glass of champagne.

By the time the party was over I'd hugged so many people and shook so many hands and laughed at so many corny jokes, that I'd almost lost my mind. Just when I thought I'd made it through the night, I walked past a group of women talking about their children.

"Hannah is getting so much better at violin. She got the solo at her recital last month," one said.

"Well my son Arthur made the honor roll again all year. His cumulative GPA is a perfect 4.0. We've already gotten calls from Harvard and Princeton."

My stomach dropped and I could feel its contents start to stir. The bathroom on the main floor was occupied so I ran downstairs to the basement. I made it to the toilet just in time, heaving out the contents of my stomach. I felt empty inside, more than usual. I remembered the feeling of having a full womb, and just like that it was taken from me. Tears ran down my face and I could feel my makeup start to run. I knew Marvin would have a fucking fit if he saw me behaving this way.

I looked at myself in the mirror and pulled it together as best I could. I needed to look presentable enough to make it upstairs to my makeup bag, so I opened the door and headed upstairs. Jonathon was on his way down. I gave him a quick smile, but he didn't return the favor.

"Kari, are you okay? I been tryna talk to you all night."

"I'm fine. Why have you been trying to talk to me?"

"I just wanted to make sure you were okay. You been lookin' sad all night."

I shook my head.

"I'm fine. And I'm not sad, but thanks for your concern," I said sounding a little bitchier than I wanted to.

Jonathon grabbed my hand and gave it a light squeeze. He looked in my eyes and bit his lip. My panties got moist and I snatched my hand away. I couldn't have these feelings.

"You're too beautiful to be so sad," he said running his hand across my cheeks. "If I had you, I would always make you smile."

I couldn't believe what he'd just said. I didn't know if it was a compliment or if he was flirting with me. Since he was Marvin's friend I knew flirting with me was out of the question. I gave him another smile.

"Thank you, Jonathon. That's very sweet of you."

He gave me a small smile and looked me up and down with lust in his eyes. I continued up the stairs and closed the basement door behind me. I avoided eye contact with anybody and headed upstairs to fix my makeup. After applying some necessary touches, I gave myself a once over in the mirror and headed back downstairs.


"Are you sure you don't want me to stay and help clean up?" Jamie asked as I put her plates of leftovers in a grocery bag.

"Yes I'm sure. I'm not even helping. I did my part. I'm about to pour myself another glass of Chardonnay and go upstairs and take a bath. Go home and get some rest while the kids are gone."

I gave Jamie a hug and thanked her again for helping me. She was a true friend that always came through for me.

Marvin was saying goodnight to some of his coworkers while Damon and a couple of his friends were helping with the cleanup. I headed upstairs just as Jonathon came up behind me.

"You headin' upstairs?" he asked.

"Yeah, I'm beat. Thanks for everything you did to help. We really appreciate it."

"It's no problem Kari," he said grabbing my hand again. I could feel him slip something in my hand, but he gave me a look that told me to be discreet.

"Well I hope you sleep well tonight Kari."

"Thank you."

Finally upstairs, I closed and locked the bedroom door

behind me. I was sure by now Marvin had gotten the hint that he wasn't welcome in our bedroom, but I locked the door just in case. I put my wine glass on my nightstand and opened up the business card. On one side it was his name title and cell phone number. On the back was a handwritten message for me:

# I want to be the one to make you smile.

# CHAPTER 7

The day of Marvin and Jonathon's competition finally had arrived. I woke up before Marvin and cooked breakfast. Good Morning America blared from the living room while I cooked eggs, bacon, grits, and toast. Marvin was gonna need his energy to beat Jonathon. I was also a little excited, only because the outcome was going to be too hilarious. Marvin and Jonathon had been going at it so tough about this game that whoever lost would never be able to live it down.

Marvin strolled down the stairs about a half an hour later wearing his blue robe and house shoes. He seemed to be in a good mood, and was extremely confident that he would win. I didn't know who would win, and I really didn't care. It was just entertaining to see them go back and forth. There was 500 dollars riding on this game, so it was the real deal.

Marvin finished breakfast and went upstairs to get dressed. He'd told Jonathon to be at our house at noon and it was almost eleven-thirty. After cleaning the kitchen, I went upstairs and sat on the bed watching the news until Marvin got out of the shower. After showering I threw on some clothes and brushed my hair up into a bun to keep it off my neck.

Jonathon and Marvin were already downstairs talking junk when I came back down. Jonathon had obviously just arrived and Marvin hadn't let him in the door before the word war began.

"Look man, I aint gon go back and forth with you, my game will speak for itself. Just have my money ready when I'm done."

"Jonathon you know you're about to lose, I don't know why you keep embarrassing yourself. Look, my wife is going to be laughing at you for the next few months after this," Marvin said after noticing I'd come downstairs. Jonathon gave me a quick smile and went back to trash talking with Marvin.

"Look, you aint showing me nothing standing here talking about it. Let's head outside and start this game. I wanna drag you on this court and make it to pick up my dry cleaning by two. No," Jonathon looked at his wristwatch. "One thirty."

"Come on man, you're talking too much shit."

I followed Jonathon and Marvin out of the house and into our driveway where our basketball hoop was and sat down on one of my lawn chairs with a bottle of water waiting for the game to begin. I didn't watch them play basketball much, but Marvin insisted I be outside today to keep score. This game was serious.

They shot around for a while, getting warmed up. After about twenty minutes of that, they started the game. I grabbed the small pad and pen Marvin had left on the table and started doing my job.

The score was close: Marvin had eight to Jonathon's six. Jonathon made a perfect jump shot, tying the game.

"You better get ready homie, I'm shootin' like this all game."

"That was a lucky shot, man. Just a lucky shot. I'm not worried."

Jonathon grabbed the ball just as Marvin's cell phone rang. He called a timeout and came over to the table to answer it.

"Marvin Fairmount... Yes... Yes I signed those and left them on my desk last night... Uh huh... They have to be sent today... I did? Are you sure? Okay.... Okay... I'll run up there and sign them really quick... Yeah, give me ten minutes... Bye."

Marvin put his cell phone in his pocket and went over to Jonathon.

"I forgot to sign something that has to be sent off today. I have to run to the office and give them my John Hancock."

"You want me to ride with you?"

"You can, or you can just stay and shoot around if you want. You need the practice."

"Yeah yeah, you just hurry up and get back. Don't try to

46

escape this ass whoopin'.'"

Marvin laughed and headed to the house for his keys.

"I hope you remember all this after I win this game."

Marvin disappeared into the house and after a few minutes the garage door came up. Jonathon moved out the way and Marvin pulled out the driveway headed towards the office. I watched Jonathon shoot around for a few minutes, then I went inside to cool off while Marvin was gone.

I was sitting on the couch drinking my bottled water and reading Vibe when I heard the front door open. Jonathon emerged seconds later, sweat traveling slowly down his face.

"Can I get a towel Kari?"

I went into the bathroom and got Jonathon a towel to wipe his face.

"Thank you."

"No problem."

I sat back down on the couch and Jonathon stood in the living room doorway staring at me.

"Did you read my note?" he boldly asked.

"Yeah."

"So why didn't you ever call me?"

"What?"

"I gave you my card for a reason. It has my number on it and I want you to use it."

"I don't think Marvin would like that."

"What Marvin doesn't know won't hurt him."

I couldn't believe what I was hearing! Jonathon and Marvin were friends, and here he was in his home trying to talk to me.

"I think it would."

"You're beautiful," he said stepping into the living room. "Sometimes when I'm here I can't stop looking at you."

I grinned even though I shouldn't have. Marvin never told me I was beautiful anymore. Hearing foreign words were like music to my ears.

"You deserve to smile Kari. You deserve nothing but the best."

I tried not to agree, but I couldn't help it. He was telling me the same thing I tried to tell myself every day.

Jonathon came closer, obviously seeing I wasn't getting offended by his words. He had balls to talk to me this way in my own home.

"What made you give me that card?" I asked curiously.

"Like I said when I'm around you I can't take my eyes off of you. At the party I noticed you were really upset. I could tell you were hiding something painful behind that smile. I want you to smile, and I wanna be the reason you do that."

Jonathon came and sat next to me on the couch and I could feel my body temperature start to rise.

"What if I would've told Marvin what you did?"

"That was a chance I was willing to take. You're worth it."

I smiled again and quickly turned my head. Jonathon grabbed my face so that I was facing him.

"Don't hide it from me. It makes me feel good that I'm making you smile."

Jonathon kept his hand on my face and looked deep in my eyes. I could tell he wanted to kiss me, but I couldn't let that happen. I was a married woman, and Jonathon was my husband's friend! That was something I could not be a part of.

I got up from the couch and walked to the other side of the room, it was better for me to get away from him. He definitely knew all the right things to say and do. That would only get me in trouble.

Jonathon got up from the couch and followed me in to the kitchen.

"Why you runnin' Kari? You don't have to be scared of me."

"I'm not scared, but this is wrong. Marvin will be back home any minute now."

"We not doin' nothin' wrong, we just standing here talking."

He made me feel stupid when he said that, like I was overreacting. I hadn't done anything wrong, so I shouldn't feel scared about Marvin coming home. If anything, Jonathon was the one that should be scared.

I leaned against the counter and stared at Jonathon. He was fine, but that was none of my concern. I was married. I had to keep reminding myself that.

Jonathon came closer to me and wet his lips.

"Can I see you smile one more time before I go back outside?"

A smile spread across my face slowly. He smiled too, showing his perfect, white teeth. He came over to me and pressed his body against mine. Frozen, I didn't know whether to push him off or let the moment pass. He looked into my eyes again as he came in closer to kiss me.

I heard Marvin's Lexus SUV pull into the driveway. Jonathon leaned down and whispered in my ear.

"Use that card Kari. Let me show you how you're supposed to be treated."

Before I had a chance to respond, he turned and walked away as if nothing had ever happened. I stood in awe in the middle of my kitchen. After a few minutes, I went back outside where Marvin and Jonathon were getting ready to continue their big game.

After he beat Jonathon 30 to 26, Marvin ordered a couple pizzas and we went inside to eat.

I sat in the living room eating a slice of pepperoni pizza and listening to Marvin brag about the ass beating he had just put on Jonathon. Jonathon was embarrassed, and kept telling Marvin he had just gotten lucky. They went back and forth some more, and I knew then a rematch would be coming soon.

After I ate my pizza, I took all of the trash into the kitchen. I could feel a pair of eyes on me, but now I didn't know whether it was Marvin or Jonathon. On my way upstairs, Jonathon's eyes locked on mine. He smiled and gave me a quick wink. He was sexy.

Once in the privacy of my bedroom I got his business card from my jewelry box where I had put it.

# I want to be the one to make you smile, I read again.

It was wrong, but Jonathon had already achieved that goal.

Calling Jonathon for the first time was terrifying because I didn't know what to say. If I called, he would automatically assume I wanted to mess around, but I didn't really understand why I was calling. Maybe it was the attention I craved, or just being able to talk to someone who would actually listen. Whatever the reason, I wanted to call him.

After giving it some thought, I decided I would call Jonathon and set him up with Jamie. That way, he wouldn't think I was looking for anything romantic with him.

I waited until Marvin left for work and called from the house phone. It rang twice before he picked up.

"Hello?"

"Hi Jonathon."

"Kari?" he asked incredulously.

"Yeah, how are you doing?"

"I'm fine, how are you?" he smiled through the phone.

"I'm pretty good."

"I'm glad you called. I been waitin' for you to call me."

"Yeah, well I was calling because I have this friend named Jamie, and she's single. She's been over my house so you've probably seen her."

He laughed.

"Yeah, I think I know who you talkin' about."

"She's pretty, and she's fun. She has two kids named-"

"Kari, stop playin'. I know you didn't really call me to talk about your friend."

"Yeah, why would you think I was playing?"

"Because it's not your friend that I want and you know that."

My breath caught in my throat. I didn't know what to say in response. There was a long pause.

"Kari, I got a call coming in that I have to take," he said urgently.

"Okay, go ahead."

"I wanna talk to you though. Give me your cell phone number so I can text you."

"I can't do that."

"You already called me. Calling is much worse than texting, so we're actually moving in reverse."

"You know that would be wrong," I said sitting down on the loveseat.

"Just let me text you today and if you don't want me to anymore, I won't."

I hesitated and I didn't know what to do.

"Get your call, I'll text it to you."

"You better, or I'm calling you back on the house phone."

He hung up and I sat there with the phone in my hand. I

didn't know if he was serious or not. I got my cell phone out of my purse and texted him just to be safe. After about thirty minutes, I got a message from him.

What do I need to do to show u that u r the one I want? it read. I stared at it. There was no safe way to respond.

I'm married to ur friend and u know that, I replied. I received a reply in less than a minute.

Then why did u really call me? Because after the way I came at u in the kitchen, u know I'm not tryna play games.

So what r u trying to do? I don't understand what u want from me, I replied.

I want u, he replied.

I don't know how long I looked at that message, but I didn't know how to reply. It was amazing how many times this man could leave me speechless.

What am I supposed to say to that? I sent the message. Immediately he responded.

Say what u want. If you like me u like me, if u don't that's cool. Whatever we say is between us.

I read the message and put my phone down. I couldn't believe this. He was in our wedding! He was Marvin's friend. How could he want me? I didn't know what to say, so I didn't respond. I needed to think about what was going on.

After about fifteen minutes my phone chimed.

So is that a no? U didn't like the way I pressed my body against urs at ur house that day?

I still didn't respond. It seemed he was asking me questions that would make me guilty no matter how I answered. He was trying to trap me.

When I didn't respond to either text message, he called. At first I didn't answer, then I thought about what he'd said about calling the house phone.

"Why aint you respondin' to none of my texts?" he asked when I picked up.

"Because I don't know what you're trying to do. How do I know Marvin didn't tell you to talk to me to see how I would respond?"

He laughed.

"I don't think any man is that stupid Kari. Marvin knows that if he did that you would never come back."

This time I laughed.

"You have a lot of confidence don't you?"

"You could say that. So are you going to tell me the truth about why you called?"

"I was curious. I didn't know what you wanted."

"I think I made it clear what I want."

"Look Jonathon, I don't know what type of woman you think I am, but I'm faithful to my husband."

"I think you are a very beautiful woman. That's my opinion. I just want to get to know you without being under Marvin's watch."

"Why is that necessary?"

"Kari, if you don't want to talk to me you don't have to. You can hang up and I will never try to talk to you again."

"Maybe that would be best."

"That's fine. I guess I'll see you later."

"Maybe you will."

I ended the call feeling like I had done the right thing. Talking to Jonathon behind Marvin's back was wrong and I couldn't let it happen.

# CHAPTER 8

It was early Saturday afternoon and once again my living room was full of hot, sweaty men. Marvin, Carl, Fred, Patrick, Damon and Jonathon were drinking beers and watching the news. Their clothes stuck to their bodies, clear evidence that they had played basketball all morning. I came downstairs wearing a long pink sundress and pink and white wedge sandals. My hair was pulled into a neat bun on top of my head. I had invited Jamie over since she wanted to meet some of Marvin's friends. I told her to come over when they played basketball to check a few of them out.

Jamie showed up a little later wearing blue jean capris and an orange tank top. She had on orange flip flops. Her hair hung down her back in big curls. She always dressed simply, but always managed to look gorgeous no matter what she wore. She gave me a hug.

"They smell so don't be alarmed," I whispered in her ear.

"Well you said they'd be playing basketball, so I kind of figured."

She followed me into the kitchen and we sat at the living room table. Discreetly she was checking all of them out.

"Who is the one in the black beater?"

"That's Patrick, he's nice. He works in construction, but he's going back to school to be a doctor."

"He's fine. Is he single?"

"I think so, I never see him with anybody. I can ask Marvin later."

She nodded her head and smiled. Patrick was good looking. He was kind of skinny, but really tall. He looked as if he could have been the basketball star in high school. He had long dreads, but they were really neat and he always kept them pulled back. He had dark skin and big white teeth. His eyes were sexy and dark, which Jamie referred to as bedroom eyes. She always had me laughing out loud and I made a mental note to invite her over more often on basketball Saturdays. There was too much testosterone in my house and she could keep it balanced.

Jonathon came into the kitchen with his empty bottle. I hadn't talked to him since I'd called him on the phone to talk about Jamie. It seemed he'd been staying away, or maybe I was avoiding him. Either way he was standing in my kitchen looking sexier than ever in black basketball shorts and a white wife-beater. He was still sweating and I could see his chest through his beater. I squeezed my thighs together to keep that sensation from coming, the same sensation I felt every time I saw him.

He didn't even look my way, but he immediately smiled when he saw Jamie.

"Hi, you must be Jamie. I don't know if we've ever met. My name is Jonathon," he said extending his hand. She grabbed it immediately.

"Yes, I'm Jamie. It's a pleasure to meet you."

"The pleasure is all mine. I know that sounds cliché, but pleasure applies when it comes to you."

I rolled my eyes. He had some nerve flirting with her right in front of my face. He had already said he wanted me and wasn't interested in Jamie.

"So what is a woman as gorgeous as you doing being single?" he asked sitting down at the table and helping himself to our fruit.

"I ask myself the same thing every morning," Jamie said giving Jonathon one of her dazzling smiles. "Thanks for the compliment."

"You don't have to thank me when it's true."

Jamie blushed and I knew that was my cue to leave. I didn't think I could stomach any more of his courtship. Politely I excused myself from the table trying to hide my attitude. I liked when Jonathon showed me attention. Hell, I wasn't getting it from Marvin these days. I just wasn't trying to take it as far as Jonathon wanted. Now, I was getting completely ignored by both men.

I went to the basement bathroom to gather my thoughts. I had no right being mad that Jonathon was flirting with Jamie. They were both single and I had made it clear to Jonathon that I didn't want anything to do with him. I was being ridiculous.

Still trying to regulate my heart rate with breathing, I heard a light knock at the door. I went over to it and opened it.

"Excuse me," I said rudely trying to push past Jonathon. He laughed as he grabbed my arm.

"What's the problem baby? Why you actin' all mad?"

"Don't touch me," I whispered as he backed me into a wall. He had a thing about backing me into corners.

"I thought you wanted me to talk to your friend. Aint that why you called me?" he asked, trying to catch me in my lie.

"Yes that's what I wanted, and I'm not mad so can you get out of my way?"

"I told you it's not her that I want."

"Then why did you even start talking to her in the first place?"

"Because I wanted to see if you would get mad. You want me don't you?"

"Can you let me go?"

"Why do you wanna act like this?" he said coming closer to me. "I told you I wanted you, I made that clear."

"Shh," I said afraid somebody upstairs might hear us. Jonathon pressed his body against mine and brought his face so close that I could feel his breath on my lips.

"If I kissed you right now, would you kiss me back?" he asked softly. I could feel my panties getting moist. The living room upstairs exploded in laughter and I jumped.

"Don't be scared," he said running his hands down the sides of my body. "You can trust me baby, I got you. I'm not gonna let us get caught."

Jonathon rubbed his lips against mine softly and I turned my head to avoid what was about to happen.

"Let me kiss you Kari, you know you want me to."

"I can't," I said trying to push him away. "You have to stop doing this in my house."

"Okay, we can go to my house, I'm good with that too."

"You have to stop this," I repeated. "You have to, or I'm going to tell Marvin."

"You're not gonna tell Marvin, I'm not worried about that."

"Why not?"

"Because you like it. That's why you ran out the room when I was talking to your friend. You were jealous."

"Look you need to let me go Jonathon, somebody is going to catch us."

"Didn't I just tell you I got you. I just want you to tell me the truth," he licked his lips and looked me up and down. "Or show me."

I looked deep into his eyes and then had to force myself to look away. I was falling under his spell. Even with my husband right upstairs, Jonathon was making it so easy to forget that I was married.

"I want you to call me again, will you do that?"

Like a school child, I nodded my head obediently. Jonathon smoothly walked away and went into the bathroom. Quickly I went upstairs before anyone had a chance to pay attention to the fact that we were down there together. As a matter of fact, I needed to avoid my basement altogether.

# CHAPTER 9

Marvin's business trip couldn't have come at a better time. We hadn't been getting along and he seemed to be angrier every day. I knew his father was showing up at the office more, but Marvin never talked to me about Fairmount Inc. It had gotten to the point that he was staying in his office all day long and late into the evening. He said it was for work, but I didn't care. The less I talked to Marvin, the more I talked to Jonathon. I would call him as soon as Marvin left for work and stay on the phone with him all day which was easy since he worked from home. He was a good listener and although we had truly built a friendship, it was starting to get harder and harder to ignore his advances.

The day before Marvin was supposed to leave for Boston, he came home early from work. I was lying on the couch talking on the phone with Jonathon when Marvin walked through the door. I hung up the cordless phone and put it under the pillow. Before Marvin could close the door, I was in the hallway.

"What are you doing here?"

"I live here."

"I know, but it's early."

"I know what time it is. I didn't realize I couldn't come home early."

The phone started ringing and my heart dropped. I could only pray it wasn't Jonathon calling me back.

"What happened? Why did you come home?" I asked trying to ignore the phone ringing. I was hoping if I pretended I didn't hear it, he wouldn't either.

"Can you get the phone!" he ordered. He was already annoyed from work, so I went into the living room and grabbed the phone from its hiding spot.

"Hello?"

"Kari why you hang up?" Jonathon asked.

"Oh hi Jonathon, how are you?"

"What's going on? He aint home is he?"

"Yeah Marvin is here, hold on."

Marvin was coming into the living room and I handed the phone off to him.

"Hello... Oh hey man, how are you? Yeah you caught me as soon as I walked in from work... Okay...Okay Jonathon, that's fine... talk to you later."

Marvin hung up the phone and put it on the table. I studied his face to make sure he didn't look suspicious of the call. He started taking off his tie and headed upstairs.

"What's up? Why'd you come home early?" I asked after him.

"I'm the boss, I can go home whenever I want to," he responded without turning around.

"So you're going to your office now?"

"I still have work to do."

I heard his office door slam and I was alone once again. I knew calling Jonathon back was too risky, so I finished up some laundry I had neglected and started dinner.

Marvin stayed in his office the rest of the day, only coming out to eat and pack his bags. I wasn't sure what his problems were, I was just glad he was keeping it upstairs.

Later that night I got a text from Jonathon when I was getting ready to get in the bathtub.

**Is everything okay?** It read.

I texted back.

**It's all good.**

In a matter of seconds my phone vibrated again.

**That was close,** I texted back.

**I know. The next time I hang up don't call back.** He replied.

**Understood. I learned my lesson on that one.**

I slid into the hot bubble bath and closed my eyes before the phone vibrated.

**What are you doing?**

Taking a hot bubble bath, I replied.

**I wish I was with you.**

I shook my head and texted back.

**Don't start that. You know I'm married to Marvin. I like talking to you so please don't cross the line.**

He didn't reply back for a minute which was fine because I was enjoying my alone time. I didn't feel like thinking, just relaxing.

My phone finally vibrated.

**I know what the deal is, but what do you want me to do? Deny how I feel about you? Deny that I want you?**

I didn't text back right away and relaxed in the bathtub. Turning the jets on high to allow my body to be massaged, I got lost in my thoughts.


I didn't text Jonathon back until I got into bed. Marvin was in the shower and I was watching TV.

**You need to do whatever you need to make sure our friendship stays as it is. Marvin doesn't deserve to be betrayed like that.**

Jonathon didn't reply to my text and he didn't need to. There was nothing he could say that would make me change my mind. After deleting all of our text messages, I closed my eyes and went to sleep.


I dropped Marvin off at the airport and although he was only leaving for a day and a half, I was ecstatic. His horrible mood was starting to take a toll on me. Maybe a change of scenery would bring him back to Michigan relaxed and happy.

After I dropped Marvin off I spent the whole day pampering myself. I got a manicure and pedicure, and even went to get a massage. It was refreshing knowing I could go home to an empty house with no Marvin stomping around.

I stayed out all day shopping and picked up a pizza on the way home. I was lying in bed with pizza, pop, and a bunch of junk food when Jonathon called.

"Hello?"

"Hey, I didn't hear from you today," he said in his sexy voice.

"Yeah I was out all day pampering myself."

"Sounds nice. Did Marvin get off okay?"

"Yeah I dropped him off around noon."

"So what are you getting into tonight?"

"Just staying home eating pizza and watching movies."

"Why don't you come over and visit me?"

I shook my head as if he could see me.

"Jonathon, I told you I can't do that. It would be wrong."

"It would be wrong for you to come over and watch a movie with me?"

"Yes."

"Why?"

"You know why."

"Marvin is out of town. He won't find out. We not gon do nothin' but watch a movie anyway."

Jonathon sounded convincing and I had been alone all day and would enjoy his company, but I couldn't allow myself to do that. It was disrespectful to my husband and far too risky.

"That's just not a good idea Jonathon. I'm not comfortable with it."

"Okay that's cool," he said like it was no big deal. "What movie you watchin' anyway? I'll tell you if it's any good."


Jonathon and I stayed on the phone all night and well into the morning. Marvin never called to tell me he made it to Boston or to check up on me. Our relationship was slowly but surely going downhill, and I had given up on reversing that.

# CHAPTER 10

The time to pick Marvin up from the airport came far too soon. I had enjoyed pampering myself, shopping, relaxing and I even met Jamie for drinks at the bar while he was away. I was not obligated to be home and have dinner done at a certain time. There used to be a time when I was counting down the hours until his plane landed, but now as I drove to the airport, I dreaded seeing him.

I sat in front of *Bishop Airport* and waited for him to arrive. He did almost twenty minutes later with his usual scowl on his face, dressed to travel wearing a black sweat suit and tennis shoes. He was carrying his suitcase and carryon bag, and still had his headphones in his ear. After putting everything in the trunk, he got in.

"Hello," he said dryly.

"Hey," I said matching his stale face.

I took off and we didn't say anything else to each other. We rode in silence listening to the smooth jazz CD he had put in.

"Did you cook anything?" he asked. I shook my head.

"Did you go grocery shopping?"

"No."

"Well what the hell did you do while I was gone?"

"I had time to myself."

"So while I was away working, nothing got done?"

I didn't even answer him. He would be unhappy no matter what I said. Even if I had cooked and gone grocery shopping, he would still find something to be unhappy about.

"Well can you stop by a restaurant so I can have something to eat?" he snapped. I bit my lip to keep from saying anything. I didn't have the energy to argue with him.

I pulled into the Burger King by our house and Marvin ordered himself some food. When we got home he left his bags at the door and went to eat in front of the television. I didn't feel like being bothered with him, so I went upstairs. If Marvin was gonna come back with his same sour attitude, he could have stayed his ass in Boston.

Marvin and I went almost two days barely speaking to each other. I didn't get out of bed the next morning until after he left for work. The way I saw it, if I avoided him I didn't have to deal with his comments and insults. It was becoming too much.

They say an idle mind is the devil's playground and that was definitely true in my case. There wasn't a day that had gone by that I hadn't thought about the abortion. I thought about it more when Marvin was away at work and I was alone. My days should have been filled with dirty diapers, bottles, and a sweet warm baby. Instead, I spent my days cleaning, cooking, running errands and taking care of Marvin, a grown ass man.

I tried not to beat myself up about the decision I'd let Marvin make for me, but I couldn't help it. As a woman there was no way I should have let a man convince me to go through with an abortion. I should have fought for my child, but I backed down, as usual, and did what I was told.

I went downstairs and made a cup of coffee before I started cleaning. Wednesdays were usually my deep cleaning days. I started in the kitchen cleaning out the refrigerator and mopping the floor. I made my way around the downstairs sweeping, mopping, dusting, and scrubbing. When I made it to the front door, I noticed Marvin's bags were right where he'd left them. I took them upstairs to unpack so I could wash his dirty clothes with the rest of the laundry.

After I took everything out the suitcase, I threw it on the floor. When I did, I noticed the corner of a purple box slide out of the inner zip compartment.

I thought my eyes were deceiving me. I knew I wasn't seeing

what I thought I was, but I went over to the suitcase, and pulled out a box of condoms. My mouth dropped open and I could feel the heat in my body start to rise. What the hell had Marvin been up to?

I tried my best to calm down and wait to confront him when he got home, but I was too mad. What the hell had he been doing in Boston and who did he plan on fucking with the condoms? I had questions that needed answers, so I called him at work.

"Marvin Fairmount?" he answered.

"Marvin, it's me. I need to talk to you."

"About what?"

"About what happened in Boston, Marvin. What the hell have you been up to?" I asked, unable to hide my anger.

"Kari I am working. I don't have time to play the guessing game."

"Why the fuck do you have condoms in your suitcase Marvin? Who the fuck were you planning to use them with?"

"Kari I don't have time for this-"

"Well you better make time for it Marvin! I'm not playing games with you!"

"Kari you shouldn't have gone in my suitcase anyway. Those weren't even mine."

"Do you think I'm stupid Marvin? Is that what it is?"

"No, look Kari, I am working. We can talk about this when I get home."

I ended the call by throwing my phone on the floor. I knew Marvin would never talk about anything like that at his office no matter how mad I was or how much I pushed.

I spent the day cleaning, trying to take my mind off of how pissed I was. By the time Marvin got home, my anger had gone to a whole new level. He had gotten home really late, but I was still up waiting for him. I was shaking I was so mad. When he opened the door I was standing there waiting.

"Why do you have condoms in your suitcase?" I asked again, throwing the purple box at him. It hit him in the chest and fell on the floor.

"What the hell? What has gotten into you Kari?"

"I want you to tell me why a married man has condoms in his suitcase for a business trip," I said, standing in his face. He looked down at me and I couldn't read the look in his eyes. "I don't know what to tell you Kari. What do you want me to say?"

"Were the condoms yours?"

"I told you no."

"Stop lying to me Marvin. If they weren't yours, whose were they? And why the fuck were they in your bag?"

"Look, I don't want to talk about this, so get out of my way."

"No! I don't give a damn what you say, we are going to talk about this now!" I yelled. "I am not moving until you tell me what the fuck you were gonna do with the condom-"

Marvin wrapped his hands around my neck cutting off my circulation and preventing me from saying another word. He pushed me into the wall and walked away from me. I stood there in disbelief. I couldn't believe he was putting his hands on me. I grabbed my own neck, feeling for marks that hadn't emerged.

"Marvin, what the hell-"

"I TOLD YOU TO MOVE THE FUCK OUT OF MY WAY! I pay the bills and make the money. You don't have the authority to question me."

"I don't know who you think you married, but I don't allow any bullshit."

"Kari shut the fuck up. You'll allow what the hell I tell you to allow. I'm the man, you're the woman. Know your fucking place," he hissed.

Marvin had done and said some hurtful things in the past, but this situation definitely took the cake. I couldn't say anything to him, nor could I stand the sight of him anymore. I got my purse and keys and jacket, ready to leave the house.

"Where the hell do you think you're going Kari?" he asked, coming into the hallway. I went into the garage without even answering. His cheating, disrespectful ass had some nerve thinking I was gonna stay in the same house with him. He had really turned into a monster and I could no longer take his abuse. If he wanted to go on a business trip and be a dog, he could do it without being married to me.

Without a destination in mind, I got into my car and drove

away. I didn't really feel like being around a lot of people and I wanted to take my mind off of the whole situation with Marvin. Picturing him romantically involved with somebody else made me sick to my stomach, but the way he had blown off my feelings infuriated me. If I was walking around with condoms, that wouldn't sit so well with him. But because he was the man and he made all the money, he could do what the hell he wanted? That's not how marriage was supposed to work.

I drove around for almost an hour before I found myself outside of Jonathon's apartment building. I didn't know what had made me drive there, and I was halfway tempted to put my car in reverse and leave, but I wanted to see Jonathon. I wanted to talk to him. The only other man I could talk to was Kevin and he would have a fit if I told him. I slowly got out of my car.

I stood at his door in my jacket trying to decide if I was going to knock or get back in my car. It was two thirty in the morning and I didn't feel comfortable showing up at his house unannounced. I hadn't even thought to call.

I knocked softly, and then snatched my hand back. I had made a big mistake. I turned around and rushed back to my car, but before I could get in, Jonathon called my name.

"Kari?" he asked sounding hopeful and unsure at the same time. He had nothing on but a pair of basketball shorts. I had never seen him with so little clothes on and all kinds of inappropriate thoughts flooded into my head.

"I was just taking a drive," I explained, completely embarrassed. "I was just driving, but I shouldn't have just shown up. I'll just talk to you later."

I got into my car, but before I could close the door, Jonathon grabbed it.

"You don't have to leave Kari," he said gently removing the keys from my hand. "Come in for a minute and talk to me. You look upset."

Jonathon grabbed my hand and led me into the house. He closed and locked the door behind us and we went into the living room.

"What's goin' on?" he asked, sitting next to me on his loveseat.

"It's just everything. Things between me and Marvin are so bad lately and... and I'm almost sure he's sleeping with someone."

Jonathon grabbed my hand and held onto it tightly.

"I'm just tired of dealing with the bullshit. I'm ready to start a family, I'm ready for kids and he won't give them to me. Anything I want that makes me happy just gets dismissed."

Jonathon continued to just look at me. He was starting to make me uncomfortable. I wanted him to say something, but he looked at me intent on what I was saying.

I took a deep breath.

"I really needed to get that off my chest, thanks for listening."

I stood up and Jonathon pulled me back down before I could even get balanced on my own feet.

"I don't think you should leave."

"I probably should go. You aren't saying much anyway. Maybe you should get some rest."

"It's late, too damn late for you to be driving by yourself, and with your state of mind. You should stay for a while."

"I don't think that's a good idea. Marvin is gonna wonder where I am."

Jonathon gave me a soft kiss on the lips. It was the first time he had ever actually kissed me. He had talked about it before, but I never thought he would do it.

"I been wantin' to kiss you for a long time," he said, kissing me again. This time I opened my mouth and allowed his tongue access. I knew it was wrong, but it felt so good. I had dreamt about kissing him for so long and I couldn't believe I was actually doing it.

I pushed Jonathon away from me and wiped my lips as if that could wipe away what we had just done.

"Come on baby, don't stop," he said kissing me again. "You know you like it, stop fighting me."

He kissed me again. The room started to spin as we sat there going at each other like high school virgins.

"I don't think we should be doing this. This is wrong," I said pushing him away again, the guilt finally setting in. I was cheating on my husband with one of his friends. This was the ultimate betrayal; I knew that.

Jonathon stood up and grabbed my hand.

"Come with me upstairs Kari."

I immediately shook my head. "No Jonathon, I have to go

Even though I knew Marvin was already up, I tried to be quiet since I was nervous. Everything I had done was written all over my face. I put my purse and keys on the kitchen counter and began to make a pot of coffee. I wouldn't be able to sleep, and Marvin would wake me up anyway. The only reason he was up early was so he could know down to the second what time I came home. I poured myself a cup of coffee then went into the living room and turned on the news.

"Where you been at Kari?" Marvin voice boomed down the stairs. He emerged, still wearing his robe and house shoes.

"I went out. It's none of your concern," I snapped.

"Everything you do is my concern Kari."

"Yeah, but obviously I shouldn't be concerned about what you do."

Marvin came into the living room and stood over me. I stared straight ahead making absolutely no eye contact with him.

The guilt is all over your face.

"Kari."

"I don't wanna talk to you Marvin. As a matter of fact, if I sat here and talked to you all fuckin' day long about how much I don't wanna talk to you, you still wouldn't understand how much I don't wanna talk to you!"

Marvin just stood there looking at me. He was standing so close. I hoped I had washed all the sex off of me in the quick shower I had taken at Jonathon's.

"Can I just explain to you what was going on?"

"You really can't explain shit to me Marvin. You weren't ready to explain anything when you had the chance to. You're caught now. I don't need you to explain what I already know."

"Kari-"

"Please go to work Marvin. Please. There is nothing you can say that I wanna hear. Go to work."

Marvin stood there for a while longer before he finally dropped the issue and walked away. He went back upstairs and I finally relaxed a little. I was tired as hell, but I waited until Marvin came downstairs dressed in a navy blue business suit before I went upstairs to go to sleep. It had been one long ass night. I took off everything but my panties and bra before crawling into my bed and falling asleep.

The sound of my cell phone ringing pulled me out of my restless slumber. I got out of bed and took my cell phone out of my pants pocket where I had stuffed it before rushing home last night.

"Hello?"

"Is everything alright? Marvin wasn't trippin' was he?" Jonathon asked, without saying hello.

"Yeah, he was but I told him I didn't wanna talk to him."

"Good. What are you doing now?"

"I was asleep, I didn't get any sleep last night."

"I wonder why," Jonathon joked. I didn't laugh.

"Jonathon what happened last night was a mistake."

"I knew this was comin'."

"I never should've come over. It was wrong."

"The only thing you did wrong was leave without sleeping in my bed with me."

I got back into bed.

"You know that would've been wrong. Everything we did was wrong."

"I wanna make you cum again," he said out of the blue.

"Stop."

"But this time I wanna make you come with my dick."

I was speechless. Did he not hear anything I was saying? Letting him make me cum once was crossing the line and he was already talking about doing it again!

"I can't talk to you anymore Jonathon. I gotta go."

"Don't start this shit Kari. The only reason you runnin' from this is because you liked what happened last night... didn't you?"

There was a pause.

"I gotta go."

"Just answer my question first. Did you like how I made you feel?"

"It doesn't matter because it won't be happening again."

"Answer me."

I took a deep breath.

"Yes," I said rolling my eyes.

"Yes what?"

"Yes, I liked the way you made me feel."

"You don't want me to make you feel like that again?"

I couldn't answer that question honestly. It was a trick question. Of course I wanted him to make me feel like that again, but it was wrong.

"I can't talk to you anymore Jonathon, I'm married, and you wouldn't know how that feels."

"Kari, you can tell me a million times that you married if it'll make you feel better, but haven't you realized by now that I don't care? I want you. I been wantin' you and I don't give a fuck about anything else you talkin' about. You in it now baby, you'll see."

"What does that mean? You gonna blackmail me if I don't fuck you?"

"Hell no, I don't get down like that. But I made you crazy last night with only my tongue. Imagine how I could make you feel with this dick."

"I gotta go Jonathon," I repeated. "I can't talk to you anymore."

"You know it's true. And you know Marvin can never make you feel like you did last night."

I ended the call. Messing around with Jonathon was a huge mistake. Marvin would kill me if he ever found out. I couldn't take the chance of losing everything I had built with Marvin because one of his friends wanted to have sex with me. I had to be smarter than that.

I put my phone on the charger and lay back down. I waited for my phone to ring, but I fell asleep before it ever did.

DeQuindra Renea

# CHAPTER 11

It had been almost a week since Jonathon and I had been together and I couldn't stop thinking about it. He was right, he had given me something to dream about and that's exactly what I was doing. I felt guilty every time I thought about being with him. I was married and yet I lay in bed every night touching myself, thinking about fucking my husband's friend.

After driving myself crazy, I knew it was time for advice from someone I trusted. Kevin would have a fit if he ever found out, and the only other person I could rely on was Jamie. I hadn't talked to her in a few days because she had been busy with work and the kids, but I knew she was long overdue for girl time. The first time I called she didn't answer so I left a voicemail. She called me back later that day while she was picking the kids up from school.

"Hey girl. I'm so sorry I missed your call I had an appointment today."

"That's okay. I was calling to see what you had planned. I need to talk to you."

"I know, it's been too long. I can see if I can drop the kids off at my Mom's house for a couple of hours."

"Okay, let me know."

"I'll call you right back."

Jamie ended the call and called me back not five minutes later. She told me her mother had agreed to keep the kids for a while and she would be over right after she dropped them off. I got up and dressed since all I had been doing was lying around watching TV. We would have to go somewhere and talk because I didn't feel comfortable telling her everything in my house.

When she got there I met her outside before she could even get out of the car.

"Well hello, I see I've been missed, you're meeting me at my car and everything."

I laughed.

"I wanna go out. I've been in the house too long. "

"That's fine as long as it's on you and you're driving. Where are we going?"

"Are you hungry?"

"A little, but I want a drink."

"We can go to *Bar Louie's*. Do they have good food?"

"Yeah, me and my coworkers go there sometimes," she said, putting her seatbelt on. I started the car and headed for the restaurant.


"This drink is pretty good," Jamie said taking a sip of her classic margarita. "I'm telling you, you should get a margarita."

"I really need a shot of something, not a pretty drink."

"This pretty drink is pretty damn strong so don't try to play me."

I took a sip of my water and looked over the drink menu. I still didn't know what I wanted and the truth was I was too nervous to concentrate on anything. I had something I needed to get off of my chest and I wouldn't be comfortable until I did so.

The waitress came over and I ordered a Hennessey on the rocks.

"Well it looks like I'll be driving home," she said eyeing me suspiciously. "What's the matter Kari?"

"Everything is fine. I just have a lot on my mind."

"And that's what you wanna talk to me about?"

"Yeah."

"I'm listening."

"Look Jamie, I know we haven't known each other that long, but you are the only person I can talk to and trust."

"I'm honored," she said putting her hand over her heart. "But seriously, is everything okay?"

"Not exactly. I did something that is... I did something horrible."

Jamie's smiled faded as she realized how serious my situation was.

"What did you do?"

"Jamie if I tell you this you have to swear you won't tell anybody. I mean, I need to talk to someone and I only trust you-"

"I know, I understand Kari. You can tell me. I swear I would never tell anybody."

I took a deep breath.

"I had... I did something with someone... someone that's not my husband."

Jamie's mouth dropped open and she closed it quickly, trying to hide her shock.

"What did you do?"

"I'm... I can't tell you. I'm too embarrassed."

"Kari, you just told me you cheated on your husband. The rest should be a cakewalk."

"I let him eat me out."

"Okay, well who is he? Where did you meet him?"

"That's the other thing... it's one of Marvin's friends."

Jamie's mouth dropped open again, but this time she didn't close it.

"Kari... I... I just don't know what to say."

"I know it's a shock. It was a mistake."

"How did it even happen?"

"I don't know. He just kept saying stuff to me, and I don't know. We've been talking for awhile, and me and Marvin got into it. I went to his house and it just happened."

"Which one of his friends is it?"

"Remember the day you came to my house and all of Marvin's friends were there after they played basketball?"

"Yeah."

"He's the one that came in the kitchen and started talking to you."

Jamie looked like she was trying to recall it in her memory. She nodded her head after a few moments.

"Jonathon?"

"Yeah. That's him and Jamie, I don't know what to do."

"If it was a mistake then you know exactly what to do."

I didn't say anything.

"It was a mistake, right Kari?"

I was grateful that the waitress came over and brought me my Hennessey because I sure needed it. I took a few swallows as Jamie placed an order for the appetizer sampler. The waitress left, and Jamie focused her attention back to me.

"Did you take a drink? Does that feel better?"

I forced a smile and nodded my head.

"Okay Kari, it's just me and you sitting here. You can be honest with me and tell me the truth. You don't have to worry about it leaving this table."

"Girl, he made me feel so good. I have never had anybody want me like this before. Marvin hasn't wanted me in so long and it feels so good to have somebody that wants to please me."

"So was it a mistake?"

"I don't know. I can't stop thinking about him. It's driving me crazy."

"Have you talked to him since then?"

"He called me the next morning."

"What did he say?" she asked, hanging on to my every word.

"He wants to make me cum again. He wants to fuck me and make me feel good."

"And this is one of Marvin's friends?"

"Yeah. But I told him that I can't see him anymore and that it was a mistake. He's called and texted me a few times since, but I haven't responded."

"Wow. This was not what I was expecting to hear."

"I know. It's crazy I know. I just dunno what to do. I can't stop thinking about him and having fantasies. I just don't know what to do."

"And Marvin doesn't have a clue about this right?"

I shook my head.

"I don't think so. I never meant for it to go this far. I wasn't thinking."

""Kari I don't know what you want me to tell you. You obviously know what you did was wrong, but the way you talk about him it's like you won't be able to resist him, and he's going to be around Kari."

"I know, that's what scares me."

"Don't get caught up Kari, that's the best I can tell you. Be careful, don't let him use you."

"What do you mean?"

"I mean you are in an unhappy marriage. You are the easiest fuck."

"Excuse me?"

"I don't mean it like that Kari. What I'm saying is women who are in unhappy relationships are a simple fuck. When they talk to the other guy about their relationship and how unhappy they are, all he has to do is do what you say your husband isn't doing. That simple."

"It's not like that though."

"You may not think so, but think about it. What does he have to lose if this whole thing blows up? A good friend? Marvin is your husband. You have to divorce him, move out, move him out, and readjust your life."

I thought about what she was saying. Could Jonathon really be using me like that? Everything he said to me sounded so genuine and real. Even though I shouldn't believe him, I did. He said he would never lie to me, but was I naïve?

"Kari, all I'm saying is if you're going to do it, don't get used. Don't let him play you for his own selfish reasons. You better make sure that if this blows up, he has just as much to lose as you do."

After I got that off my chest, Jamie and I enjoyed our lunch, drinks, and then went back to my house. She had to pick up her kids and I wanted to go shopping, but I was too buzzed from the Hennessey to drive. I decided to go into the house and sleep it off before I went to the store.

After sleeping for a couple of hours, I freshened up and headed to the mall. I was glad I wouldn't be home when Marvin arrived. Our relationship seemed to be broken beyond repair and these days I would much rather be away from him than stay home and be miserable all day.

When I got home from shopping, Marvin, Jonathon, Carl, and Fred were watching TV and relaxing. I put my bags on the floor and closed the door behind me.

"Hi Kari," they greeted, when I walked in and sat my purse and keys down. Jonathon gave me a discreet smile to let me know he was happy to see me. I said hello to everybody and went upstairs

I hadn't been upstairs five minutes when I got a text from Jonathon.

**Where did you go?** It read.

I typed in, **Up to my room,** and sent the message. It was hard to ignore his messages while we were in the same location. After a few minutes my phone chimed again.

**Come back downstairs. I wanna look at you again.**

A smile spread across my face and I quickly forced it away. This was too close for comfort and I told Jonathon just that when I sent my reply.

He texted back

**I'm not gonna touch you, even though I want to. I just want to look at you.**

I read that text five times. He made everything sound sexy. Just the thought of his eyes on me sent chills all over my body. This man wanted me. I had never in my life been told by a man that he just wanted to look at me. That alone made me feel beautiful.

Before going back downstairs, I looked in the mirror to make sure my appearance was in check. It was hard to not pay attention to the way I walked knowing Jonathon's eyes were on me. After getting myself a bottle of water out of the refrigerator, I headed back upstairs. I made eye contact with Jonathon when I walked by. He was glaring at me, and biting his lip. He was looking at me like I was completely naked.

When I made it back upstairs to my room I had a message from Jonathon. It was only four words long. It said:

**I wanna fuck you.**

The juices started to flow between my legs. Jonathon had made me cum countless times only using his mouth. My mind raced as I imagined the things he could do to me with his dick. I squeezed my legs together to stop the tingling. I wanted him badly, but was too scared to go through with it.

I texted him back two words: **we can't.**

I put the phone on the nightstand and sat waiting for a reply. I knew he wouldn't be happy with my answer, but we'd already discussed this. My phone chimed.

**Just leave and go to my house. I'll leave like fifteen minutes**

later and meet you there.

I shook my head. Was that his game plan? For him to damn near follow me out of the house? He was just begging for us to get caught. He might as well just come upstairs, drag me downstairs by my hair, lay me on the living room table, and fuck me right there in front of my husband.

That's not happening. It's too obvious, I texted back. I waited for a reply and after a few minutes I heard footsteps coming up the stairs. I didn't know what to do. I couldn't believe he had the nerve to come upstairs to my bedroom.

"You left your bags downstairs," Marvin said bringing them into the room and setting them on the floor. I let out a sigh of relief.

"Thank you."

Marvin looked at me for a minute, then turned and went back downstairs. I put my hand on my chest and took a few breaths to calm myself down, then began putting my new clothes and purchases away. My phone chimed again.

Why are you doing this to me? His message read.

What are you talking about? I texted back. I tried not to wait for my phone to chime again, but I couldn't help it. After a few minutes it did.

I can't stop thinking about you and you act like you don't give a fuck.

I quickly replied back,

I'm married! You act like I can do something about that.

My phone chimed.

You did something about it the other night.

I had to think before I texted back.

I told you the other night was a mistake. It can't happen again.

This time it took him a few minutes to text back. I could hear them talking and laughing downstairs. I pictured Jonathon sitting on the couch texting me discreetly while talking to my husband. It was scary but sexy in a weird way.

I finally got a reply.

If it was a mistake why can't you stop thinking about me? I replied.

I never said I was thinking about you. He replied.

You didn't have to. You been avoiding me. You don't wanna be around me because you're scared.

I'm not scared. I just know it was a mistake that can't happen again. I texted back, defending myself.

Did it feel like a mistake? the text said, and I could almost hear him whispering it in my ear. It felt so good there was no way it could be a mistake. But I couldn't tell him that. I couldn't tell him that I thought about it every day, no matter what I was doing. I couldn't tell him that I fantasized about doing more with him. There was no way I could tell him that I touched myself, pretending it was him. That I moaned his name softly when I reached my orgasm. I couldn't tell him that stuff, there was no way.

I couldn't respond to Jonathon's text message because if I did, he would win. He sent a reply before I could.

See you can't even answer. You know what I did to you felt right and you know you wanna feel like that again. So let me do it for you. Just come see me tonight.

I didn't know what to do. My body was telling me hell yes, but my conscience said no. I was putting myself in a position I knew I wasn't prepared for if I said yes. My phone chimed again.

We don't have to do anything you don't wanna do. We won't even go to my room. I just wanna talk to you. I wanna be able to look at you and talk to you. Is that cool?

I still didn't respond. Jonathon had to know that all he had to do was get me over there and he could seduce me right out of my panties. My phone chimed again.

You can trust me baby. I won't make you do anything you don't want to do. I promise.

I finally texted back, Okay, and hit send before I had the chance to change my mind. I didn't know what the hell I was getting myself into. My phone chimed again.

Leave now and meet me at my house.

I texted back.

You said tonight.

My phone chimed again.

I don't want you trying to use the excuse that it's getting late. It's seven now, you'll be back at a decent hour if you leave now. And if you wait you have to come up with a lie about where you're going. Just trust me.

I hated when he told me to trust him because it always made me want to. I couldn't forget what Jamie had told me though, and I wasn't about to get used.

I went downstairs and grabbed my purse and keys off the counter where I'd left them. I was trying my best not to make eye contact with Jonathon, and I was almost out the door when Marvin called my name.

"Where are you going?" he asked, barely looking at me.

"I'm bored, I'm going out for a while," I said easily.

"If you're bored you can come downstairs. You don't have to stay locked up in the bedroom."

"It's just nothing about Sports Center really interests me. Sorry I'm a woman."

I rolled my eyes and left the house. Marvin should have just let me leave. He got on my nerves always treating me like a toddler. I knew I could come downstairs if I wanted to, it was my house.

I left and headed for Jonathon's house. I couldn't believe what I was doing. I knew the best thing for me to do would be to turn around and go back home to my husband, but I had convinced myself I was just going to talk to Jonathon. I could control myself, and if things got out of hand, I would just leave.

I pulled into Jonathon's apartment complex and parked a few buildings down from him. It was already too risky for me to be parked in his complex in broad daylight and I wasn't about to be stupid enough to park right in front of his apartment. I turned my car off and waited patiently for Jonathon to pull up. After about twenty minutes he rolled right by me not even noticing my car. He called me a few minutes later.

"Where are you?"

"I'm coming," I said getting out of my car. "I parked down a few buildings. It is the middle of the day."

"True. Well my door is open so just come in."

I ended the call and walked quickly to his apartment. It felt like someone's eyes were on me and I was scared somebody that knew Marvin would see me. When I made it to Jonathon's apartment, he was in the living room waiting for me.

"I'm glad you came," he said with a sexy grin on his face. I dropped my purse on his table.

"I only came to talk. You said you wanted to talk to me."

"I do."

"About what?"

"About why you been ignoring my calls and text messages."

"You know why Jonathon."

"Come here and sit down."

Slowly I walked over and sat down next to Jonathon. He looked at me for a minute before he started talking.

"I never expected you to show up at my door Kari. I wanted you to, but I never expected it."

"I shouldn't have come over here that night. I told you that was a mistake."

"I don't know why you keep saying that when you know you liked what I did to you."

"That's not the point, Jonathon. I am married, and Marvin is your friend! How can you act like that doesn't matter?"

"Because to me it doesn't, and I know that's fucked up, but I want you Kari. I don't think you really understand that."

"What am I supposed to say to that?"

Jonathon touched my face and ran his fingers along my lips. The heat in my body started to rise.

"I told you before Kari. Whatever happens between us, whatever we say or whatever we do, that's between us. Nobody is gonna ever find out."

I shook my head slowly and took a deep breath.

"I can't do this with you. You are his friend. That's wrong."

"So what you want me to do? Stop talking to him? Because I will. If that means you'll let me touch you like I want to I won't be friends with him anymore."

"No, you can't stop being his friend Jonathon, you have to stop this with me. You have to stop talking to me."

"I'm not gonna stop talking to you Kari."

"Why not?"

"Because I like the way you make me feel. I get turned on by just looking at you. I like talking to you. I don't know. I can't explain it, it's just a feeling I never felt before."

He ran his fingers through my hair and down my neck. A chill ran up my spine the way it always did when he touched me.

"I'm telling you baby, Marvin just don't know what he got," he said softly. "I would never treat you the way he treats you."

I could feel his breath on my neck and he kissed me gently. I was frozen.

"I know what you're doing to me Jonathon," I whispered. I was scared if I spoke too loudly I would let out a sound of pleasure.

"What am I doing to you baby?"

I opened my mouth to answer him, but my breath caught in my throat when he ran his tongue along the nape of my neck. It was time to go, things were starting to go too far.

I tried to move and get up, but Jonathon wouldn't let me. He continued to kiss and lick my neck as his hands started to explore my body. First my collarbone and shoulders, then his warm hands traveled onto my breasts.

"Stop Jonathon. You said you wouldn't make me do anything-"

"That you didn't want to do," he finished. "You don't want this baby?" he asked putting my hand between his legs. His dick was hard.

"I can't do this... I can't," I moaned.

"Nobody is gonna know but me and you," he whispered.

He kissed my lips and slipped his tongue in my mouth. I still had my hand on his dick and he put it inside his pants and wrapped my hand around it. He continued to kiss me and put his hand up my shirt.

"You have to let me leave. We can't do this," I whispered getting more scared.

"Stop fighting me baby, please. Nobody is gonna catch us. Nobody is gonna find out. Just do what you want to do."

Jonathon pulled my shirt up over my head and I knew I was fighting a battle I had already lost when I opened his front door. He laid me down on the couch and straddled me. He expertly took my lace bra off and started sucking my nipples. I could feel them growing hard under his tongue. He licked a trail down my belly and unbuttoned my pants. I lifted my hips and he pulled them down, stopping only to unhook my sandals. I lay on his couch wearing red lace panties.

Jonathon looked down at me and ran his hand up and down my body. He squeezed my breasts, then put his hand down in my panties. I moaned in my throat when his fingers began to play with my clit.

"You like that baby?"

85

I nodded my head and as soon as I did, Jonathon slipped a finger inside.

"That pussy is getting so wet. See, aint it always better when you stop fighting me?" he asked fingering me. I nodded my head again.

"You gonna let me put this dick inside you baby?" he asked, leaning down and whispering in my ear. I nodded my head again. He was making me feel so good with his fingers, I couldn't wait to feel his dick. There was no turning back, I had already crossed the line.

Jonathon took his fingers out of me and left the room. My coochie was tingling from the finger fucking he had just given me and I wanted more. He returned with a gold package and climbed back on top of me.

"I told you you don't have to worry about nothing," he said sliding off my panties. He threw them on the floor and covered his body with mine.

"Take off your clothes," I said, finally finding my voice. He smiled and climbed off me again. I bit my lip in anticipation as I watched him remove all of his clothes. When he pulled off his drawers, his dick jumped out and pointed straight at me. He mounted me and I could feel his throbbing dick on my leg.

"What you want me to do now baby? I like when you give me orders," he said kissing my neck again.

"I want to feel you inside of me."

He smiled. I closed my eyes as I heard the wrapper tear. After a few moments, Jonathon opened my legs wide and I could feel his dick at my opening. I opened my eyes and he was looking down on me with this sexy smirk on his face. When he entered me, he closed his eyes and let out a low moan.

"You feel so good baby," he said stroking in and out of me. I grinded into him, closing my eyes. He felt so good inside me that I forgot about feeling guilty. What he was doing to me didn't feel wrong at all, but I didn't have to tell him this time. I was showing him every time I brought my pussy down matching his thrusts. I pulled him down and kissed him this time putting my tongue in his mouth. He sucked on it gently and kissed me in the same rhythm that we were fucking. I was so turned on that I could hear my juices gushing every time he went inside of me.

"God damn baby! This pussy good as hell!" he said, slowing

his pace to keep from exploding. He pulled out of me and turned me over on the couch so that I was on my hands and knees. He entered me slowly from behind. I threw my pussy back at him and fucked him like my life depended on getting him off. Jonathon grabbed my shoulders and went deeper inside of me and I let out a shriek with every stroke. This man was working me so good I was losing my mind. He grabbed my hair and pulled my head back and kissed me, never stopping his stroke. He let out moans as he kissed me, sucking on my bottom lip.

"Ooh Kari... Damn baby! This pussy is so damn good! You gonna make me cum."

Jonathon slapped my ass and the pain and pleasure felt so good. I could feel my orgasm coming. I held on to the arm of the couch and threw it back at him some more.

"Go deeper baby. You gon make me cum, fuck me harder," I pleaded. I could feel the pleasure creeping up; I was almost there. Jonathon grabbed my shoulder again and matched my thrusts hitting the bottom of my pussy. I yelled aloud in ecstasy as he continued to fuck me. He pumped a few more times before he, too, reached his climax. He fell on top of me on the couch and we both lay there for a minute, too exhausted to move. Jonathon got up after a few minutes to get rid of the condom and I turned over and lay on my back. My body was covered in sweat, my hair stuck to my face and back. Jonathon came back with a glass of water and lay back on top of me still naked.

"Don't you stay away from me that long again," he said with his eyes closed.

"You know why I stayed away."

"And you know that was some bullshit. What we did last time was not a mistake and what we did this time was not a mistake. You are not a mistake so don't let me hear you say that again."

I didn't know how to respond.

"Don't ignore my calls and texts either."

"I'm married Jonathon, what do you want me to do?"

"Make time for me, that's what I want. I wanna be able to have you to myself just like this."

# CHAPTER 12

After I had sex with Jonathon for the first time, I couldn't get enough; I was addicted. We met up anywhere, at any time, whenever we could. Whether it was in the parking lot of a department store in the middle of the night, or a hotel room, I didn't care. If he wanted to see me I was there, and vice versa. And the sex was damn good! That man had me damn near crawling up walls when I was with him. I felt so inexperienced at times, but it didn't matter to Jonathon. He was always happy to teach me and that made me want him more. He never caused me to feel inferior or stupid. He liked me for who I was, not for what he wanted me to be.

I was in the house packing up some clothes to take to the Salvation Army when I got a phone call from him. Every time his number popped up on my cell phone screen, I got excited.

"Hello?"

"Hey baby, can you talk?" he asked.

"Yeah, I can. How are you?"

"I miss you. Why you making me wait this long to see you again?"

"Because I told you Marvin is starting to get suspicious. I mean he doesn't know it's you, but he suspects I'm having an affair with somebody."

"I just wanna see you for a second. Just come give me a kiss."

"I can't," I said almost sure he could hear my smile over the phone.

"So what are you doing for Valentine's Day?"

"You know I'm going to be with Marvin on Valentine's Day."

"Well can you sneak away, I got somethin' special planned for you."

"Jonathon, you know I can't. Valentine's Day too? Are you trying to get us caught?"

"Can you try? I just wanna spend a little bit of Valentine's Day with you."

I smiled again. I swear this man made my jaws hurt from smiling so much.

"Okay, I will try baby, I promise. I miss you too."

"You lyin'. If you missed me you would come see me right now. Come and sit on Daddy's lap."

"You know how bad I wanna come, but we gotta slow down. If we keep up the way we been doin', Marvin is going to figure it out. He's smart as hell and when he gets to snoopin', he won't stop until he finds something."

"I don't want you worryin' about that. If he ever does find out, I'll handle everything. You just pack your bags and head on over to my house."

I laughed. He was always making jokes about me leaving Marvin, but I never took him seriously. I knew his kind. He was a player; he always made his woman feel like she was the only one he wanted to be with, even though she wasn't.

"Yeah I'll be there."

"You know I'm serious don't you?"

"Jonathon Marvin is not going to find out."

"So you are gonna come see me on Valentine's Day right?"

"I said I would think about it Jonathon. I'll let you know."

"Alright baby. Text me later when you get a chance."

"I will."

I ended the call and continued tugging the garbage bags full of clothes down the stairs. There was something about being wanted that always put a smile on a woman's face, and nothing could get me down that day.


Later, I got a call from Marvin while lying on the couch watching a movie.

"Kari, I'm working late tonight so don't wait up."

"I thought you said you were done with that deal and you would have more time off."

"Well something came up and I have to do some extra work. I'll be home as soon as I can."

"Okay."

Marvin hung up and I was left alone in the house once again. Staring at my phone, I tried to stop myself from doing what I was about to do. I had an itch that needed scratching and only Jonathon could do it. I opened a new text message and sent him a text.

Marvin is working late again.

A reply came within the next couple of minutes.

Come over for a little while and keep me company.

That was all I needed to see. I texted Jonathon back and told him I was on my way, then threw on some jeans and a hoodie. It was cold outside and although staying home and lying underneath my warm covers sounded tempting, lying underneath Jonathon outweighed that.

About fifteen minutes later I pulled into his apartment complex and he met me at the door. He was wearing a pair of sweatpants, no shirt. His body was cut and muscular, and a tattoo of a cross with a crown adorned his chest. He gave me a kiss on the lips.

"What's up baby?"

"Hey," I said setting my purse on the counter. After taking off my shoes, I followed Jonathon into the living room. The TV was on Sports Center, but he was focused more on the work he was doing on his laptop.

"You can turn it if you want to," he said handing me the remote without ever taking his eyes off of the computer screen. I grabbed it and browsed the menu before I turned to a Lifetime movie. Jonathon laughed and shook his head.

"What's so funny?"

"I knew you was gonna turn it to some sentimental show. Watch you gon be cryin' in 10 minutes."

"I won't," I said laughing and slapping him playfully on the arm. "Just keep working on your computer, don't worry about me. What are you doing anyway?"

"I'm tryna decide what logo to use for my company. Wanna help me pick?"

Excited, I nodded my head. He put his arm around me and I lay on his chest looking at the computer screen.

"Okay, first is this one," he said pulling up the screen. It was a small animation of a hand holding a cell phone which displayed the words Bradshaw Innovative Designs.

"I thought this was cool since the world is so technology based," he explained. "Everybody does everything on their cell phones. This logo shows that my company is up to date with the changing world and its technology. I just hate that it's so basic."

I nodded my head as he pulled up the second design. It was a laptop computer and the words Bradshaw Innovative Designs jumped out of the computer screen.

"This one is different, but might be a little too much. I really want to work on it more, make it a little less three-dimensional."

"Or make the other one a little more three-dimensional and see how that comes out."

This time Jonathon nodded his head.

"I'm proud of you. Your business will be big in no time."

"I hope so. I can't go back to working for a company. The hours are too long and the pay isn't as good. I like having control of what I do and when I do it," he said.

"At least you have something to do."

"What you mean?"

"Everybody around me is so successful, or has plans to be. I'm just stuck. Marvin won't let me do anything."

"You can do whatever the fuck you want. Don't wait on no nigga to give you the okay. Not Marvin or nobody else. Don't let him keep you stuck under his money. You too good for that."

Jonathon wasn't focused on the computer anymore, he was looking right at me. He put his computer on the table and faced me.

"What do you wanna do? What would make you happy? Tell me more about your dreams."

I told Jonathon all about how I loved cooking and wanted to start my own catering company, even have a cookbook and a show on TV. I also told him how I wanted to have kids and raise them with knowledge about business and how to run one. He never once interrupted or told me I sounded stupid. He just listened to me talk about my dreams and encouraged me to make them come true with or without Marvin.

92

After we talked we watched a little TV. Then I felt his hands start to roam my body. His hands squeezed my butt and I could feel his dick growing through his sweat pants. Feeling his erection on my stomach got me excited and I could feel the heat through my jeans. I pulled off his shorts and stared at his hard dick. Licking my lips I took his length in my mouth and he moaned in delight. He grew in my mouth. My head bobbed up and down. He looked into my eyes and bit his lip. Holding my breath I took all of him into my mouth until my lips were touching his stomach. I could feel him hitting the back of my throat. We locked eyes again and he moaned aloud, ecstasy evident on his face. I came back up, running my lips along his shaft.

Jonathon pulled his dick out of my mouth. And I smiled. He was ready to explode, but he would never do so without making sure I came first.

Jonathon sat up and pulled me up too. He took off my jeans, then panties and I stood there naked from the waist down. He pulled me onto his face and went to work on my pussy.

"Mmhmm," I moaned as he sucked on my clit. My sweet nectar ran, and Jonathon lapped it up before it even had a chance to fall.

I squealed in delight when he slid his tongue into my coochie and fucked me with it like it was a dick. The rhythm of my hips followed perfectly with his mouth. My orgasm was building.

"Oh yes baby!" I said as it got closer. He pulled me off of his face before I had a chance to cum. My wetness glowed on his beard and mustache.

"I don't want you to cum yet. I want you to cum on this dick."

Jonathon handed me a condom. I took off my shirt, put the condom on him, then climbed on. Even though I didn't like to ride, Jonathon did. He took off my bra as I bounced up and down. I closed my eyes and bit my lip as I rode to get that good feeling he always gave me. He grabbed my hips and thrust inside of me and I came instantly.

Jonathon reached his orgasm, his eyes closed and face sexily distorted. My eyes closed and I fell into a light slumber. I didn't wake up until he finally moved and put his hand on my bare back.

"What time do you have to leave?" he asked.

"I don't know. Marvin said he was working late, but he didn't say what time he was going to be home."

Jonathon laughed.

"What's so funny?" I asked, finally opening my eyes.

"Why do you talk like that?"

"What are you talking about?"

"Why do you try so hard to talk proper?"

"What do you mean try so hard?"

"I mean, when we sit and talk regular you try to talk all proper. But when we have sex or you get mad all that proper shit goes out the window. I thought you were from Swartz Creek?"

"Marvin says I talk ghetto. He hates to take me around his friends because I embarrass him," I said avoiding the question about my past.

"How does that make you feel?" Jonathon asked, grabbing my hand and intertwining our fingers. I shrugged my shoulders.

"I don't know. It used to hurt my feelings, but I'm used to it now."

"Well you don't have to talk like that around me. I just want you to be comfortable and be yourself."

I didn't answer. I just lay there and listened to his heartbeat. I didn't know what it was about him, but he made me happy.

"Did you hear what I said?"

"Yeah I hear you."

"Why didn't you say anything?"

"Because if you really knew me you wouldn't say that."

"You don't know what I would say."

"Just trust me."

Jonathon lifted me up so that I was looking into his eyes.

"What is it that I don't know about you? Tell me."

I shook my head.

"Kari I don't think anything you tell me could make me want to stop fucking with you."

"Well we still have to lay low. I don't want Marvin to get more suspicious."

Jonathon kissed me.

"Just do what I tell you to do baby. We won't get caught."

I stayed at Jonathon's house all day and left around six thirty. I didn't know what time Marvin was coming home, and I really needed to beat him there. He had been questioning me too much about where I'd been and what I'd been doing. I wasn't prepared to have him breathing down my neck.

I got home and Marvin's car still wasn't there. I took another shower and went downstairs to start dinner. I knew Marvin would not be happy that dinner was not ready when he got home so I tried to put together something quick. Marvin got home not even an hour after I made it home.

"Hey Marvin, how was work?" I asked over my shoulder.

"Fine. Is dinner ready?"

"Not yet, it will be in about twenty minutes."

"So you been home all day and I still gotta wait for my dinner?"

"I fell asleep."

Marvin shook his head.

"You worthless, you know that. You sit here all damn day long and I go out and bust my ass. The least you can do is have dinner ready when I get home."

"And I usually do, but today I fell asleep," I snapped getting annoyed.

Marvin threw his briefcase on the table and I dropped the fork I was holding.

"I'm so tired of your fucking mouth," he said loosening his tie. It was obvious he had a bad day at work, but I was tired of him coming home and taking it out on me.

"Then why don't you find something else to eat," I said taking the skillet off the stove and turning off the heat. I walked past him and snatched away when he tried to grab my arm.

"Kari, get your ass down here and finish cooking."

"Fuck you!" I yelled storming upstairs. I went into the bedroom and locked the door. Marvin needed to stay away from me for the rest of the night. He was not stepping foot in the bedroom. I didn't care where he slept or what he wore to bed. I could feel myself getting fed up and I knew it wouldn't be long before I was ready to walk away.

# CHAPTER 13

The more Marvin buried himself into work, the more I buried myself into Jonathon. My sexual relationship with him quickly turned into a full blown love affair. I found myself falling for him. When we were apart I missed him; I spent the whole day checking my phone so I wouldn't miss any calls or texts from him. When we first started messing around it started out being all about sex, but the more time we spent together, the more we talked, and the more we enjoyed each other's company. Things with him quickly turned emotional before I realized.

I wasn't aware how real my feelings for Jonathon were until Valentine's Day. A nice intimate dinner was waiting for my husband. Things still weren't going well with us, but I was going to try to make it work. Jonathon and I had made plans to get together later that night and he had been texting me to confirm everything was still a go.

I'll c u @ 9, the text message read. Quickly, I closed my phone and threw it back in my purse. I flipped through my CD collection for the perfect music. It had to be soft, sweet and slow. I put the Sade CD in and let it play.

Everything was ready. Candles were lit throughout the house, the music was playing, and on the stove: steak, shrimp, steamed vegetables and rice, red wine, and for dessert, my world famous peach cobbler.

Walking into the bathroom, I took one final look at myself. My brown skin seemed to glow from the cocoa butter I'd put on.

My makeup was flawless, and Manuel had my hair flowing in big curls down my back. My little black dress hugged my body just right, and I was sure my husband would be pleased.

After pouring myself a glass of Merlot, I sat at the table and waited for all of twenty minutes before I heard his keys at the door. I jumped up and met him.

"Happy Valentine's Day!" I said excited. I wrapped my arms around him and kissed his lips. Things between us hadn't been good, but it was Valentine's Day and I wanted to try to enjoy my husband.

"Hey Kari," he said walking past me. "Why is it so dark in here?"

"Wait, come sit down," I said grabbing his hand and leading him to the table. He took off his coat and reluctantly sat at the table.

"I cooked dinner."

"I appreciate that Kari, but I'm really tired."

"It's Valentine's Day, Marvin," I said getting annoyed. Any other day he was pissed if dinner wasn't ready.

"Business still goes on, babe."

"So I did all this and you're not going to eat?"

Marvin exhaled hard. As he loosened his tie,

I couldn't help but give him an evil look. I mean, it was fuckin' Valentine's Day. You would think after seven years of marriage I deserved at least an evening, just a few hours of his time. It was really sad that I was sitting in the room with my husband and I still felt lonely.

After fixing our plates, I sat down with Marvin at the table. He poured himself a glass of wine. As we ate, all you could hear was Sade's mellow voice. Neither of us said anything. After seven years we had nothing to talk about.

"So how is everything at work?" I asked in an attempt to make conversation.

"Same. It's still pretty slow, but the few jobs we have are pretty intense."

There was another long pause. I swear, talking to him was pulling teeth, not easy like it used to be.

"The food is excellent, Kari."

"Thank you."

We finished our meal in silence. When he was finished he got up and put his plate in the sink.

"I made dessert," I said hoping he would sit back down.

"I'm going to hop in the shower. Maybe I'll have some later."

I rolled my eyes as he reached in his pocket. He pulled out a long, slim box and set it in front of me on the table.

"I didn't forget, baby. Happy Valentine's Day."

He kissed the top of my head and left the room. It was always like this. He probably felt if he bought me something I wouldn't want his time and attention. He was so predictable.

After staring at the box, I finally opened it and there lay a diamond tennis bracelet. It was beautiful and I loved it. As a matter of fact, I loved it just as much as I did when he'd given me the same one two years ago. Instantly, I was enraged. Nothing he did for me meant anything. We were going through the motions. I closed the box and left it sitting on the table. There was no use of me wallowing in sadness. Nothing would change anyway.

The slow music came to a halt when I cut it off and blew out all the candles before putting on my coat and grabbing my purse. My exposed legs were freezing from the cold weather, but I didn't care. Getting out of that house was my only priority. I let my car warm up, and then sped away. A lone tear slipped out of my eye as I watched our house fade from view in my rearview mirror.


Jonathon opened the suite door and scooped me up in his arms. He began showering me with kisses all over my face and neck before I could even say hi. I couldn't help but notice the three dozens of red roses, and basket of all of my favorite things on the dresser. He sat me on the bed next to a huge teddy bear that held a heart with the words, I love you.

"Happy Valentine's Day baby," he said kissing me once more and handing me a card. A huge smile spread across my face.

"My life has been so much brighter since the day I met you," I read aloud. "Your smile, your laughter and everything about you makes me so lucky to have you in my life. Happy Valentine's Day."

I tried to stop the tears from falling from my eyes, but it was too late. Before they had a chance to grace my cheeks, Jonathon wiped them away.

"Don't cry baby. You're too beautiful to cry."

"Thank you."

"I love the red highlights in your hair. When did you get that done?"

"Today. Marvin didn't even notice."

"Of course he didn't. He doesn't deserve you Kari."

"Thank you for everything Jonathon. You always know how to make me feel special."

"I got you something too," I said smiling eagerly.

"You did?"

"Yeah, but I left it in the car. Let me go get it."

"Hold on," Jonathon said grabbing my arm. "I have something else for you."

Jonathon pulled out a small box and opened it. Inside was the most beautiful diamond ring I had ever seen.

"Jonathon," I gasped. "It's beautiful!"

"I knew you would like it."

"I do, but you know I can't keep this."

"Yes, you can."

"Let me go get your gift," I said trying to leave.

"I don't care about that gift Kari. There is one gift you can give me to make this day special."

"What?"

"You. Leave Marvin and marry me."

I looked at Jonathon in awe. He couldn't be serious.

"I can't do that Jonathon, I can't marry you."

"Why not?"

"Because you're Marvin's friend."

"Kari, I don't know what you think been going on here, but it's not just fun anymore. This is serious, what we have is serious. I'm not playin' fuckin' games no more. I'm tired of always having to hide you and stay in the house. I love you and we gotta do somethin' about that."

My legs started shaking I was so nervous. I knew I loved him and I thought he might love me, but I never thought he would take it to this level.

"Let me go to the car and get your gift," I said getting off the bed.

"Stop tryna leave this fuckin' hotel room Kari. I want you to sit down and talk to me." He grabbed my arm and pulled me back on the bed.

"So what, I'm alone in this? You think this shit is just all fun and games?"

"That's not what I'm saying. But you are asking me to walk away from the man I have been married to for seven years!"

"You still love him?"

"Why are we still talking about him?"

"I didn't talk about him, you brought him up."

"Why are you doin' this today? Can we please just enjoy tonight? Why you wanna piss me off too?"

"I'm pissin' you off because I'm tellin' you I wanna be with you?"

"No, you pissin' me off because you are expecting me to react to this right away. I just need time to think about everything."

"And I'm just supposed to sit here and wait for you to think about whether or not you gonna keep goin' home to him?"

"Okay if this is what today is gonna be about I can spend Valentine's Day by my damn self," I said getting off the bed and grabbing my purse. I was fed up with the bullshit.

"Then get the fuck on then Kari, cuz you like being treated like you aint shit. So stay with that muthafucka."

I slammed the hotel room door. Jonathon was helping ruin my Valentine's Day and I couldn't believe it.

The car ran for a while before I took off. I drove for a minute with no real destination. Home definitely wasn't an option.

My phone rang fifteen minutes after I left the hotel. Jonathon's number popped up, but I ignored him. I didn't have time for his whining.

Jonathon called right back and I knew he would keep calling until I answered because he thought I was going home to Marvin.

"Why the fuck are you calling me?" I answered.

"I don't give a fuck about yo attitude Kari. I know you better bring your ass back to this hotel room."

"Fuck you Jonathon, because I don't need you."

He didn't say anything and I knew I was pissing him off more.

"Like I said, bring your ass back to this hotel before you piss me off more."

He hung up before I had a chance to respond, driving a while longer until I realized I had nowhere to go. I stayed put a little while longer just to piss him off then made my way back to the hotel. Jonathon opened the door and let me in without saying anything. I put my purse back on the nightstand where it had been before and sat down. Silence consumed us as we stood watching each other.

"Did you call me back here to just look at me?" I asked, irritated.

"Maybe."

Jonathon came and stood over me. He pushed me back on the bed and got on top of me.

"Do you love me?"

I nodded my head and he kissed me. We didn't say anything else. We undressed each other and started making love. Jonathon and I might have disagreed about where we were headed, but sex was always the one thing we agreed on and we were both fine with that.

# CHAPTER 14

I didn't go home the next morning until I was sure Marvin was at work. Jonathon had put my body in so many different positions that I couldn't even walk straight. If Marvin was home when I walked in the house he would definitely know I had been doing something, I needed to soak in the hot tub and get my body right before Marvin came home.

After letting my body soak for an hour, I lay down to take a nap. Jonathon didn't let me get much sleep the night before and I was exhausted. I was just getting into a good deep sleep when my phone started ringing.

"Hello?" I answered, confused, because I didn't recognize the number.

"Hey Kari, how are you?" an unfamiliar voice said in my ear.

"I'm fine. Who is this?" I asked regretting I answered.

"Tara, from Applebee's."

"Oh, hey girl, what's going on?" I said wiping my eyes and trying my best to keep the sun out of them.

"Hey look, I know we're not really friends like that or anything, but I just thought you might want to know what's going on."

"Tara, what are you talking about?" I asked sitting up and opening my eyes wide.

"My guy friend took me out to Red Lobster last night for Valentine's Day and I saw your husband there with another woman."

"Are you sure it was him?"

"I'm sure. I worked the evening shift yesterday and my friend took me out right after work. It was around nine maybe. I'm really not the type to start anything, but I would want to know if it was me."

"No thank you for telling me."

"I'm really sorry Kari, and I'm here for you if you ever need anything."

"Thank you Tara."

I ended the call and sat in the bed staring at my phone. I wasn't surprised Marvin was cheating, he'd done it before. But for him to take her out on Valentine's Day in public meant things were far more serious than a quick fuck. He didn't have any time to spend with me, but he had time to take somebody else out to dinner.

I got out of bed knowing I would be unable to fall back asleep. This had happened too many times to count. There were constantly calls from women in the past and I couldn't count how many text messages and emails I'd found from others.

After much thought I pulled my suitcase set out of the closet. If Marvin didn't give me the answers I wanted about Red Lobster, I was through. Someone else wanted to be with me and I deserved more than Marvin was giving. I had been through too much.

Marvin got home late again that night. It was almost nine when he walked through the door and I was sitting in the living room with the TV on waiting for him. I turned it off as soon as I heard his briefcase hit the floor.

"Marvin, come here."

I waited and after a few moments he came into the living room. He stood there looking uninterested in me and whatever I had to say. That pissed me off more.

"Where did you go last night?" I asked.

"Where did I go? You stayed out all night last night. Where did you go?"

"Who the fuck did you take to Red Lobster last night Marvin."

He wasn't expecting me to ask that question and the look on

his face told me so.

"I didn't go to Red Lobster last night."

"You lyin' Marvin, you fuckin' lyin to me again."

"How the hell can you question me when you didn't come home last night?"

"Come home to what? To you ignoring me and the nice night I tried to put together for us?"

"I told you I was tired Kari."

"Yeah and you sure didn't want dessert." I got up and walked over to Marvin making sure I was face to face with him and looking him in the eye.

"You can stop lying to me Marvin because I already know the answer. So I am gonna ask you one more time: Did you go out to dinner at Red Lobster with a woman last night?"

"Yeah Kari, I did. I went out to dinner with a coworker. It was business."

I laughed right in his face.

"You must think I'm stupid Marvin. A business dinner on Valentine's Day?"

"Yeah. And how would you know if I'm lying Kari? How many businesses have you worked for? You don't talk to me about anything unless it's cleaning this house and what to cook for dinner. You let me worry about everything else."

"I'm so tired of you talkin' down on me just because you have a job and I don't. I asked you can I have a job, you said no, then you wanna belittle me every day for not having one."

"Because you would never make it in the corporate world and I'm trying to spare your feelings. You can't even talk right. You went to a public school and you don't know shit! You should be thanking me for not letting you make a fool of yourself."

My legs started shaking and I tried to fight back tears. I couldn't believe the man I had been married to all these years thought so little of me. I didn't say anything more. He thought he was so much better than me and I was tired. I took off my wedding ring and threw it as hard as I could at his chest. I wanted to slap the shit out of him, but his pathetic ass wasn't worth it. He didn't say anything as I went upstairs and packed my suitcases, taking everything I knew I would need down to my cleaning supplies and makeup. I tugged the suitcases downstairs and past Marvin without even looking at him.

I checked into the Holiday Inn just in time to catch one of my favorite movies on the television. As I lay back in the bed I couldn't help but feel relaxed. I now had time to think with a clear mind.

Later that evening I got bored and decided to go get a drink. After straightening my hair, I put on some skinny jeans and a sexy red top. My six inch, red stilettos clicked when I walked, introducing me before I entered a room. My confidence was high as I made my way to the bar; I knew I looked good. It felt kind of weird going out by myself, but I didn't care.

Sitting at the bar relaxing, I sipped my apple martini. The music was nice and mellow, and the bar wasn't very crowded. As I looked around I realized how out of place I was. Everyone was either young or in a company or crowd. No one was alone, and all of a sudden I didn't want to be either. I pulled out my phone and called Kevin. He was off work by now and if he wasn't out on a date or at the gym, I knew he was available.

"Yo!" Kevin answered.

"Where are you?" I asked, smiling just from the sound of my brother's voice.

"At home on the toilet checking my email."

"Ugh! Too much information!" I laughed. "Well wipe your ass, jump in the car, and come up to *Buffalo Wild Wings*."

"Tonight? Kari, why do you always have to be last minute?"

"I don't know Kevin, but you aint doin nothing else! Now get up, wipe your ass and come get drunk!" I said as loud as I could without being noticed.

"Who's the big brother Kari?"

"You."

"I'm on my way."

Kevin arrived about twenty minutes later looking handsome. He had the whole casual businessman thing happening with a nice pair of black slacks, a button up shirt, and dress shoes. We looked alike. We were both brown skinned with light brown eyes and light brown hair, his was cut real short.

Kevin pulled me up out of my seat and gave me a big bear

hug. We were so happy to see each other. We were inseparable and now that we had different schedules, it was hard to link up, so when we did we were grateful.

"What's up little one?" he asked, joining me at the bar. He put in an order for a Corona.

"I just wanted to get out. Tired of being all cooped up. I'm so happy to see you."

"Me too. You're looking beautiful lil sis. I see Imma have to kill a nigga out here."

"Kevin stop, I hate it when you talk like that," I pouted.

"Just making sure you know. So tell me what's up. What's goin' on with you?"

"Kevin it's a crazy situation to be in. Things haven't been right for a long time. Part of me is tired of fighting and part of me thinks it may be worth it this time. I just have other people..."

I stopped and cleared my throat. I couldn't slip up and tell him about Jonathon.

"...I have other things in my life that I'm trying to pursue. I can't have him and the negativity of that relationship holding me back."

"I understand, but I believe in you. You'll figure it out little one. We've been through a lot...a whole lot. You always bounce back. You manage to do it even better than me. "

"Yeah, but Kevin I'm not all that strong. People lose their parents every day. "

"Yeah, but you need to talk about it," he said softly. "Kari, it was —"

"I don't want to talk about it."

"Kari, it's been twenty years since the fire. We need to talk about it."

"Kevin I love you to death, I do. On November 20th, I will go to the cemetery with you just like I do every other year, but I won't talk about the fire with you. Not now or ever again."

Kevin quickly dropped the issue. He knew I didn't want to talk about the fire. It was too painful. It had been twenty years, but I could still remember everything about that night no matter how I'd tried to block it out of my mind. All I had left were memories and pictures that I kept locked in a box in my basement that no one would ever find. That is what hurt the most.

My phone rang and Jonathon's number popped up on my caller ID. Immediately I got chills all over my body.

"Kari," Kevin said waving his hand in my face.

"Huh?"

"I been calling your name for ten minutes. You're not mad at me are you?"

I cracked a smile.

"I could never be mad at you Kevin. You know that. Just don't bring it up again."

"I know. I won't."

I took a sip of my apple martini.

"So where is Jayla? You haven't talked about her much lately."

"Jayla and I are taking a break."

"A break? You've been with her four years and all of a sudden you're taking a break."

"She gave me an ultimatum."

"Which was?"

"Marry her or move on."

"So are you moving on?"

"I don't know. I really think she's the one Kari. I really do."

"Then what is the problem?"

"I don't know. I just don't think I can make that kind of commitment. I mean, think about it Kari, we've lost a lot. A lot. I don't want to lose anything else. What if something happens, what if something goes wrong?"

"Then you get through it. Kevin, you can't live your life running from good things because you're scared of failure. Yeah, sometimes you will fail. But that's when you learn, and that's when you get up, dust yourself off, and try again."

"I don't know Kari," he said shaking his head. "That's a huge step."

"Kevin, your love for her should be stronger than any doubt, fear or anything else. That's what should make it worth the risk. I know you love her Kevin. I know you do. Don't let fear drive a good woman away."

"I understand what you're saying Kari, but I just need to think about this."

"Okay. But really think about it big brother. I want your happiness. That's what's important to me. So no matter what you decide I will be there for you and love you anyway."

"I know you will. That's why I love you so much Kari. You're the best person I ever had in my whole life."

Kevin and I hugged and had to stop ourselves from sharing a too emotional moment in the bar. We had been through so much together and I knew that he would go to the grave before he let anyone hurt me. It takes a lot to be able to trust someone with your life, but I trusted him with that and everything in between.

We had a few drinks and talked for a couple of hours. It felt so good to be in his presence. Being around him made me forget about my problems. Jonathon and Marvin were put on pause in my mind while my brother was present. He deserved all of my attention and that was exactly what I was going to give him.

When we left the bar, Kevin walked me to my car. Once he made sure I was safely in and my engine was running, he leaned his head into my window and gave me a kiss.

"I love you little one. Call me when you make it to your hotel room."

"I will Kevin. I love you more."

Kevin left me alone in my car and my mind raced back to Jonathon and Marvin

I didn't expect to stay that long at the bar with Kevin, but we had a lot of catching up to do. It was good seeing him and it did help me feel better.

I picked up the phone and returned Jonathon's phone call.

"Hello?" he answered.

"Hey baby."

He laughed.

"What's up baby? I just called you."

"I know, I'm sorry I missed your call."

"It's cool. But I been waiting on you to call me all day."

"I know."

"So why didn't you call?"

"It's just been a lot goin' on. I'm staying at a hotel."

"A hotel? What's goin' on? Marvin didn't find out did he?"

"No, it's not that. Some other stuff," I said, turning the radio down since the conversation seemed to be getting intense.

"Kari, you know where I'm staying. You could have stopped by or at least left me a text message and let me know what's going on."

"I just didn't want to call anybody. I just want to be by myself."

There was a long pause.

"Alright Kari."

"Alright what Jonathon?"

"Nothin' Kari, I'm just gonna call you back after while."

"Are you mad?"

"Nah I'm not mad I'm just gonna call you back."

I ended the call and turned up the radio. I didn't understand what everybody wanted from me. I was spending time with my brother and I wasn't obligated to answer my phone.

I drove back to the hotel with soft jazz playing. Once I realized what I was listening to, I rolled down my window and threw the CD out. Marvin liked jazz, and there was no way I was letting him invade my life anymore. I listened to hip hop the rest of the way there.

When I got back to the hotel I decided to take a long hot bath. I put the do not disturb sign on the door and cut off my cell phone. After the day I'd had, some time alone was definitely overdue.

After my bath, I threw on my favorite pair of pajamas and climbed into bed. It was 2 a.m. and I was exhausted.

My phone rang loudly and woke me out of my sleep. I looked at the digital clock on the nightstand and it read 3:10 in the morning. With my eyes still closed, I answered the phone.

"You sleep?"

"Who is this?" I asked, confused.

"Jonathon baby. Wake up."

"I'm up."

"I'm sorry about the way I acted. I wasn't mad. I was just wondering what was going on. I didn't hear from you all day and that's not like you."

"I didn't do it on purpose Jonathon I had a lot on my mind."

"I know."

There was silence. I didn't really have anything to say. It was so out of the ordinary for Jonathon to be so pressed about me calling him. It was usually the other way around. I guess the situation we were now in changed things.

"What are you doing in the morning?"

"I didn't have anything planned," I said yawning.

"Well I have a surprise for you. Can you meet me somewhere?"

"You can come pick me up if you want to."

"What hotel are you in?"

"Holiday Inn room 314."

"Okay, I'll be there around eight."

I ended the call and drifted back to sleep.

DeQuindra Renea

# CHAPTER 15

Jonathon was at my hotel room door at exactly eight the next morning. He looked sexy in his blue jeans and loose fitting white button up. He had on crisp white air force ones, and of course, a white fitted hat. Jonathon looked good in a suit and tie, but I especially liked his style. He was always dressed casual and relaxed, so different from Marvin who was always dressed up.

"Good morning sexy," he said giving me a kiss on the lips.

"Hi Jonathon, you look really good. "

"You look better."

I blushed as I looked in the mirror. I didn't have on anything special, just a pair of jeans, a red sweater that hugged my body tightly and a pair of red stiletto boots. My hair was flat ironed straight down my back and I had spent nearly an hour putting on my makeup. The way I looked was important to me, but I always felt my best when I was around Jonathon.

"Are you ready?" he asked, grabbing my hand.

"Yes," I said grabbing my purse and room key.

As I walked to Jonathon's' car, I was a little hesitant. The last thing I needed was someone Marvin knew seeing us leave the hotel together. It would start more drama that we didn't need. We had enough of that going on without anyone else's help.

Jonathon took me for a drive to Bay City and we went to lunch at a tavern on the water's edge. It was nice to be out with him without having to worry about being seen by someone. We could kiss and hug and hold hands when we wanted to. It was such a nice day and it was good to be with him.

We held hands the whole way back to the hotel. I let my seat back and looked at him on the ride home. He was so damn sexy that my pussy began to throb. I couldn't wait for him to get me back to the hotel so he could give me some more of what he had given me on Valentine's Day.

When we pulled up to the hotel, Jonathon parked the car, but neither one of us got out. I sat there looking at him.

"You comin' upstairs?" I asked, hopeful.

"You want me to?"

"You know I do."

Jonathon smiled and took the key out of the ignition. I got out and went in first, and he followed behind a few minutes later. We were back home now, and anybody could recognize us at any time. It didn't really matter because Marvin was cheating, but Jonathon was his friend and I was still embarrassed.

When Jonathon made it up to my room I was already undressed and ready for whatever he planned to do to me. He laughed when he saw me.

"I remember when I used to have to damn near tear you out of your clothes."

I laughed.

"Yeah I remember that too. That was when I used to be a good girl."

"So what you sayin' I turned you into a bad girl?" he asked, sitting on the bed and taking off his shoes, never looking away from my naked body.

"I think so," I said crawling into his lap. "Because I used to be shy and timid and I used to say no."

"I like it better when you tell me yes," he said grabbing my head and kissing my lips. "You can't tell me no anyway."

I pulled his shirt over his head and pushed him back on the bed. He knew this time it was my turn to be in control and he was always happy with that.

"You know your hands look so pretty without that ring on it," he said bringing my hands to his face and kissing them. "My ring will look much better on your finger anyway."

Jonathon stayed at the hotel with me for a couple of days, only leaving to attend meetings with potential clients that he couldn't reschedule. Being with him for three days straight was a real treat and I was starting to get a taste of what life could be like now that I was no longer with Marvin.

While it was nice to be with Jonathon all day and night, I knew the time would come for him to leave and for me to really think about what I was going to do next. If I did plan on leaving Marvin, I had to get my stuff out of his house. I would go looking at apartments later in the week. For now I just needed a few days to clear my head and relax somewhere I didn't have to worry about cooking, cleaning, or making anyone happy.

After a week and two days at the hotel, I finally got a call from Marvin. He had to know this time I wasn't playing. I almost didn't answer, but I just had to know why the hell he was calling me.

"Kari, how you been?" he asked softly.

"I'm great Marvin. What do you want?"

There was a long pause. I could tell he was trying to find something to talk to me about.

"Have you seen my red button up shirt? The one I wear with my black suit."

"Bye Marvin. Don't call me with these fuckin' games."

I was about to end the call, but I could hear Marvin calling my name.

"Okay Kari, I just want to talk to you."

"So talk."

"Can I see you? When are you coming home?"

"For what Marvin? Do you not understand that I am done with your bullshit? Go be with the bitch you spent Valentine's Day with."

"Why do you have to take it there Kari? I'm not trying to argue with you."

"Well what do you want Marvin?" I asked getting annoyed. I had better things to do with my time than sit and talk about nothing with Marvin."

"I just want to talk to you about what happened. Can I take you out somewhere?"

"I don't know Marvin, I'm a little busy today," I lied. He deserved to beg a little for the way he degraded me.

"Well what about tomorrow? I can get off of work a little early if I need to."

"Now all of a sudden you can get off of work early, huh?"

"Kari, please don't do this. I'm not trying to fight," he reminded me.

"Okay call me tomorrow, we can probably do something then."

"Okay."

I ended the call and continued watching TV. Marvin had something up his sleeve, but if he thought he was just going to be able to make up for the things he said to me and how he treated me, he had another thing coming.


Marvin took me out to dinner at *Lucky's* the next night. It was my favorite restaurant. He was being extremely nice, opening doors and making sure I had everything I needed. He hadn't been this attentive since we'd first dated. I didn't know for sure what he wanted to talk to me about, but I could almost guess it had something to do with him wanting me to come home.

We ordered our food and waited for our drinks to come. It was silent at the table. Marvin had changed so much from the person he used to be that I didn't know what to talk to him about. We used to be friends, but now we were strangers sitting across the table from each other.

"Kari, I wanted to take you out to dinner because I wanted to talk to you about our argument."

"What about it?" I asked, taking a sip of my drink.

"Did you mean what you said about wanting a divorce?"

"Yes."

"Why?"

"Are you seriously asking me that question?"

Marvin took a deep breath. I knew what was coming next.

"Kari, I'm sorry."

"I'm sure you are, but Marvin you know you've done some fucked up things throughout this relationship, and honestly I can't do it anymore."

"Kari I said I'm sorry."

"That's not enough Marvin. Don't be sorry now that I'm done. You should've been sorry a long time ago."

Our conversation came to a halt when the waitress came back with our food. She sat the plates down in front of us, made sure we had everything we needed, and left us alone again.

"I know I messed up and I know I did a lot of disrespectful things in the past, but I love you so much and now that I know what it feels like to lose you I don't want to do that," he said looking into my eyes.

"Marvin it's too late. I don't want your apologies."

"What do I need to do to make you change your mind? You want to have children? Let's have a baby."

"I don't want you to get me pregnant to make me stay with you. I want you to get me pregnant because you're ready to start a family."

"I am Kari. I've been ready to start a family. But you know how much my father worked when I was a kid. I never really knew him. I didn't start getting a relationship with him until I was eighteen. All he cared about was the business. It took over his life. I don't want to put my kids through that. I want to be home and make breakfast and teach my children how to drive. I don't want to miss their life like my father missed mine."

"Why didn't you just tell me that?"

"You and I don't talk about our past a lot. We both kind of had it hard in different ways. But when I think about our marriage and all of the terrible things I've done and said to you it makes me sick. It reminds me of how my father treats my mother. I always hated to hear him talk down to her and now when I think about the things I've said to you, I realize I sound just like him. I'm turning into him. His workaholic ways, narrow minded way of thinking… everything. And that is scaring the hell outta me. I don't wanna be like that."

Marvin had never talked to me like this before. For the first time I felt like his apology was sincere.

"Kari, I am truly sorry about the way I treated you, and I mean that whether we stay together or not. You are such a beautiful woman and you have always been so good to me. I would be a fool to let you go."

I tried not to smile, but Marvin was saying all the right things. It didn't repair all the things he'd done to me throughout our relationship, but it was definitely making me second guess rushing into a divorce.

I enjoyed my meal and ultimately, Marvin's company. He was starting to remind me of the way he was when we'd first dated. He wasn't being so uptight and was actually listening to what I was saying. We sat there for hours talking, drinking, and enjoying each other's company. We even split a piece of cheesecake for desert.

Marvin paid the bill and we sat waiting for his change.

"So how long were you planning on staying at the hotel?"

"Not too much longer. It's expensive. I been looking at some apartments. It's cheaper to just do that."

"Kari you can come back home whenever you want. I never asked you to leave."

"I needed to leave, and I really don't think it's a good idea to come back yet. We had a good night Marvin, let's not take it there yet."

"But if you get an apartment you have to sign a lease and that's too much. I don't plan on you being gone long enough to sign a lease."

"You don't plan on it?'

"No. Just stay at the hotel for as long as you need to and I'll pay for it."

"You don't need to do that."

"I want to, because I realize that I have to start somewhere. I have to show you that I'm serious about making our marriage work."

I really didn't want Marvin to pay for my hotel stay, but he was right, I had to let him start somewhere. Divorcing Marvin was becoming harder and harder by the minute.

We left the restaurant and Marvin walked me to my car. He opened the door for me and I started the car, then rolled down the window.

"Thank you for taking me to dinner Marvin. I actually had fun."

"I'm glad you had fun. I want to take you out again soon."

"Then you better be callin' me soon."

Marvin smiled and kissed me on the forehead.

"I'll call you tomorrow."

I watched him walk to his car before I drove off. My mind

was in a million different places. Before dinner I was so sure of what I wanted, but now I wasn't so sure. Starting our relationship over with a clean slate sounded good, but it also meant I had to come clean too. My infedilitely would be harder to forgive because of the relationship he had with Jonathon. What man would forgive a woman who gave what belonged to him to his friend? That alone was making it impossible for me to confess. However, I had put up with Marvin's bullshit for seven years. If he was really ready to shape up and make it work, I owed it to myself to give him another chance. I had begged him to love me for years and now he really wanted to. Was it really too late?

DeQuindra Renea

# CHAPTER 16

While I was busy thinking about what to do about my marriage, Jonathon was left in limbo. It had been days since we'd talked because I had started feeling guilty again. The several nights I'd spent with Jonathon since my fight with Marvin had me wondering if my affair with him was the real reason I was giving up on my marriage.

I was lying in bed watching the rain fall from the window. Today was a bad day. Rain made me depressed. It was three in the afternoon and I was still in the hotel bed in my pajamas.

My phone rang for the fourth time that day and I didn't pick it up. It was only Kevin calling to check up on me and I really didn't feel like talking to anybody. I put the covers over my head and closed my eyes when my phone started to ring again. I ignored it, but it started ringing again not even two minutes later.

"Hello?" I answered, not hiding my irritation.

"Kari I was just calling to check on you," Kevin said.

"I figured you were that's why I didn't pick up."

"It's raining. I just wanted to make sure you were feeling okay."

"I feel fine Kevin. I was lying down before you started blowin' my damn phone up like a fuckin' bill collector."

"Well you wasn't picking up!"

"Bye Kevin. Don't call me no more."

I ended the call and lay back down. My phone started ringing again immediately.

"Stop fuckin' callin' me, I told you I'm fine!" I answered.

"This is my first time calling you, calm down. What the hell is your problem?" Jonathon said.

"I'm just not having a good day. What's up?"

"I was leaving a meeting and I wanted to call and see if you needed anything."

"No I'm fine."

"You sure?"

"Yeah."

"You want me to come by?"

"I'm not in the mood. Call me later."

"Okay," he said confused.

Tears started to sting my eyes as I ended the call and lay back down. I didn't want to cry, so I put the covers back over my head and shut the world out.


Later I awoke later to someone banging at my door. Jumping up in a panic, my heart racing, it took me a few seconds to get myself together. I got out of bed and snatched the door open. Jonathon was standing there carrying a bunch of bags.

"Why the fuck are you bangin' on my door like that?"

"I been knockin' fa damn near five minutes," he said.

"Well I was sleep. If you would've called first you would've known that."

"I did call you Kari, twice. What the hell is wrong with you?"

"I told you I wasn't having a good day."

"Well are you gonna let me in or not? I just came to drop you off somethin' to eat I can leave."

"Well you done already woke me up so you might as well stay."

Jonathon pushed past me and turned on the lights.

"Why you sleep in the middle of the evening? What got you so tired? And why the fuck do you got all the damn mirrors covered?"

"Cuz I don't wanna look at myself."

"Why not?"

I shrugged my shoulders.

"I told you I was having a bad day."

Jonathon dropped the issue and started taking the stuff out of the bags. The room immediately began to fill with delicious smells of food and my stomach growled. I had been in bed all day and hadn't eaten.

"I got you some catfish, macaroni and cheese and greens," he said, handing me a Styrofoam box and a plastic fork. I sat on the bed and started eating in silence. Jonathon left me alone, obviously sensing my bad mood. I finished my food and sat the empty box on the nightstand. Before I could ask, Jonathon brought me a cold bottle of water.

"Thank you," I said quietly. I drunk half of the bottle and sat it next to my empty box.

Neither of us said anything for a while. I wasn't really in the talking mood. I didn't know if he was scared to talk to me because I was in a bitchy mood, but I could tell he had something on his mind. I turned on the TV and after a while he came and sat next to me.

"What's wrong?"

"Stop asking me that please," I answered without looking at him. He didn't say anything else for a minute.

"How long you gonna do this?"

"I told you I was having a bad day. You still decided to come over."

"I'm not talkin' about that. How long are you gonna stay in this hotel room? You can't live here."

"I know. I'm still thinking and trying to decide what I'm gonna do."

"What you mean by that?"

"I mean that's my life. That's been my life for the last seven years. I need to think before I just walk away."

"You took the ring off Kari, what else is there to think about?"

"Did you not hear what I just said?" I snapped.

"If you gon keep snappin' at me I can leave."

I bit my tongue really hard to keep from saying what I wanted to say.

"Have you talked to him?"

"He took me out to dinner the other night and we talked."

"Why you aint tell me that?"

"Because it was none of your business."

"So what, you thinkin' about going back home?"

"I really don't wanna talk about it right now."

"Kari I gave you a ring," he reminded me. "So how can you sit here and act like whatever you decide doesn't affect me?"

"I didn't know that I needed to tell you when I went out on a date with my husband."

"That's what it was? A date? So what happened?"

"It aint none of your business."

He was starting to piss me off. I was already having a bad day and here Jonathon was trying to force me to make life decisions.

"You know what, I don't know why I fuckin' bother with this bullshit."

"What did you say?"

"You heard me."

"Yeah well I know how you feel because sometimes I wished I would have never started this thing with you," I said angrily.

"Oh that's how you feel?"

"Yeah because you don't give a damn about what I have to go through. What do you think his family is gonna think of me? You must've forgot, I'm the bitch that's fuckin' her man's friend. I'm the one everybody is gonna be talking about."

"That's what you worried about? What everybody think. That's the difference between me and you baby because I don't give a fuck what people think. The only thing that's stopping me from going and telling Marvin about us is you."

I didn't say anything. There was nothing I could say. I wasn't ready to make a decision yet and Jonathon was just going to have to understand that.

"He's my husband, I can't just walk away that easy. I need time to think."

"So you gonna stay here?"

"For a while. I looked at a few apartments while I was out the other day."

Jonathon laughed.

"So even if you don't go home to Marvin, you still won't come to me."

"Why does everything have to be about you? Don't you understand other people's feelings are involved?"

"Look Kari, I'm tired of playing games. I told you how I felt about you, I put it all out there. Now either you wanna be with me, or you don't. I'm tired of all this bullshit."

"I can't give you an answer right now."

Jonathon shook his head.

"You know what, go back home to Marvin, I don't give a fuck no more."

"You act like you didn't know I was married! You came on to me, remember? You started this."

"And I made a mistake. I shouldn't have let shit go this far with you," Jonathon said getting off of the bed. "I fucked around and fell in love with my friend's wife. I can't do this any more Kari. You been telling me this whole time you were somebody else's, but I thought I could make you mine. We don't belong together like I thought."

My heart dropped when he said that. I knew he would be mad, but I never thought he would take it this far.

"What do you want me to do?" I asked, fighting back tears.

"Do what you wanna do Kari, cuz I know it's not bein' with me. I don't know what else to do to prove to you that I love you."

"I know you do."

"Then leave him," he said easily. "I'll take care of everything else."

Jonathon looked down at me, but this time it wasn't so sexy. He was mad, hurt, and angry. I could see it all in his eyes. I didn't want to hurt him, I did love him and I wanted him, but I wanted the old Marvin back, too.

"I can't just leave like that."

Jonathon nodded his head.

"So you just don't give a fuck about you and me?"

Jonathon didn't wait for a response.

"It's cool. Go on home to him then," he said grabbing his keys off the table.

"Can you please stop this?" I pleaded.

"Yeah, I can."

Then he left, just walked out and left me in the hotel room by myself. I didn't know if he was seriously done or just pissed off, but I had a feeling that I had let him walk away.

# CHAPTER 17

Jonathon must have really been mad at me because I didn't talk to him after our argument. He hadn't come back to my room, he hadn't even called. The last thing I was going to do was call him. I hadn't done anything wrong. My second thoughts about my marriage had nothing to do with him and it was something I needed to decide on my own.

Marvin was calling me every day, taking me out and showering me with gifts. I was seeing the old Marvin more and more, and I was seeing the change. One evening he came to my hotel room dressed in sweat pants and his college sweat shirt. I opened the door with a smile on my face.

"Are you happy to see me?" he asked, kissing me quickly.

"Yeah and it's good to see you relaxed."

Marvin looked down at his clothes.

"I'm not working."

"That never mattered."

He laughed.

"I'm trying not to be so uptight. I don't have to dress up all the time, it's just how my father raised me. I got used to it."

"Well I'm glad to see the change."

I sat with Marvin on the loveseat and he grabbed my hand.

"Kari, I have something I want to give you."

Marvin reached in his pocket and pulled out a small black velvet box. He looked at me and forced a smile. He was nervous like he was the night he asked me to marry him. I was only eighteen years old, and he being seven years my senior, had every reason to think I would say no. I didn't know what he had up his sleeve tonight.

He opened the box and in it lay a platinum princess cut diamond band. It was the most beautiful ring I had ever seen and it put my wedding ring to shame. I didn't know how things had been going at work, but it must have cost him well over ten thousand dollars. My mouth dropped in awe at its beauty.

"Kari, I know being married to me has been hard and there is no excuse for how I treated you. But you leaving has reminded me of how lucky I am to have you as my wife and how I never want to lose you. I love you, you are my wife, and I want you to be home with me. I miss seeing your beautiful face every day."

Marvin took the ring out of the box and placed it on my finger.

He grabbed my face and kissed my lips tenderly. My panties got moist. For the first time in a long time, I wanted to make love to my husband. I slid my tongue in his mouth and climbed on top of him.

"Are you going to come home?" he asked, looking into my eyes. I nodded my head and kissed him again. He truly loved me. He would never walk away from me or let me walk away. We had been through hell and would make our marriage work.

Jonathon walking out on me was the best thing he could have ever done. It made me realize I didn't belong with him, or at the hotel. I didn't belong anywhere else but home with my husband.

Marvin picked me up off of the couch and carried me over to the bed. He didn't waste any time taking off all of my clothes and kissing me all over my body. My skin tingled as he ran his tongue down my stomach.

"Take your clothes off Marvin," I ordered. He continued to kiss my body and didn't respond to my request. Instead of waiting, I pushed him off of me and started taking off his clothes myself. At the moment I wasn't interested in making love, I wanted to get fucked. I needed him to penetrate me and let me be in control. For a brief moment Jonathon flashed in my mind because he always listened to what I asked him to do.

Once Marvin was nude, I pulled him on top of me again. Taking control, I grabbed his dick and put it inside of me. He looked so good, and he felt even better. I missed this Marvin, not the one that was turning into his father. I missed wanting my husband, and only thinking of him when we were together.

Once I got the ball rolling, we didn't have any problems with our lovemaking. Although there was no talking between us, the passion was enough this time. It had been so long since we were together and you could tell that he missed me as much as he said he did.

Marvin put me in every position I wanted to be in and I was excited. It was the first time he had ever been this open and spontaneous. Maybe his age made him insecure, but it definitely didn't feel like that this time. From now on he needed to make love to me like he missed me, even though I was coming back home.

DeQuindra Renea

# CHAPTER 18

Marvin was still working as much as he was when I'd left. I knew he couldn't help it so I didn't complain. Besides, with my birthday coming up I was busy planning my party. It was only three weeks away and I needed to make sure I got things together. I knew the day would come sooner than I thought.

Besides planning my party, the house also needed to be cleaned from top to bottom. It was clear I'd been gone and Marvin hadn't maintained the house's usual shine.

For the first couple of days I cleaned and did laundry, but by the weekend, I was ready to rejoin the world. Besides, if Jonathon was coming over to play basketball, I definitely didn't want to be around.

I called Jamie to see if she wanted to meet for lunch. She said she wouldn't be off until three, but would meet me right after. That gave me enough time to take a quick shower and do something to my hair.

I heard the boys as soon as they walked in. They were loud and hype of course, and I knew they were getting bottles of water out of the kitchen.

Pulling my hair into a neat bun, I threw on some jeans, a cream polo shirt, and got ready to leave.

My heart pounded as I descended the stairs. I was expecting to see Jonathon's face among the small crowd of sweaty men, but he wasn't there. As scared as I was, I had to admit I was looking forward to seeing him. Marvin came over to give me a kiss and I tried to hide my disappointment.

"You okay? Where you headed?" he asked out of breath.

"I'm meeting Jamie for lunch."

"Are you going shopping after that?"

"No," I answered, confused.

"You should."

"Are you gonna give me some money?"

Marvin went and got his wallet and gave me his credit card.

"Buy something nice for your party and something nice for the bedroom."

"So this is about lingerie?" I smiled, taking the card.

"No it's about me treating you how you deserve to be treated."

I gave Marvin a nice long kiss before I left to meet Jamie. He had been really spoiling me since I'd been home and I was loving every minute of it.


I brought Jamie up to speed with everything that had been going on in my crazy life. It had been awhile since we'd talked, so she filled me in on her love life. I had missed her, and after a salad and a couple of drinks, I dreaded saying goodbye to her.

"I'm so glad we had a chance to catch up," she said pulling some money out of her purse to tip the waitress.

"Me too. Sorry I didn't call you."

"Obviously you had your hands full," she joked.

"That is the truth. But now I'm focused on my marriage. Jonathon was a huge mistake."

"Have you talked to him?"

"Not since the last time I saw him at the hotel."

"And he hasn't been by your house yet?"

I shook my head.

"That's why you feel that way. Do you think you can tell him that to his face?"

"Absolutely. I'm over him. He gave up on me. He walked away first."

Jamie nodded her head like she didn't believe me. I didn't care what she thought, and I wasn't going to waste my time convincing her.

We walked outside together to our cars. We reached hers first and she turned and smiled.

"Thanks for lunch. Call me soon or I will come knocking at your door."

"And I will welcome you with open arms."

We hugged and parted ways. I went to my car and headed to the mall in search of a dress for my party.


I made it home that evening with more bags than I could carry in one trip. Not only had I found a dress for my party, I had caught some great sales. Marvin would surely be happy because I hadn't forgotten about his request for lingerie.

"Should I be scared to ask how much money you spent?" Marvin asked, carrying in the last of my bags. Thankfully he had showered and had on his pajama pants and robe. He looked so sexy, I wanted to tear him out of it.

"No you shouldn't be scared. You know I try to bargain shop."

"Since when? I remember you buying a thirty five hundred dollar pair of shoes."

"But I had to have those. And I didn't hear you complainin' when I modeled them for you later that night."

"That's because the shoes were all you had on. Who would complain?"

Marvin dropped my bags in the hallway where I'd left the ones I carried and sat next to me on the loveseat.

"Do you have some shoes to model for me tonight?"

"Oh, I got somethin' better than shoes."

I grabbed a bag out of the sea of others and went into the bathroom. I'd bought four lingerie sets, one black, one red, one hot pink, and one white. I'd prepared to put on a show for my husband, but I hadn't had the hot pink one piece on for three minutes before it was taken off of me and thrown on the floor. I ended up with my legs in the air screaming as Marvin feasted on my clit. He was pushing his tongue in and out of me and it was driving me wild. My mouth was wide open, but no sound would come. What he was doing to me felt so incredible. He brought his hands up and pinched my nipples as he sucked my clit. My breath caught into my throat. He bit it lightly and I screamed out. I felt my juices start to flow and my body shook. Marvin kissed the insides of my thighs and looked up at me and smiled. The Marvin I loved was back and it was good to be home.

Weeks went by and I didn't hear from or see Jonathon. Since he hadn't been to the house, I wondered if he and Marvin had gotten into it. I was too scared to ask about him because I didn't want Marvin to get suspicious. All I could do was wait.

I didn't have to wait very much longer. Jonathon came over a week later. Marvin, Damon, and I were all watching the basketball game in the living room. My heart dropped as soon as he walked into the room. He looked so good. He had on jean shorts and a black beater. He had on black socks and black Nike sandals. I fixed my eyes on the screen hoping he wasn't looking at me. My heart was beating out of my chest. It was the first time I saw him since he had left the hotel and I wondered what he thought seeing me home with Marvin.

"So who in the lead?" he asked. I wasn't looking at him, but I knew he was seated on the couch with Damon. His legs were spread wide and his arms were folded across his chest. I didn't have to look at him to know what he was doing, or to know he was looking at me.

"Chicago," Marvin answered.

"Man, they can't win. I got money on this game," Jonathon said.

"Oh you put your money on the wrong team because Chicago is about to win," Damon said.

"Yeah, we'll see about that."

I sat there for as long as I could pretending to pay attention to the game. Being in the same room with Marvin and Jonathon at the same time was uncomfortable.

"I want something sweet, what do you want to eat?"

"You," Marvin whispered in my ear. I forced a sexy giggle.

"I'm serious, what do you want?"

"I don't care. Snicker doodles."

I should have known. Snicker doodles were Marvin's favorite. I got up and went into the kitchen to start baking them.

Marvin and his company were arguing over the game. It was a good one, and I was mad I was missing it, but there was no way I was going back into that living room. I would finish watching it in my room when the cookies were done.

Jonathon came into the kitchen just as I was putting the cookies in the oven. He stood there for a long time just looking at me. I knew he wanted to get me alone, but I didn't think he would be brave enough to come into the kitchen with Marvin right in the next room.

I stood there waiting for him to say or do something, but he just stared at me. Finally he spoke.

"Nice ring," he said. He looked at me again before he got a bottle of water out of the refrigerator. He left the room without saying anything else: alone and confused.

It was obvious that Fairmount Inc. was doing extremely well, but I didn't know if Jonathon was trying to say that was the reason I had come back home. I waited anxiously for the cookies to get done, put a few on the plate and went upstairs to finish watching the game.

I had gotten myself in a world of trouble. Jonathon was Marvin's good friend and he wasn't going away anytime soon. I didn't know where we stood and didn't know what type of hell our relationship could later cause my marriage.

DeQuindra Renea

# CHAPTER 19

"Happy birthday Kari!"

Marvin kissed my lips waking me out of my sleep. I opened my eyes slowly. Marvin sat down at the foot of the bed with a tray of food.

"Thanks baby."

I sat up slowly and forced a smile. Marvin was dressed in one of his tailored business suits and I knew without asking he was going to work.

"My Dad called. I have to go into the office. I'm sorry baby, I really wanted to take you out."

"Don't worry about it. Kevin is taking me out to lunch."

"I'll try to come home early to take you out somewhere."

"If not, don't worry. The party is the weekend and we've been going out a lot anyway. Go to work, I don't want your Dad giving you any more hell."

Marvin kissed me again and put the tray in front of me. It wasn't much because cooking wasn't Marvin's forte', but I thought the fruit, croissant, and cup of coffee was an excellent gesture.

I watched the news while I ate my breakfast and when I finished, I took the tray downstairs. When I made it, the kitchen table was full of gift bags, jewelry boxes, flowers, and a birthday card. I didn't know if Marvin had an accomplice or he knew my taste that well, but everything was to my liking. My birthday was getting off to a great start.

"Well doesn't my little sister look good!" Kevin said when I walked into the restaurant. He was referring to my long pink and yellow sundress. I had just left the hair salon, so my locks were freshly flat ironed and hanging down my back.

"Thanks big brother, but you don't have to make a scene," I said hugging him. I was referring to the group of old ladies that were waiting to be seated. They smiled at us. Although it was positive attention, Kevin knew I was shy.

"Oh don't be like that Kari. You always have attention. You're beautiful."

"Stop," I said blushing. Kevin always had been charming.

The hostess led us to our table. He was taking me to the Olive Garden. It was his favorite restaurant and he always took me here when we went out... even when it was my birthday.

"Why didn't Jayla come?"

"I told her she couldn't," he said easily, opening his menu."

"Why? That's mean, she loves Olive Garden."

"She been irritating me lately."

"So she couldn't come to eat on my birthday lunch because she irritates you?"

"Damn right."

"It's my birthday."

"If you say so. Either way I left her ass at home."

"You are so mean to her."

"No, I treat her like a fucking queen. You sound like her, I'm not mean. I told you she irritates me."

"Okay we are done talking about Jayla, I see that's not putting you in the best of moods."

"It's not, thank you. Change the subject."

"What are you eating Grinch?"

Kevin tried not to smile.

"I don't know."

"Well I think I want the Sicilian Scampi."

"I was looking at that, but since you're getting it I can just eat off yours and get something else."

"Yeah that won't be happening."

"You can share. I'm getting a couple of bites."

The waiter came and took our order and came back with our

salad and bread sticks. Kevin stopped talking and dug in, clearly enjoying his favorite part of the Olive Garden experience.

We chatted briefly between bites about Kevin's job and my plans for the party.

"It's good to see you happy Kari. I didn't like you living in that hotel."

"I know, but Kevin you can't always take care of me. You have to let me do that on my own."

"I'm used to taking care of you. I did when you were a kid, then when I found you when you were twelve. You my baby sister and I know you had it hard. I feel responsible."

"Us getting separated wasn't your fault. We were kids when the fire happened. Nobody would step up and take us. Nana was already gone."

"Finding you was the best thing that ever happened to me. I thought I had lost you in the system."

"I thought you wanted to."

Kevin and I were separated after the fire and I didn't see him again until I was twelve years old. He got custody of me when he turned eighteen; I was fourteen years old.

"Is that why you didn't look for me?"

I shrugged my shoulders. Kevin was bringing up old wounds, but since I wouldn't talk to him about the fire, I let him take the lead of the conversation and play twenty-one questions, his favorite game.

"I was scared. The last thing I remembered was passing out as the house burned down. When I woke up I was in Mrs. Rawling's foster home and you had been adopted out."

Kevin looked confused.

"Kari, you were awake after the fire. I used to come to your room and try to talk to you, but you were mute. You just laid there and stared, remember that?"

I tried to think back, but I didn't recall seeing Kevin anymore after the fire until six years later when I was twelve years old.

"No, I don't remember that," I answered honestly.

"So it's like you blacked out almost a year of your life. We were together for almost a year at Mrs. Rawling's house."

I didn't understand what Kevin was talking about. I did not remember being with him at all at the Rawling house. He had to be mistaken.

"That can't be right."

"Kari think of how you celebrated your sixth birthday. That was the one you had before the fire."

I thought back and it seemed as if my brain had recovered lost memory. However, I was remembering things I didn't want to remember.

"I don't wanna talk about this any more Kevin."

"Just answer me, do you remember that?"

"Yes."

"Now how did you spend your seventh birthday?"

I tried to recall, but I was drawing a blank every time. I was starting to get scared. Why hadn't Kevin brought this up before?

"Do you remember?"

I shook my head confused about everything. Maybe I was crazy. All I knew was Kevin was ruining what was supposed to be a happy birthday lunch.

Apparently Kevin didn't know either because he was quiet after that. He ate his food and didn't mention anything else about what happened after the fire. I was grateful. I would rather it be quiet than talk about that.

Marvin made it home in time to take me out to eat at Red Lobster. There, he had more gifts for me. I could tell he was genuinely happy to be able to spend some time with me on my birthday, and I was too.

Every year I threw a party for my birthday. Since June 16th had fallen on a Wednesday, we waited until Saturday to have it. We invited over a few of our closest friends and family to enjoy the weather and celebrate my day. It was also a chance for me to show off my cooking skills. Marvin knew how much I loved to cook, and he loved giving me the opportunity to do what I did best.

With my birthday quickly approaching, I rushed around getting some things for the BBQ. I was leaving *Sam's Club* when I got an incoming call on my cell phone.

"Hello?" I turned down the *Pointer Sisters* on the radio to hear who it was trying to reach me.

"Hey Kari, are you busy?" my friend Jamie said on the other end.

"No girl, just out getting some last minute things for the BBQ. What's going on?"

"I was actually calling to see if you needed me to bring anything."

"Just bring yourself and your appetite. I have everything taken care of."

"Well I'll bring a couple bottles of wine. I can't just come empty handed."

"That's fine. Thank you."

"No problem girl! So what have you been up to?"

"Nothing much, just trying to get everything together for my birthday."

"And what about everything else?" Jamie asked trying to cut through the crap and get to the real.

"No Jamie, I still haven't spoken to him."

"Did you call him?"

"I'm not calling him. He walked out on me. Why would I call him?"

"Because you love him and you miss him."

"It's over between us Jamie, and that's what's best. If he wanted to talk he would call me. He has my number."

"You are so stubborn Kari. Do you really think you're going to be with Marvin forever?"

Jamie was not a fan of Marvin at all. She thought that I could do so much better. She could tell Jonathon made me happy.

"We're working on it Jamie. One day at a time."

"So you don't miss Jonathon?"

"I don't think about him anymore. He doesn't come over anymore, he and Marvin always go out. He has completely removed himself from my life."

"So he won't be at your party?"

"I doubt it. Marvin hasn't mentioned it."

"Well I'm bummed. I wanted to see him."

"Well maybe next time."

"Yeah, maybe. Well I will be there with my bottle of wine and a date."

"A date? Who are you dating?"

"I guess you'll find out, won't you? Bye doll!"

I laughed.

"Bye Jamie."

I ended the call and turned the radio back up. I had lied to Jamie. I thought about Jonathon all the time and the truth was I hated the way he had just dropped out of my life. We were friends, and he just decided that meant nothing if he couldn't have all of me to himself.

After I finished running errands, I stopped by Marvin's office to take him lunch. He had really been treating me good lately and I was starting to think things between us were going to work out.

I knocked softly on his office door and peeked my head in just as he was wrapping up a telephone call.

"I think that sounds like a pretty good idea. I'll get my secretary to set up a meeting… Well that's okay because what I am going to offer him is going to be three times better than what Anchorsoft is offering, it'd be wise for him to take my offer… Yeah… I'll let you know how it goes… Alright, you too sir."

Marvin hung up the phone and walked over to me. He looked good in his three piece navy blue suit. He licked his lips in a sexy way and pulled me into a hug.

"Hey baby, I'm glad to see you."

"Are you?"

"You know I am."

"I brought you lunch," I said holding up the bag of food. Marvin gave me a soft kiss on the lips and took the bags.

"Thanks baby, I'm starving."

"What time do you think you'll be home tonight? Are you working late?" I asked sitting in one of the leather chairs in front of his oak desk.

"I don't plan on it. I plan on coming home to you. What do you have planned tonight?"

"Planned? The only thing I've been doing is planning this party."

"Baby nobody really plans a BBQ, they just throw one. Don't you think you're putting too much thought into it?"

"But it's my birthday. I want it to be perfect."

"And it will be. Stop worrying baby, everyone is going to have a great time, they always do."

I watched as Marvin ate his lunch. I loved to see him so happy and positive. It was one of the reasons I fell in love with him.

"How many people did you invite?"

"A couple of people from here and their spouses. My sister Christina will be there and my parents said they were going to stop by. Steve, Mark, and Henry are coming too."

My heart dropped when I didn't hear Jonathon's name.

"That's it?"

"I might invite a few more people but yeah, that's it on my side. What about you?"

"Kevin and Jayla, Jamie said she's bringing a date, Kelly and Kim are coming, a couple of Kevin's friends and... I'm forgetting somebody."

"So what's that a good thirty people. We always want to have extra. People can always take food home."

"That's fine. I almost have everything I need, when are you going shopping for the meat?"

Marvin pulled out his Blackberry to check his schedule. That was one thing that annoyed me. Everything revolved around that damn phone. He couldn't survive without it.

"I can go Thursday after work. That way I'll have time to let it marinate real good."

"Okay cool."

"So tonight, you want to go out. Wanna see a movie?"

"A movie sounds perfect. Which one were you thinking?"

"I hear that new Denzel movie is pretty good. You wanna catch that?"

"That sounds good baby," I said getting up and grabbing my purse. "I'm gonna head home, I was just stopping by to drop off your lunch."

I went behind the desk and planted a long, passionate kiss on Marvin. I could taste the French salad dressing, but I didn't care.

"I love you. I'll see you when you get home."

# CHAPTER 20

The jazz music from outside flooded into the bathroom as I stood in the mirror putting the finishing touches on my makeup. It was the day of my party and I knew I looked damn good. I had on a sexy strapless sundress that was tight and hugged my curves in all the right places. The low cut white and pink dress made my cleavage look nice and full, and stopped right in the middle of my thigh. My hairdresser had laid my hair out as well. It was straight and hung down my back. It was full of body and showed of my new honey brown streaks and layers. I wore pink eye shadow to match my dress and my golden caramel skinned glistened from all the baby oil I'd put on after I showered. I threw on some MAC lip gloss and looked at myself one more time in the mirror. I knew I was fine. It was my birthday and I was feeling more like myself lately. I had already had two glasses of wine while I was cooking so I was a little buzzed: my small eyes showed evidence of that.

I left out of the bathroom and walked into our bedroom where Marvin was sitting on the bed looking through his Blackberry. Immediately I rolled my eyes.

"Can you put the business on hold for one day? It's my birthday."

"I know baby. I am just sending this email and then it is all about you."

Marvin finished sending his message as I put on my pink stilettos. He walked up behind me and wrapped his arms around me.

""You look good enough to eat right now Kari. I think we might miss the party," he whispered kissing my neck.

"Stop," I giggled, cocking my head to the side to deny his lips access to my sensitive spots. "After all the cooking I've done, we are having this party."

Marvin ran his hands up and down the front of my body. His hand stopped, resting on my flat stomach. He kept it there for a while without saying anything.

"You know I love you baby, you know that right."

"Yes I do."

Marvin kissed my cheek and released me, finally allowing me to finish strapping up my shoes. Smiling to myself, I followed him downstairs. The aroma of good food filled my kitchen. In addition to the BBQ Marvin had been grilling all day, I had cooked macaroni and cheese, baked beans, yams, dirty rice, crab cakes, peach cobbler, sweet potato pie, and cheesecake. I had taken it easy this year making sure that I didn't cook too much so that I would actually be able to enjoy the party.

Henry, one of Marvin's coworkers, covered all the food and carried it outside. We put burners under everything so the food would stay warm. Jacob, one of Marvin's friends from work, had brought over his DJ equipment and was playing Teena Marie, one of my favorite singers. The backyard was landscaped beautifully with a fountain being the focal point of the yard. The tables were all set up under a huge tent in case any rain decided to make an appearance. So far it was sunny and hot, and the weatherman predicted it would be that way for the rest of the day.

After we got the food outside, I poured myself another glass of wine and sat in the house waiting for the guests to arrive. Marvin got the last of the meat off of the grill and came into the house.

"This won't all go out Kari, I'll put it in the oven," he said carrying a big pan of ribs in the house.

"Okay."

"Oh, do you think it will be enough food for Jonathon to come by? I finally got in touch with him. He said he's coming. Is that cool?"

My heart dropped into my stomach.

"Yeah, there's more than enough. It's cool if he comes."

Marvin poured himself a glass of wine and sat next to me on the couch.

"Everything looks so nice Marvin, thank you for setting it all up."

"Anything for you baby."

Marvin kissed me on the lips just as the doorbell rang. We got up to greet our first guests. Always punctual, Jamie was at the door with her date.

"Hi Kari!" she yelled as Marvin took the wine bottles from her. "This is my date, Matthew. Matthew, this is my friend Kari."

Matthew and I shook hands and I had to admit Jamie had done well this time. He was gorgeous, like he had stepped straight out of an Abercrombie magazine. He had blonde hair and blue eyes and tan skin. He showed me his perfect Colgate smile as he greeted me.

"It's nice to meet you. Do you guys want anything to drink?"

"Wine is fine for me," Jamie replied.

"I'll take a beer if you have one," Matthew said following me into the kitchen. I introduced Marvin to Matthew and they both grabbed a beer and headed outside. I poured Jamie a glass of wine and we followed.

"It looks beautiful out here girl, happy birthday," Jamie said linking her arm with mine and taking a sip of her wine.

"Thank you. It is beautiful out today. I'm glad it didn't rain; I was crossing my fingers."

"I know you were. Did you cook some crab cakes?"

"Yes I made some crab cakes, and I made you your own pan to take home."

"Did you? See that is why I love you, you keep me nice and fat."

We both laughed and sat together on the lawn chairs next to the garden. Beyonce was playing now and Jamie and I both rocked to the music. Marvin and Matthew were sitting at one of the tables looking as if they were having the most interesting conversation in the world. I was glad her date seemed to be enjoying himself.

Jamie and I sat and talked for a few minutes until more guests began to arrive. I got up and did my duty greeting and mingling with everybody. Many of them had brought me gifts which I thought was extremely thoughtful. I made a mental note to mail thank you letters to everybody in attendance.

After eating a small plate of food, Marvin and I talked to Marvin's friend Andy and his wife Kelly. It had been a while since we had all got together and we stood there catching up. We laughed and made a promise to all get together soon for drinks.

Marvin grabbed my hand and led me over to his parents. His mother wore a pair of blue jean shorts and a red tank top. Her salt and pepper hair was in soft curls on her head. We hugged and she handed me a card.

"Thank you Paulette, you didn't have to get me anything."

"Nonsense dear, a birthday only comes once a year. Even though you don't look a day older than you did when I first met you."

"Oh that's just the makeup," I blushed.

"I know a natural beauty when I see one," she said shaking her finger at me. "You are a natural beauty. You don't need that make up."

I smiled at her compliment. She never failed to tell me how pretty I was, but Paulette wasn't a bad looking woman herself. She had been a fox back in her day.

"Would you like a glass of wine Paulette?"

"Oh no thank you sugar, but I am going to make myself a plate. I haven't had any of your cooking in so long."

"Well help yourself and let me know if you need anything."

Malcolm gave me a hug and shook Marvin's hand.

"Since you both throw a party out here every year, why can't you throw a company dinner out here? The change of scenery would be nice," Malcolm said without even bothering to tell me happy birthday.

"I don't know Dad, that's something to think about."

Malcolm and Paulette made their way to the food table and I made my way back over to my friends. Before I could take a step, Marvin grabbed my hand. I must have really looked good because he didn't want to let me out of his sight

We walked around the massive yard talking with our guests. I was really enjoying myself. Marvin and I were getting along really well and having a good time together. He was acting like he used to when we were dating and I loved it. This Marvin, the outgoing, fun, carefree Marvin was the one I had fallen in love with.

Marvin and I sat at the table eating dessert and talking to a couple of his coworkers when Jonathon walked in. He looked good. He had on a pair of blue jean shorts and a blue and white short sleeved button up. On his feet was a pair of crispy white Jordan's. His hair was cut into a low fade, making his newly grown goatee stick out more. He looked good, more mature with the facial hair. My whole body was hot and I couldn't understand how this man, who was not my husband, had the power to control my body without even trying. My panties were already wet and he hadn't even looked in my direction.

Marvin noticed that new guests had arrived and grabbed my hand to go and greet them. It wasn't until I was walking over that I noticed Jonathon had brought a date. My heart dropped as I looked at the golden exotic beauty, with long flowing black hair and gray eyes. Her full lips were perfect and went along with her other exotic features. She was beautiful, and as I walked over to them and saw him holding her hand, I could feel the jealousy heating in my heart.

"What's up man?" Marvin greeted Jonathon. They gave each other a handshake and a half-hug before Jonathon acknowledged me.

"Hey Kari, happy birthday!" he said in the most normal tone I had ever heard. It seemed so distant and insincere I almost forgot to thank him.

"Thank you Jonathon," I said just as dryly as he had. He was trying to make it completely obvious to me he had moved on.

"Marvin, Kari, this is my girl Leilani. Leilani, this is my friend Marvin and his wife Kari."

Marvin and I took turns shaking hands with the exotic princess. Her beauty put mine to shame and I wanted to go upstairs and hide under the covers until the party was over.

"It's very nice to meet you," she said in a thick accent. I tried my best not to roll my eyes. I never thought Jonathon would become the typical accent guy.

"Help yourself to anything. Food is out on the table, wine is in the kitchen. Jonathon knows where it is," I said finally looking into his eyes. We made eye contact for a brief second, then Marvin started talking.

"Where are you from?" he asked trying to make conversation.

"Puerto Rico. You ever been?"

"No not yet. Kari has always wanted to go."

This muthafucka is trying to be funny! I thought to myself. I had told him before I had always wanted to go to Puerto Rico.

"You should! Lots of fun there!" she said giving us a dazzling smile.

"So we've heard. Where did you meet Jonathon?" Marvin asked.

"Met him on a business trip. He has to go to New Jersey often and sometimes he stays with me," she said shrugging her shoulders like it was no big deal. I had to remove myself from the situation as soon as possible.

"I really hate to be rude, but my brother just got here. It was really nice to meet you Leilani and I hope you enjoy yourself."

"Thank you."

I walked away from them and made my way over to Kevin and Jayla. She was wearing a long purple sundress with purple and black accessories. Her medium length hair was pulled into a beautiful up do style with curls coming down the side. My brother had on a pair of basketball shorts, a beater, some socks and Nike sandals. He looked happy as he paraded Jayla on his arm like she was Miss America.

"Happy Birthday Little One!" he said lifting me up in the air and spinning me around.

"You two act just like kids when you see each other," Jayla laughed.

"I feel like a kid when I see him," I said as Kevin put me back on my feet. I gave Jayla a hug and admired her dress.

"I love this dress. When you gonna let me steal it."

"I will trade you, let me have that one you're wearing and the body to go with it!"

"You look gorgeous, stop it," I said slapping her arm playfully.

"Well I been working out with your brother so I will be in shape soon. He is wearing me out."

"And she is not talking about at the gym."

"Ugh, T.M.I.," I said, as we all laughed. My brother always felt it was important to tell me inappropriate things. He thought my reaction was hilarious.

"It's beautiful back here Kari, thanks for inviting me," Jayla said, scanning my backyard.

"You are welcome anytime Jayla, don't be silly."

"Yeah Jayla, don't be silly," Kevin mimicked.

"Well you know we have plenty of food so help yourself," I said motioning toward the food. "You want a glass of wine?"

"Yes please."

"I'll take a glass also," Kevin said.

"Yeah I know you will."

I went into the house and poured two glasses of wine. I swear I had done it almost a million times that day, but I didn't mind. I enjoyed playing hostess, and it was also an opportunity for me to have a drink without looking like a lush. Hell, it was my birthday, I wanted to get tipsy, but I didn't want to have a glass of wine the whole damn party.

I took Kevin and Jayla their drinks and went to find Jamie. After walking the yard three times I found her with Matthew talking to two other couples. She had a glass of wine in one hand and a plate of crab cakes in the other. I gave an apologetic smile as I pulled her to the side.

"Okay listen closely I'm only gonna say this once. Jonathon is here."

"He is? Where?" she asked, looking around, breaking her neck to find him.

"See, you already about to blow it. Stop looking so obvious."

"Nobody knows what we're talking about, stop worrying."

"He came with someone."

"Who? Jonathon?" she mouthed.

"Yes. How dare he bring a woman to my house?"

"That you share with your husband," she said bringing me back to reality. "Is she pretty?"

"No she's not, she's a damn goddess! She's gorgeous!"

"Kari don't let that ruin your birthday. Enjoy the party."

I smiled and allowed her to go back to the group. She was right. I shouldn't let that ruin my day.

I found Marvin sitting at a table talking to his friend David. He had a half eaten piece of sweet potato pie in front of him as he laughed aloud. I took the seat next to him and he grabbed my hand and kissed it. It was times like this when I truly loved this man and it again gave me hope for our future together.

The sun set over my backyard and the smooth jazz blaring out of the speakers seemed to match the mood. It was beautiful outside and I lay against Marvin's chest as he reclined on one of our lawn chairs. He was having a debate with Carl and it was getting pretty good. We all laughed as they insulted each other's opinions. I didn't know much about politics, but it was always entertaining to hear men argue.

"I'm gonna go in for a minute, I'll be back out," I whispered in Marvin's ear.

"Bring me back a glass of wine," he said giving my butt a gentle squeeze. I got off the lawn chair and went into the house. After using the bathroom, I went into the kitchen to get Marvin and I both a drink. I washed some dirty glasses I brought in from outside, humming to myself as I finished cleaning and drying the two glasses.

Feeling someone's eyes on me, I turned around to find Jonathon watching me in silence.

"Can I get you something?" I asked turning back around, grateful for the two empty wine glasses so I wouldn't have to look him in the face.

"I just wanted to say happy birthday and thanks for inviting me. I hope you don't mind that I brought my friend."

"Your girl, not your friend," I said using his words against him.

"Kari, I don't want you to be mad-"

"No you just brought your girl to the party to introduce her to us. No big deal."

I turned back around and focused on opening a new bottle of wine. I wished he would just go away. Anytime I was in his presence I felt nervous and this time was no different.

"Kari, it wasn't like that-"

"You don't have to explain anything to me Jonathon. Trust me. I am not your woman, I get it now. Do what you want, I don't care."

I could feel him just standing there not moving as if there was something else he wanted to say. After a moment he walked away. I just stood there for a minute trying my best to get myself together before I went back outside to my husband. After downing one of the glasses of wine, I poured another one, took a few more seconds, then picked up the glasses and headed outside.

I was almost out of the door when somebody grabbed my

arm and pulled me into the bathroom. The wine glasses shattered at my feet. Jonathon closed and locked the door behind us, then threw me against the wall. He kissed me roughly before I had a chance to say anything. He forced my mouth open and tongued me down with so much passion it made my head spin.

"I missed you baby. You know I missed you," he said stopping and looking into my eyes.

"We can't do this. Somebody is gonna catch us-"

"I don't care," he said kissing my neck. My eyes dropped in pleasure as I tried my best to ignore what he was doing to me. He needed to stop, I wanted to make him stop, but I couldn't. I had missed him too.

Jonathon lifted me up as if I didn't weigh a pound and I wrapped my legs around him. Using the wall to hold me up, he moved my thong to the side and slid two of his fingers inside of my wet pussy.

"Ooh baby, you are so wet. You missed me didn't you? I knew you missed me."

Without responding I bit my lip to keep myself from moaning.

"Damn, I miss you baby. I want to fuck you right now, right here, and make you scream loud enough for everybody in the fucking party to hear you."

"Your girlfriend is here."

"I don't give a damn about her. I lied to you. We do belong together baby. "

"Shh. Stop. We gotta stop," I said trying to close my legs. Jonathon fingered me harder and shut me right back up. If I opened my mouth I was going to scream, Jonathon was going to make sure of that.

"I wanna see you. Come tonight," Jonathon said kissing me again. I shook my head no.

Jonathon pulled his fingers out of me and in one quick motion put three in. I bit down on my lip harder as he pushed them in and out of me.

"KARI!" I heard Marvin yell into the house. The back door was literally ten feet away from the bathroom so he was close. I grabbed Jonathon's hand to stop him and put my finger over my lips to signal him to be quiet.

"Come see me tonight. Promise me you will come see me

tonight or I will make you scream so he will hear you," he whispered.

"Okay, okay I will."

"I said promise me you will."

"I promise. I swear I will, now stop before we get caught."

We waited until we heard the screen door slam, and then Jonathon pulled his fingers out of me and let me down. I fixed my dress as he went to the sink and washed his hands. He looked at me one more time before he left out the bathroom.

"Text me later," he said in a tone that told me he meant business. "We need to talk."

I nodded my head and he gave me another kiss. He cracked the door and made sure no one was around before he slipped out of the bathroom and left me in there alone.

I stood there for a few minutes unable to believe what I had just done. It was wrong and we had absolutely crossed the line. We were lucky that nobody caught us.

I took one final look at myself in the mirror making sure there was no trace of my infidelity and opened the door. As soon as I did Marvin was walking into the house.

"Kari, where you been? I been looking everywhere for you. Did you hear me calling you?"

"No, I didn't," I lied.

"What happened? Why is it glass all over the floor?"

"That's what was taking me so long, I was trying to clean up in here. I tripped and almost fell and dropped the wine. I'm sorry."

Marvin laughed.

"You and them damn heels," he said shaking his head.

"Let me clean this up," I said trying to walk past him. I couldn't look him in the face after what I had just done.

"It's okay baby, I'll get it. Go ahead and enjoy your party."

Smiling. I almost ran out of the room and back to the party. Jonathon was standing near the speakers talking to Jacob. When he saw me he gave me a concerned look. I nodded my head to let him know everything was okay and got as far as I could away from him.

"The food was so good Kari! Oh my goodness! You have to

give me the recipe for your sweet potato pie! You put your foot in that!" Jayla exclaimed giving me a hug.

"Did you take a couple of pieces to go?"

"No, it's okay Kari. I already had two pieces."

"Well have two more. Kevin go get her some pie to go."

"Oh so ya'll just gonna make me do everything," Kevin said, giving Jayla the to-go plates he was already carrying and making his way back into the house.

"I had a lot of fun, thanks again for inviting me."

"Anytime girl, and I'm glad you had fun."

"So you should come to church with Kevin and me Sunday. He said he thought you would really like it."

"You know what, call and remind me and I might go. I promise."

"I will."

We chatted for a couple more minutes until Kevin came back with the plates. I told them to be careful and urged Kevin to call me when they made it home.

"What do you need me to do to help?" Jamie asked coming over to me a few minutes later as I sat on the couch with my feet up.

"Girl go home and get some rest. Marvin is making his friends help him clean up, don't worry about it."

"Okay girl, well I had fun," she said leaning down to give me a hug.

"I'm glad you came. Don't forget your crab cakes, they're in the oven."

"Thanks girl, cause them are so good! You get some rest."

"I will. Thanks for coming."

I walked Jamie to the door, then went outside to say goodbye to the rest of my guests. It had been a lot of fun, but I was glad it was over! It was time for me to relax.

After everyone was gone I went upstairs and ran me a nice bubble bath. It was the perfect way to end my night and as I lay there with my eyes closed, I shut the outside world out and had some me time.

Marvin walked in while I was sitting on the bed with my

pajamas on watching a movie. He looked tired, and I knew he was considering how hard he had worked today. I really appreciated how much he had done to make my birthday party such a success. He was truly stepping up and showing me he could be a better man.

"You look tired baby," I said, as he sat on the bed and took his shoes off. He lay down beside me and closed his eyes, finally able to rest for a few minutes.

I let him lie there and have his much needed moment of silence and continued my movie.

"Did you have fun?" he asked, sitting up and stretching.

"I did. I had a great time, thank you so much for all you did."

"You're welcome baby, you deserve it. You know I was watching you all day right?"

"Yes," I said hesitantly not knowing where he was going with that comment.

"Yeah. You were looking fine. Did you pick that dress out?"

"Yeah."

"Well if you wore that for your birthday, I can't wait to see what you wear for mine."

Marvin leaned down and kissed me sliding his tongue into my mouth. He lay down and pulled me on top of him sliding his hands up my shirt.

"I been wanting to get you up here all day baby."

"I know, I can tell. You wouldn't let me get away from you for five seconds."

"Well I didn't want to give anybody the opportunity to snatch you up."

You failed, I thought.

"I'm about to hop in the shower and then come back out and show you what I've been trying to do to you all day."

Marvin went into the bathroom and started the shower. I couldn't believe how he was acting. There was a time during our relationship where he barely wanted to be around me, now it was like he couldn't stay away.

I lay back down in the bed and continued watching my movie. It felt good to finally be in the bed. My phone chimed just as I was starting to doze off. I grabbed it off of the nightstand and I squinted my eyes as they adjusted to the bright light from my phone. I had a text message from Jonathon.

I told you to text me later, it read.

I texted back:

Sorry I was wrapping the party up.

After a few minutes my phone vibrated again.

It's cool. What time u comin ova?

I took a deep breath and texted him back.

I can't come tonight, I'm really tired.

I sent the message and lay back down. Before I could even get comfortable again my phone rang. Already knowing it was him, I quickly answered.

"So we breakin' promises now?" he asked, as soon as I answered the phone.

"Jonathon I'm not, I just can't get away tonight. I'm sorry, I know I promised."

"You damn right you promised, and we don't break promises remember?"

"No we don't break promises, but I really can't tonight," I said leaving out of the bedroom and going downstairs to make sure Marvin couldn't hear me.

"You need to find a way Kari. I don't give a damn if you gotta wait until he goes to sleep, but I want to see you tonight."

"Jonathon I can't," I said again going into the downstairs bathroom and closing the door.

"Kari, if you don't come over here tonight I promise I will come over there tonight and tell Marvin about us. I promise."

Immediately I got pissed off. I couldn't believe Jonathon was blackmailing me.

"Kari, did you hear what I said?"

"Yeah I fuckin' heard you Jonathon!" I said in the loudest whisper I could. I cracked the door to see if I heard water running, but it had stopped.

"Where the hell am I supposed to tell him I'm going at this time of night?"

"You should've thought about that before you made that promise Kari."

I couldn't believe this. Was I really supposed to think all of that while he had his fingers inside of me threatening to make me scream with my husband standing only feet away?

Marvin's footsteps shook the ceiling over my head and I knew it was only a matter of time before he came downstairs to look for me.

"Okay I'll fuckin' come see you Jonathon," I said. I ended the call and stood in the bathroom. I didn't know what the hell I was going to tell Marvin that would make him comfortable enough to allow me to leave at this time of night, but I had to come up with something.

"I don't know what happened all I know is Jamie called me and she needs me. Maybe she drunk more than she thought she did or something. But I can't just leave her out there."

"What happened to her boyfriend, that model guy, where is he?"

"I don't know Marvin, I didn't get all the details, she was too upset. I will be back as soon as I get done with her I promise."

I stood there in a t- shirt and jean shorts and flip flops. I didn't plan on being gone long, but I damn sure had a thing or two I was about to tell Jonathon. I tried my best not to show how pissed off I was.

"Okay, be careful. And call me and let me know what the hell is going on."

Nodding my head, I jetted out of the house. It was definitely about to be on!

When I made it to Jonathon's house, I pulled into the carport and cut the car off. Jonathon was already at the door and as soon as I saw him, I slapped the taste out of his mouth.

"What the fuck is wrong with you? Huh? What the hell do you think this is? Are you trying to get caught? What the hell were you thinking pulling me into the bathroom like that today?"

"I didn't hear one complaint about what I was doing fall from your lips."

"I told you to stop."

"But you didn't try hard to stop me, did you?"

"When did we start blackmailing each other? You'll tell Marvin if I don't come over? That's how we fuckin' playing it now?"

"I was never gonna come tell him shit, I just knew that was the only way to get you over here. We have to talk Kari."

"We could talk on the phone."

"So it's like that now?" he asked, coming closer to me. "You didn't miss me?"

I moved away from him and he came closer. If he touched me, it would be over. He knew it, too. So he came closer to me. We danced around the room for a few minutes. I was trying my best to stay away from him. I did miss him, and I'd be lying if I said I didn't, but I wanted my marriage to work. Marvin had really gotten better and it wasn't fair to him if I just gave up after begging him for years to get it together.

"Why you actin' like this Kari?" he asked, finally getting annoyed.

"I'm not acting like anything Jonathon, I'm just trying to do what's right."

"And what's that?"

For a moment, I hesitated. The right thing to do would be to stay with Marvin and let Jonathon move on, but being with Jonathon felt right and I couldn't just ignore my heart's desire.

"To make my marriage work," I finally said softly. Jonathon gave me a look that would've made me drop dead if looks could kill.

"So that's what you wanna do?" he asked.

"That's the right thing to do, we both know it."

"Well I'm starting to not give a damn what's right Kari."

"You should. Marvin is your friend and he's a nice guy."

"But he doesn't deserve you. We both know it and we already talked about it."

"But it's different when you're in the relationship, and you're not Jonathon."

"I don't give a fuck about your relationship with Marvin anymore Kari. I love you and I wanna be with you and we both know we deserve each other."

I stood against his white living room wall and we just stared at each other. He wasn't touching me, but he might as well have been. My body tingled just looking into his eyes.

"I watched you all day today Kari. I couldn't keep my fuckin' eyes off of you. I watched you walk around with Marvin and the way he touched you. It pisses me off, that's how I know I'm still in love with you. I tried to tell myself I didn't care about you, but I do."

Jonathon walked over to me and I didn't move. I let him kiss me and it felt so good.

He pulled me off the wall and into his chest. I opened my mouth to allow his tongue access as he ran his fingers through my hair. It would be best to stop him, but this man was my weakness. I desired him in a way I'd never felt before. He had the power to make me forget everything that was important to me by just kissing my lips. At this point my mind was blank and the only person that mattered in my world was Jonathon.

"I love you too, Jonathon, I do. This is just hard for me."

"I know baby, and I'm sorry. I don't want to stress you, but it's time. It's time for you to be with me."

"I can't-"

Jonathon kissed me again before I could finish my protest. He led me over to his brown couch and laid me down.

"We can't Jonathon-"

"Shhh," he said kissing me once more. "Lay here and let me make you feel good."

Jonathon slid off my shorts and panties, and I lay there naked from the waist down. Jonathon went into the kitchen and came back with a cup of ice chips. He put some in his mouth then went straight to work.

As soon as his mouth touched me, I let out a shriek. His cold mouth on the most sensitive parts of my pussy was driving me crazy. I bit my lip and let out small cries as Jonathon nibbled on my clit.

"You taste so good baby," he said pulling me down so I couldn't get away.

"I could eat your pussy all day long."

I moaned loudly as his cold tongue teased my clit. My walls started to contract as an orgasm began to build in my body. I was almost there…

"Oh my God, yes! Yes! Just like that baby, I'm about to cum," I said to him. Before I knew it, Jonathon had stopped eating me out and I could feel his length push into me.

"Damn baby, damn this pussy… oh my God."

He had done it. I had tried not to let it come to this, but he had done it. At this point he owned me, and I was willing to do or say whatever he told me. He had the best dick I had ever had in my entire life. There was no way I could turn this down; all I could do was wait until he told me what to do.

"Get on top baby."

We switched positions like he said. At this point I was thinking of no one but Jonathon. I was his genie in a bottle; his every wish was my command.

I started to ride Jonathon in a slow motion, my wetness running with every stroke. He was filling me, and all I could do was moan.

"You know you can't leave me baby," he said looking into my eyes. "You aint gonna leave this dick are you?"

"No, no baby. I'm not going anywhere," I panted. I could feel that orgasm building back up and the harder I rode him, the closer it came.

"You promise?"

"I promise. I swear I'll never leave you Jonathon, I swear."

"That's right baby. You want me to make you cum?"

"Yes baby," I cried. "Make me cum."

Jonathon turned me over on the sofa and started to pound into me. The feeling of pleasure and pain was just what I needed. I was on the brink of orgasm.

"Whose pussy is it baby? Mine or Marvin?"

"Yours!" I screamed, caring about nothing but the orgasm I so desperately needed.

"What's my name?"

"Jonathon!! OH MY GOD!! JONATHON!"

I closed my eyes as the orgasm shot through my body. Jonathon kissed me and I moaned into his mouth. At this moment he was my man and I loved him. There was no Marvin and no marriage. There was just me and him. He was the love of my life. It wasn't complicated at that moment; my life was perfect. He had just given me a body tingling orgasm and I went limp. I couldn't even open my eyes.

Jonathon wasn't quite done. He took about three more pumps and reached his orgasm as well. He came hard, professing his love for me. We laid there in each other's arms exhausted from our lovemaking. He was so warm. I never wanted to leave and go back home. At that moment, if I was brave enough, I would just leave my life behind. I could run away with Jonathon and never look back.

But the reality was, I was married and home was where I belonged. Marvin and I had agreed to try to make our marriage work and he was trying. He had been treating me so well. I needed to try too.

We lay there in silence for awhile, neither of us wanting to face the reality of what was about to happen. I had to get up and leave, and I knew Jonathon didn't want that.

I tried to get up, but Jonathon was like dead weight.

"Let me up Jonathon," I said, trying to push him off of me.

He got up, so I sat up and stretched.

"Where is it?" I asked, looking in between my legs.

"Where is what?"

"The condom. Where did it go?"

"Oh shit, I forgot to put one on."

My heart dropped.

"What do you mean forgot? How could you forget that?"

"You didn't remind me either."

I wanted to slap the shit out of him again! I couldn't believe he would just have sex with me raw like I wasn't a married woman.

I didn't say anything else to him. There was no time. I grabbed my clothes and went upstairs to the bathroom and got in the shower.

I couldn't stay in long, and I just had to make sure there was no trace of sex on me. Luckily I had taken a shower a little before I left so it wouldn't be a red flag when I came home smelling fresh.

Just when I was about to get out of the shower, Jonathon got in. He tried to grab my arm to make me stay in the shower with him, but I really didn't want to see him. I was so mad about what he had done. After I got out the shower, threw my clothes back on and combed my hair. I was putting on my shoes when Jonathon came downstairs wearing nothing but a towel.

"So you just gonna leave without saying bye?"

"You were in the shower and I have to go. Marvin has already called my phone three times," I explained grabbing my purse and looking for my car keys.

"So what does this mean?" he asked, leaning against the arm of the couch.

"I don't know Jonathon," I said, unable to focus on much but getting home before Marvin came looking for me.

"So you just gonna leave without talking to me?"

"I don't wanna talk right now Jonathon, I have to get home.

We'll talk later."

Jonathon let me out and I walked down to my car. I backed out of the parking lot and sped towards home.

"Where the hell have you been?" Marvin asked holding his cell phone in his hand. He was waiting for me at the door when I got home. "I called your phone three times. I don't have Jamie's phone number otherwise I would've called her."

Thank God for small miracles, I thought.

"I'm sorry baby. Her and that model guy got into a fight so she was really upset. I just lost track of time and my phone was on vibrate," I said repeating the excuse I had rehearsed on the way home.

"I told you to call me and let me know what was going on," he said slowly as if he was speaking to a child.

"I know. I'm so sorry. I know you were worried."

Marvin didn't say anything, he just sat there and stared at me the way he always did when I did something wrong.

"I'm sorry," I repeated.

Marvin nodded his head and turned around and went upstairs. I let out a long sigh of relief when I saw that he was going to get off of my case. It had been a long day. I looked at my phone and saw that it was three thirty seven in the morning. After setting my purse and keys on the table, I poured myself another glass of wine to end my birthday.

# CHAPTER 21

Marvin had been acting weird ever since the night of my birthday. I knew he was growing suspicious, so it was important that I kept my distance from Jonathon if I wanted to make my marriage work. Marvin was making that impossible though. Since it was summer, they played basketball together constantly. I had figured out how to plan around their basketball days so I would not be around. He had called me a couple of times, but Jonathon was not really one to chase. He would only go so far before he would back away.

I finally got off the couch and went upstairs to run myself a nice, hot bath. It was Saturday and after cleaning the entire house, I needed to soak in a hot tub and relax. After turning on some Sade, I stepped into my large Jacuzzi tub and closed my eyes. Sade's beautiful mellow voice relaxed me and the jets massage all the nerves in my body. It had been a while since I had gotten the chance to be alone with my own thoughts. It was bittersweet.

I was ashamed at the woman I had become. I had never been one to cheat and here I was having a full blown affair with one of my husband's good friends. The first time I had sworn would be the last time, but things got complicated. Neither of us planned to fall in love. There came a point when I craved him and I would get out of bed with my husband at any time of night to go and be with him. I couldn't get enough of Jonathon, and he damn sure couldn't get enough of me.

After soaking in the bath for close to an hour, I got out and threw on my robe. I put on my body cream and then threw on blue jean shorts and a tank top. It was a lazy day, and my mood was definitely deteriorating. It always did this time of year. I could feel the depression start to come over me, but I was keeping myself busy. The only person I felt comfortable talking to was Kevin and I didn't want to bother him. It would only make him upset and I didn't want to do that. He looked so happy with Jayla at my party.

Not knowing what to do with myself, I called Jamie. She was always able to lift my spirits.

"Hello?" she answered.

"Hey Jamie, what are you doing?"

"Nothing. I was meaning to call you. I hope I didn't upset you by what I said at the party. You know, about Jonathon."

"Oh no! No, I appreciate you telling me the truth. I was tripping. You're my friend, that's what you're supposed to do."

"Good. I thought about it later. I didn't want to come off all bitchy because I didn't mean it like that."

"I know, don't worry about it. I have thick skin. What are you up to?"

"Just running a few errands. Bills bills bills, you know how it is."

"I do."

"What are you doing?"

"Sitting here at home. Marvin is at work and I just got done cleaning."

"Well get dressed and come ride with me. Cheer me up a little while I give away all my hard earned money."

"I'm already dressed all I gotta do is throw on my flip flops. I'm at the door when you get here."


"So he fucked you in your bathroom during your party?"

"No we didn't fuck Jamie."

"Well almost! Kari," she said in a disapproving tone.

"Okay don't do that. Don't be judgmental. I don't tell you for you to judge me," I snapped instantly getting annoyed.

"I'm not judging you, but come on Kari, you know that crossed the line."

"I do and that's why I don't need you to tell me. I didn't mean for it to happen at all. I didn't plan for it."

"I know you didn't, but what if somebody would have caught you? His family was there, his coworkers. That could have been extremely embarrassing for you both."

"I know."

"I'm not preaching Kari, I'm not. I'm just worried about you. Do you think this little thing with Jonathon has gone too far?"

I shrugged my shoulders. What Jamie didn't understand was what I had with Jonathon was not just a thing. It was more than that. I had fallen head over heels in love with him, and now I was struggling to fall out. To love someone and not be able to love them was hard, and getting caught by somebody with Jonathon in the bathroom was the least of my worries.

We sat in silence for a minute, the sound of the radio providing just enough noise to keep it from being uncomfortable.

"Kari, I just don't want you to get hurt, that's all. Please be careful."

I nodded my head and looked out of the window. I was ready to change the subject and was starting to second guess my decision about coming along.

"Don't be over there pouting girl, you know I got your back no matter what," Jamie said nudging me playfully. I smiled at her and instantly started feeling better. I couldn't be mad at her for telling me what I didn't want to hear. That's what friends were supposed to do.

"I'm not pouting," I said, poking my lip out. She laughed.

"Hey if anything hats off to you. I have to admit I'm a little jealous. My sex life sucks."

"And it will get better. I told you, you have to get out more. What happened to pretty boy you brought to my party?"

"Nothing, we still talk here and there, but he's a little immature when it comes to relationships. He's not ready to be a stepfather to my kids. He's in the prime of his fine ass life. You know how much sex he's probably having?"

"Yeah and speaking of sex he's having, what about you? Would you fall under the sex he's having list?"

"I fall under the sex he's had list. We had sex once, after the party."

My mouth dropped open dramatically.

"And you didn't tell me? See this is what I mean about trust

Jamie. How can we be together if we don't have trust?"

Jamie laughed.

"I didn't tell you because it wasn't a big deal. When I have some big deal sex, I will call you before his penis exits my vagina."

"You don't have to take it that far, trust me. Just tell me if it was good."

"Not really. I mean, I had drunk a lot that night, but it just wasn't good," she said making a funny face.

"Well he had been drinking too, maybe that was the reason. Don't make that a deal breaker. He might actually be the one you've been looking for."

"Yeah, I doubt that."

"Don't doubt it. He might surprise you."

"Okay first of all, you're talking like we're dating exclusively. We're not. We just hang out from time to time."

"And that's fine, but you never know what that can turn into."

Jamie stopped at a red light and gave me a serious look.

"He's a nice guy, but so far that's it. Don't try to force it to be something that it's not."

"Yet," I corrected her. "Something that it's not yet. I thought he was a nice guy too, and you should give him a chance. Don't let one night of bad sex decide whether or not you'll take him seriously."

"He's immature Kari."

"Okay, give me an example."

Jamie thought about it for a minute.

"He watches Cartoon Network every night until he falls asleep."

"And that's your big problem?"

"One among many."

"You know what, you find a problem with every guy you date."

"I do not."

"Yes you do Jamie, and I think I know the reason."

She paused as she waited for my answer.

"I think you're still in love with your ex-husband."

"Okay, now you're talking crazy."

Jamie had been married to her husband Fernando for almost ten years before they got a divorce. They didn't have any major problems, and she just said they grew apart. Financial stresses had taken a toll on their relationship.

"So you don't miss him?"

"No I do not miss him," she said with a straight face. I could tell she was flat out lying, but I just let her have it. She had to admit to herself first that she missed him before she would ever be able to say it to me.

"Can we stop talking about men now? They give me a headache," she said putting her hand on her forehead

"Yes we can stop talking about men now that I have put you in the hot seat."

Jamie laughed and pulled into her credit union to get money out of her account. We drove around running errands and going in and out of stores. Jamie only had two days off a week, so she had to squeeze everything into those days.

After all the running around we went to The Olive Garden to have lunch. We placed our orders and sat there drinking and talking. Jamie talked to me about work and all the mess she had to deal with. I didn't see how she did it. Working all of those hours and having to squeeze in time for your children, but somehow she made it happen.

"I'm seriously considering looking for another job," she said taking a bite of her salad. "I don't know how much longer I can deal with the bullshit up there. Too much stress."

"What else would you do?"

"Well if you would hurry up and open that catering business, you can hire me and I can quit. But other than that I would like to do a job where I get to sit down and have enough time to go back to school and get my degree."

"I didn't know you wanted to go back to school. What do you want to go for?"

"Health care administration."

"That's a good field. You should really start to put that in motion. What school do you want to go to?"

We chatted some more as we enjoyed our meal. It was good to catch up with her and being out and about all day did take my mind off of things, but I knew that eventually I would have to get back to my life, my reality, and my problems.

DeQuindra Renea

# CHAPTER 22

Jonathon had called me twice the day after my party. I didn't answer and I didn't return his calls. Truthfully I didn't know what to do anymore. Things were easier when I was dealing with old Marvin. Now, he was being so loving and caring and I was falling in love with him all over again.

I gave myself a few days to think before I called him back. It was the middle of the afternoon and Marvin was gone to work. He didn't answer at first, but I called right back.

"Hello?"

"Hey, how are you?"

"I'm good. What's up?" he asked urgently.

"I know I haven't been answering the phone, I just needed to think."

"It's cool. What's up?" he asked again.

"You busy or something?"

"Yeah, can I call you back later?"

I paused for a minute and I could have sworn I heard a woman's voice in the background. Jealousy crept into my heart.

"Yeah, I guess," I finally answered barely able to find my voice. He hung up without even saying goodbye.

I sat with my phone in my hand for a minute feeling like a damn fool. Here I was jeopardizing my marriage for him and he didn't have time to talk to me because he was entertaining some bitch.

Before I knew it, I was calling again. He didn't answer and

that pissed me off more. I couldn't help but imagine him spending time with another woman and it infuriated me. I got up and started cleaning the house to keep myself from driving over his house and getting us both caught up.


Jonathon called me back almost four hours later after I'd finished cleaning and was making myself something to eat. I answered immediately.

"Sup, can you talk?"

"Yeah, what were you doing earlier?" I asked, wasting no time.

"I was busy."

"Did you have a girl over there?"

"What?" he asked, sounding annoyed.

"You heard me. Were you with a girl?"

"Why does it matter?"

"Just answer my question. Tell the truth."

"Yeah."

"So you just have a different woman over every night huh?" I asked, pissed.

"What?"

"You actually got me over here thinkin' about leavin' my fuckin' husband and you over there fuckin' some girl?"

"Are you serious? You married remember? You with somebody else every night!"

"You knew that already so that's not my fault."

"'Yeah, it's my fault."

"What? What you tryna say?" I asked, finally getting off of the couch. I looked outside to make sure Marvin wasn't pulling up.

"I'm just tired of this shit. I'm a single man I don't need to hear you bitchin' at me about seeing somebody. You aint my fuckin' wife!"

"Yeah, and I'm glad. You wanna fuck everybody that's why I would never marry you. You a fuckin' dog!"

"You know what, I'm done with yo crazy ass. You a damn fool if you think I'm finna be sittin' over here by myself waitin' on you. I can get a bitch ten times badder than you anyway."

"Then get one you sorry muthafucka and don't call me no more!"

"Don't worry, I won't, bitch."

Fuming, I ended the call and slammed my phone down on the table. He had just pulled me into my bathroom two days before and now he was already fucking somebody else? That really showed me how much he wanted commitment.

Deep down I knew it was time to let Jonathon go. It would be hard since I did love him, but I was being unfair to Marvin. He was his friend and what we were doing was wrong. I had to be the one to draw the line.

After gathering my thoughts, I got up and started cooking a steak dinner for Marvin. I didn't know if it was guilt or just my wanting to do something nice for him. Either way I needed to show my husband I was all in. If he was giving his all, it was only right that I gave my all too.

DeQuindra Renea

# CHAPTER 23

I woke to the blaring of the radio. Marvin's alarm had gone off. It was 6:05 a.m. and I was wide awake. I hadn't been sleeping much, never really did. The guilt was weighing me down and my depression was starting to sink in. In two months it would be November 20, the anniversary of the fire. Every year was worse than the previous. The dreams were worse, I cried more, and every year it seemed my depression sunk in further. Marvin sat up and went to turn off the radio, but I motioned for him to leave it on. I loved The *Tom Joyner Morning Show* and listening to them joke and laugh for a couple of hours might lift my spirits. Marvin gave me a kiss on the lips and got in the shower. I lay there with my eyes closed. I didn't feel like getting out of bed. Today would be a horrible day. I could already feel it. I already knew it would be. Tears slid down the side of my face and I turned over to hide them from Marvin. I didn't want him to see me crying. I didn't want him to call in to work. I needed alone time today. Him hovering over me every five seconds would not help me feel any better. Not today.

I heard the shower turn off and I lay there pretending I had fallen back to sleep. He probably wouldn't fall for it, but it was worth a try anyway. The door opened as he came back into the room. He was getting dressed, but I never opened my eyes. After about twenty minutes of him running back and forth to the bathroom, he was finally ready.

"Kari," he called softly. I didn't answer.

"Kari?"

"Hmm," I said in more of a moan.

"You sleep?"

"Yeah."

"I'm about to go to work. You okay today?"

"Yeah."

"Why don't you call somebody to come over and sit with you today?"

"Maybe."

I felt the bed shift as Marvin leaned over to give me another kiss. I didn't move, hoping he wouldn't feel the tears on my face. Keeping my eyes closed, I waited for him to leave. When I finally heard the front door slam, a small weight left. It bothered me when people worried about me, so I tried to hide my pain as much as I could. That was the reason I still hadn't called; he was the person who worried about me the most.

Marvin had been gone almost a half hour before I crawled out of bed. I didn't want to go to the bathroom because it was hard for me to look at myself in the mirror. I didn't want to see my face today. It was like that for me sometimes. Usually when I grew depressed, I made Marvin cover all the mirrors in the house. As I descended the stairs, the sound of music coming from the radio faded away behind me. The sun was starting to come up and peek through my curtains. That even made me cry. After making sure Marvin was gone, I headed downstairs into the basement. I went to my hiding space and pulled out my wooden black box. It was about the size of a shoebox and inside it held everything I had collected about the fire. It also held pictures of my family before the fire. It was what my life was like before it was destroyed. My life before everything was taken from me.

My loud sobs filled the basement as I pulled out all of the contents of the box. My chest heaved as I struggled to catch my breath when pain of that day came back to me. I didn't know why I did this to myself, reliving that day over and over again in my head. My heart was breaking again. I could feel the fire, I could still smell it as it burned up my life and loved ones. That was the day I died.

Lying my head on the floor amongst all of my photos and newspaper clippings, I cried, a cry that seemed to come from the depths of my soul. I couldn't stop. I lay there crying until I cried myself to sleep on the bathroom floor.

"KARI! KARI!

I awoke to my front door slamming and footsteps running through my house. Marvin was running through the house yelling my name. I didn't know what the hell was going on. Jumping up, I locked the bathroom door and began to gather all of my pictures off of the floor. Marvin was running around upstairs checking for me in every room. I could hear him running down the basement stairs before I could get everything in the box. Marvin shook the door handle and knocked on the door.

"Just a minute," I said trying my best to sound normal.

"Kari, open the door," he said shaking the handle again. Slipping the box in the cabinet under the sink, I wiped my eyes and opened the door.

"Kari, what are you doing? Are you okay?" Marvin asked, looking deep into my eyes.

"Nothing. What's wrong? Why are you running through the house hollering," I asked pushing past him not wanting to linger in the bathroom too long. The last thing I wanted to do was talk to him about the fire.

"Why haven't you been answering your phone? I been calling you and your brother has too. He's on his way over here."

I could've smacked myself. I knew Kevin would be calling me today and now he was going to come over and want to play fifty two thousand questions.

"Well I'm fine as you can see, so you can tell my brother he doesn't need to come over here."

"I already did. He's on his way. Kari, you gotta pick up your phone! You got everybody worried about you," Marvin said following me upstairs.

"I'm fine! I wish ya'll would stop worrying."

"Have you called your therapist? Maybe you can go in today and talk to her."

"I don't want to talk to anybody, all I want is for you to go to work, Kevin to go home, and ya'll just let me have some space! I don't need ya'll breathing down my neck every second of the day. I'm fine!"

"You pushing everybody away is not making them care any

"Oh it's me? I'm pushing you away? Where was all this concern when I was having my nightmares? Did you care then? Because I remember having to go and sleep in the guest room by myself because of your job, and now you're so quick to stay home? Go back to work Marvin," I said through gritted teeth.

Marvin didn't say anything for a minute, we just stood there in the kitchen staring at each other. He knew I was right. Just because he had been playing nice for a few months didn't change the past.

"Kevin is still going to come over."

"I'm sure he will."

Marvin left without saying another word. He knew when to leave me the hell alone and this was one of those moments.

I went into the kitchen and poured myself a glass of wine, not caring it was only nine in the morning. Hell I was going through. A buzz was needed today.

I sat there sipping on my wine and waiting for my brother. I would never be able to convince him to go back home because he knew me too well. He had to sit and look at me in my face himself for six hours before he believed I was okay. He would never take Marvin's word on my emotional state.

Silence enveloped me as I sat alone. It was doing nothing for me. I really needed something stronger, but if I reeked of alcohol when Kevin got to my house, he would have a heart attack. He would then start to worry about my drinking on top of everything else.


"Please take that concerned look off your face," I said opening the door for Kevin. "Just like I told Marvin, I'm fine."

"You're always fine let you tell it. I wish you would just tell me the truth. Look at you. You look like you been crying all morning."

"I don't care what I look like."

"Don't start that Kari, please. And don't even think about covering all these mirrors."

Kevin gave me a hug and followed me into the kitchen. He frowned as soon as he saw the glass of wine sitting on the table.

"How much have you been drinking Kari?"

"Don't start asking me a million questions Kevin, I'm not in the mood."

Kevin sat across from me at the table and looked at me. I got up to make a pot of coffee so he wouldn't be able to just stare.

"Tell me what's going on Kari," he said as he took a sip of his hot coffee when I brought it to him.

"I told you I'm fine. I don't understand why you keep asking me."

"Because I know you're lying. Is it the fire?"

After taking a sip of my wine, I nodded my head.

"Why didn't you just tell me? You act like we didn't go through that together."

"But you're fine, you grew out of it, the nightmares and stuff. That shit still haunts me, like I didn't-"

My voice trailed off. The tears were coming and I was trying my best to stop them.

"I feel like I didn't make it out of the fire," I confessed.

"But you did Kari. We made it out. I know it's hard but we have to go on. We have to try to let it go."

"That's real easy for you to say Kevin. Real easy."

"Kari, I'm trying to help you. I'm trying to tell you what helped me."

"We are not the same person Kevin. You have no idea what that fire did to me."

"Have you been in the box?"

I nodded my head again and took another sip of my wine.

"Let me take that box home Kari. You don't need to have it here. Look what it's doing to you."

"No. That box is going to stay right where I put it."

I jumped up from the kitchen table and ran downstairs. Kevin followed me. I had forgotten I put the box under the sink when Marvin came home. I returned it back to its hiding place.

"You need to let me take it to my house Kari. You can come over there anytime you need it."

"I said no Kevin, now stop asking me."

Kevin followed me back upstairs and into the kitchen. We sat at the table in silence. The radio was still blasting from my room. They were jamming so early in the morning and had my mood not been on zero, I would've probably been dancing around the house.

"Where is Jayla?"

"Work. She told me to tell you hi."

"Tell her I said the same. And tell her I'm sorry I haven't made it to church."

"She knows what's going on. She understands."

Kevin didn't say anything else. He just sat there staring at me like a fool. As much as I loved my brother, I was ready for him to leave. I understood he was worried, but he knew I needed alone time.

"Kevin you do not have to sit here and babysit me all day. If I need you, I will call."

"Yeah, I really believe that."

Kevin went into my refrigerator and warmed up some leftovers I had cooked the other night. There would be no getting him to leave.

I sat and talked to him while he ate his food. Gladly we had gotten off the topic of me and my problems. Talking to my brother did make me feel better when he wasn't harassing me about my emotional state.

"Did you ask Jayla to marry you yet?" I asked, turning the heat on him.

"I told you I was thinking about it."

"And I told you if you loved her there was nothing else to think about."

"I'm not ready to give my life up yet. I'm still young. I didn't plan on getting married until I was almost fifty."

"And when you're fifty nobody's gonna want your old ass."

Kevin laughed and got up to get a bottle of water out of the refrigerator.

"Yeah you always got jokes no matter what your mood is."

"Yeah that's me, the jokester," I said, without cracking a smile. I lifted my wine glass to let Kevin know I was empty. He shook his head.

"It's too early Kari. You don't need to be drinking."

"Just be glad I didn't pour myself a shot of Patron like I was going to before you got here."

I waited for Kevin to move, but he didn't budge.

"I can get up and pour it myself Kevin. It is my house."

Kevin shrugged his shoulders and filled my cup. I got up from the table and stretched.

"Well you can stay here if you want, but I'm going upstairs to lie down."

"Lie down?"

"Yes, lie down Kevin, people do that sometimes when they get tired. Get off my back today, I'm warning you."

I left the kitchen and headed upstairs. I turned the radio off and got under the covers. I lay there for awhile just thinking about my past. Traveling down memory lane was one of the hardest things I could do. Trying to wipe the past out of my life and move on like Kevin was impossible, so I would forever be haunted by the fire in my dreams, in my mind and in my heart.

# CHAPTER 24

The smooth voice of *The Five Stairsteps* sung in my ear through the clock radio. I felt like God was playing this song just for me. Today was not going to be a good day. My heart was already in my stomach.

Marvin came out of the bathroom wearing his robe. He looked over and noticed I was up so he got in the bed and lay next to me.

"You okay baby? You need me to get you anything."

I shook my head no, wiping the tears from my eyes.

"Can you please just cover up all the mirrors for me?" I asked turning over. I appreciated Marvin being so sweet and concerned, but I really just wanted to be by myself.

Tears slid down my face before I could stop them. Today was November 20th, the day I lost everything. It was the hardest day of the year, every year. All I wanted to do was lie in bed, but I knew Kevin would be over bright and early for me.

I sobbed into my pillow softly so Marvin wouldn't hear me. I didn't want him over my shoulder today. Kevin would man that position with no problem.

I could hear Marvin moving around in the bathroom covering the mirrors just like I'd asked him to. I let myself cry for a few more minutes then, when I was sure Marvin had covered every mirror in the house, I wiped my eyes and forced myself out of bed.

I didn't really feel like getting dressed, so I just threw on some sweatpants and a hoodie. After throwing my hair up in a ponytail, I found a pair of sunglasses to cover my puffy eyes. Today was not a day for pretty. Today was a sad day.

I went downstairs to force myself to drink a cup of juice. Marvin was already downstairs drinking his cup of coffee and reading the newspaper. He gave me a small smile and poured me a glass of orange juice before I had a chance to. Sitting across from him, I nursed my cup.

"What time is Kevin coming?"

I shrugged my shoulders.

"Soon I guess."

"Do you want me to go with you to the cemetery?"

I shook my head. Every year Marvin took November 20th off of work and asked me if I wanted him to go to the cemetery with me. Every year I refused. Marvin didn't even know where my family was buried, and that was the way I wanted to keep it. He would never understand the loss I felt so it was no need for him to even try. I didn't even want to go to the cemetery with Kevin, but I had promised him I always would when I was twelve.

"Are you sure?"

"I'm sure."

We sat there in silence for a while. I wasn't in the mood to talk. I really wanted to leave the room, but I wanted to prove to Marvin he had nothing to worry about.

"What do you want me to make you for breakfast?"

"I'm not hungry."

"You have to eat something Kari."

"Kevin is going to take me out to eat later like he does every year."

"That's later Kari, you need to eat breakfast."

I grabbed a banana out the fruit bowl to get him off of my back.

After eating my banana, I sarcastically opened my mouth to show Marvin it was gone. He dropped the newspaper and shook his head.

I finished my juice and made myself half a bagel so Marvin could see I was trying.

The doorbell rang and I went to answer it knowing it was Kevin. He stood at the door wearing a pair of black sweatpants and a black and grey coat. He had on a pair of black gloves and a black hat. It was cold outside and he came in quickly to stop the air from invading my warm house.

"Hey little one," he said forcing a smile. The sadness in his eyes almost made me cry again.

"Hi big bro," I said wrapping my arms around him. We held in a tight embrace for a few minutes. I was trying to hold him together and he was trying to do the same for me.

Kevin walked into the kitchen and started talking to Marvin. I grabbed my coat and Marvin stood up and gave me a kiss.

"Call me if you need me for anything," he urged. "I love you."

"I love you, too."


"I really hate doin' this," Kevin said putting the car in park. I sat in the passenger seat with the flowers in my lap. My heart was beating fast. I knew exactly what Kevin was feeling because I was feeling it at that moment too.

"I don't think I should get out Kevin," I said softly.

"What? What are you talking about?"

"I just... I can't do it..."

Closing my eyes tight the tears started to sting my eyes.

"I don't wanna get out!" I cried, letting the tears flow. Kevin unbuckled his seatbelt and reached over to give me a hug.

"Okay Kari, it's okay. You don't have to get out. You came. This is enough. I know how hard it is for you."

I cried softly into Kevin's shoulder. He was always supportive.

Kevin took the flowers off of my lap and gave me a brave smile. I watched through my window as he walked to the graves. He laid flowers down and got on his knees. He was crying. His shoulders were going up and down. I cried as I watched him. I wanted to go and give him a hug, but I couldn't get out that car. I couldn't take it.

Kevin stayed out for thirty minutes, then came and got back in the car.

His eyes were puffy red. He was biting his lips, trying to stop the tears. I knew he didn't want me to see him cry, but it was too late. He put the car in drive and took off without saying a word. We rode in silence, him focused on the road, and me staring out of the window.

"Kari, can we please talk about it?" he asked, breaking the

silence.

"No."

"Why? It's been twenty years."

"I know how long it's been Kevin."

"So we need to talk about it."

"No we don't."

"Kari-"

"Kevin, leave me alone," I warned. He was really pushing it.

"I need to talk to someone about what happened."

"That's what therapists are for."

Kevin didn't say anything. He just kept driving. I didn't understand why he wanted to keep arguing about something that would never change. There would never be a time when he and I sat down and had a heart to heart about the fire. It just wasn't going to happen. The sooner he understood that, the better off we both would be.

Kevin drove to Bob Evans and we went inside to eat. I ordered a bowl of oatmeal, that way Kevin wouldn't notice when I picked all over it instead of eating it.

Breakfast seemed to drag on. Kevin talked the whole time. I just wanted to go home. I wasn't in the mood to be around people, see people, or be seen. Kevin trying to cheer me up was nice, but this year I just wasn't feeling spending the whole day together.

After breakfast Kevin took me bowling. He always thought it was important for us to do something fun to try to take our mind off of the whole situation. It never worked, but he tried every year anyway. We spent the day together, and it was a quiet one. Neither one of us had too much to say to each other, but he felt it was important to be with me.

When I got home later that evening I went straight upstairs to my bedroom. Marvin was in his office with the door open, and I walked right by without saying anything to him. He followed me into the bedroom.

"How was it? You okay?" he asked with genuine concern.

"I'm fine," I said, quietly getting back into bed.

"Do you need anything baby? You wanna talk?"

I shook my head, took off my clothes, and lay under the covers in only my panties and bra. Marvin stood there for a little while longer before he left to go back into the office. He left the bedroom door open so I had to cry silently.

Late that night after I was sure Marvin was asleep, I went into the basement and got my black box from underneath the floorboard. It had officially been twenty years and I needed time to myself to grieve. I would only let myself walk down memory lane two times a year and it hurt worse every time.

# CHAPTER 25

I hadn't left the house in almost three weeks. I was barely eating and I couldn't stop crying. My depression was getting worse and I knew part of the reason was because of the fight I'd had with Jonathon. And to make matters worse, I had some type of stomach flu that made me want to do nothing but stay in the bed. Marvin had taken a week off of work because he and Kevin thought I needed "looking after," which basically meant he hovered over me all day asking me if I was okay. Today was no different.

"Kari I really think you need to go talk to somebody," Marvin said.

"I don't wanna talk to anyone. I just wanna be left alone."

"You've been alone Kari and you're not getting any better," he said concerned. "I don't think that's working."

"Technically I haven't been alone, you've been here irritating the hell outta me. That's not working either."

"I'm worried about you Kari, you've been depressed for a long time. You really need to talk to someone. It might make you feel better."

"I don't think so," I said, pulling the covers up to my neck. "I told you and Kevin I like to be left alone when I get like this. Ya'll know that yet ya'll insist on somebody being in my face twenty four seven."

"Because we care about you. And Kevin told me about your suicide attempt when you were eleven."

Instantly angered, I sat up in bed.

"Well Kevin can't tell you a damn thing cuz he wasn't there. And I told you leave the fuckin' past in the past."

"I just don't want you to hurt yourself."

"Well I appreciate you being concerned, but I'm fine," I said, laying down and turning with my back to him, hoping he would catch the hint that I was done talking.

"I'll bring you something to eat in a little while," he said before he left our bedroom.

I waited until I heard him downstairs before I pulled out my cell phone and called Kevin.

"Hey little one, everything okay?"

"No, why the fuck would you tell Marvin I tried to kill myself?"

Kevin took a deep breath.

"Because he needed to know."

"So you make that choice? Because if that's how it is I know a few things Jayla might need to know about you."

"Kari calm down, I was just trying to protect you."

"I don't need you to do anything for me. As a matter of fact stay the fuck outta my life. You always in my fuckin' business."

"'Kari, do you not see how depressed you are? I think you need to get some help. I'm worried about you."

"You're worried about me? No, I'm worried about you because I can't understand how you of all people can walk around every day and act like the fire didn't happen."

I hung up on him and turned my cell phone off. Going back and forth with Kevin was irritating. I really just wanted everybody to leave me the hell alone.


Marvin woke me up later with lunch on a tray. He had made a sandwich and brought up an apple and a bottle of water. I took a few bites of my sandwich and lay back down. Not even half an hour later, I was in the bathroom throwing up.

"That's it, I'm making you a doctor's appointment. You are making yourself sick."

He left the room before I could say anything. Leaning against the toilet, I fanned myself. I was burning up.

Fuck it, I thought. If going to the doctor will get them to leave me the hell alone that's what I'll have to do.


When Marvin told me he was going to make me a doctor's appointment, I thought it would be with my therapist. But he had somehow arranged for me to have two appointments the next day: one in the morning with Dr. Tipton my therapist, and one in the afternoon with Dr. Armstrong, my primary physician. He woke me up early and made a day of it starting with breakfast at Golden Gate. I ordered pancakes and bacon, but I was hardly eating anything.

"Do you feel a little better being out in the sun?"

I faked a smile and nodded my head, forcing myself to swallow a mouthful of pancakes. It tasted like sand going down my throat, but I knew I needed to eat.

"I really think you are going to feel much better after you talk to Dr. Tipton. Maybe she can give you some medicine that will make you feel a little better."

"I don't want any medicine."

"But you might need something."

"I don't need anything but time. And to just be left alone."

"Well we'll see what the doctor says."

Marvin drove me to Dr. Tipton's office and she called me back after only a couple of minutes of waiting.

"Your husband called me yesterday because he is very concerned."

"Yeah he made me come here today and talk to you. He thinks it might make me feel better."

"Well you usually come see me this time of the year anyway. Why didn't you give me a call?"

"Because I can get through this on my own."

"That's what you say every year Kari, but when you have suffered a loss like you have, you may be unable to fully get over it."

Tears started to roll down my cheeks and she passed me a Kleenex and gave me a warm smile. She was an older woman, maybe in her late forties. She had mahogany skin, brown eyes, and long legs. Her graying hair was pulled into a bun at the top of her head. She had on red lipstick, which didn't compliment her much. I wondered if she had children, or someone to tell her that was a bad color choice.

Dr. Tipton sat back and crossed her legs.

"Do you want to talk about the fire?"

I shook my head no. She asked that question every time I came, and the answer was always the same.

"Okay, why don't you tell me how you've been feeling."

"I'm just sad. And tired. It rained for like three days straight and rain really gets me down. I've been trying to eat, but I can't keep anything down."

"Have you been out anywhere or done anything?"

"I haven't left the house in a couple of weeks. I just don't feel like going anywhere or being around anyone. I just need to be by myself."

"Has there been anything else going on that might be taking a toll on your mood? Any fights between you and Marvin? Fights with your friends?"

Deep down inside I knew my fight with Jonathon had something to do with it, but I couldn't tell her that. The only person I'd ever trusted with that information was Jamie, and even though there was patient and doctor confidentiality I didn't feel comfortable telling her.

"Things have been going great between me and Marvin, better than it's been for a long time."

"Do you feel like you may need some medication?"

"I don't want to be put on medication Dr. Tipton, I told you that."

"I know Kari, but when I talked to Marvin he said things seem to be more extreme than normal. He said you're keeping all the mirrors covered in the house?"

I nodded my head.

"I thought you said you were done covering up the mirrors," she said scribbling some notes in her tablet.

"I just don't like to look at myself sometimes."

"Does it have anything to do with what you told me about your foster mother?"

I shuddered at the thought of Mrs. Rawlings. Me and Kevin were sent to her house after the fire. I was really messed up and she seemed to want to make sure I stayed that way

"That's part of it."

"Do you want to talk about that?"

I shook my head again. Dr. Tipton was a nice woman, but I didn't talk about my past with anyone. That was a dark road that I never wanted to go down again, and I didn't care how many degrees she had framed on her wall, there was nothing she could do to change the hell I had gone through. She wrote more notes in her tablet.

"You said you've been feeling sick, you want to tell me about that?"

"I just can't keep anything down. Even when I eat a little I throw it right back up."

"You'd be surprised the symptoms that come along with depression. I know it's hard, but you still have to take care of yourself because you can make yourself sick."

"I'm trying to take care of myself. I've been trying to eat and get rest, but I can't sleep! Every time I try to go to sleep I wake up. I close my eyes and all I see are flames."

"I can give you something to help you sleep-"

"No medication! I don't want to be put on anything! I'm dealing with enough without side effects."

"Kari I would never give you anything you didn't want to take. I can give you something that can help you get a little sleep at night, that's it."

"No, I'm fine. I have a doctor's appointment later. They'll probably give me something that can make me feel better."

"Well if you change your mind let me know. I can send the prescription to your local pharmacy."

When I left Dr. Tipton's office I didn't feel any better than I did when I came. Marvin went and got himself some ice cream, then drove me to my next appointment.


Marvin and I waited in the doctor's office for him to come back. I liked Dr. Armstrong because he never made me wait long and he took his time with me when I got back in a room. I lay in the bed in a gown with my eyes closed and Marvin sat in a chair reading Forbes. Dr. Armstrong came back in with a big smile on his face.

"Well Mrs. Fairmount, I can't give you any medication for the stomach flu," he said leaning against the metal sink.

"Why not?"

"Because you don't have the stomach flu. You're pregnant."

My mouth dropped open. With everything that had been going on, I hadn't even noticed I missed my period. Marvin looked sick.

"Let's call and make an appointment with your gynecologist so they can get you started on some prenatal vitamins. In the meantime you need to start eating and taking better care of yourself. Understand?"

I nodded my head and he smiled at me.

"Anymore questions for me?"

"No."

"Well I will see you in January for your checkup. Take care of yourself."

Dr. Armstrong shook both of our hands and left the room. I got dressed and Marvin and I left the office.


The ride home was a quiet one. I was scared to look at Marvin because I didn't know how he felt. He was against babies until he felt he had more time for them. I hated that I was going through all this at once. I couldn't feel as happy about being pregnant and that depressed me more.

When we got to the house, I headed straight upstairs to the bedroom.

"Kari, don't you think we need to talk?"

"No. You know how to make abortion appointments all by yourself. I told you I didn't want to go to the doctor anyway."

"You're still pregnant whether you would have went or not. I'm trying to change Kari," he said following me upstairs.

"So what you want to have this baby?"

"Of course I do."

I undressed and got ready to get back into the bed. This time, instead of trying to get me out of bed, Marvin laid down with me.

"You gettin' ready to take a nap?" I asked.

"No I'm lying down with you."

"You really don't have to."

"I know. But I want to help you and I can't do that sitting in another room."

"I really do prefer to be by myself."

"I won't bother you. I just want to be next to you."

Turning my back to him, I pulled the covers over my head. He could stay in the room as long as he didn't annoy me.

Marvin put his hand on my stomach as I was drifting off to sleep.

"I love you Kari, and I'm sorry about everything I did. But I'm happy about this baby. I'm glad you're pregnant."

DeQuindra Renea

# CHAPTER 26

It had been a while since I had stepped foot in a church. A lot had happened in my life and for that reason I saw no reason to worship God. He had taken so much from me. If He loved me, He could have prevented a lot of pain in my life. But Kevin had fallen in love with Jayla, who was strong in her faith. If Kevin was willing to give God another chance, I could see what it was all about too. Also finding out I was pregnant was really a blessing, even if I was depressed. I figured this was my way of thanking God for that gift.

Jayla was waiting for me at the front door just as she had promised; she was wearing a beautiful crème colored suit with red accessories. She looked absolutely stunning. The suit seemed to compliment her smooth chocolate skin. Dark red eye shadow accentuated her almond eyes. Her hair was curled in big Shirley Temple Curls that hung to her neck. She grabbed my hand and smiled as soon as I walked in the door.

"Good morning Kari," she beamed. "You look beautiful!"

"Thank you," I said feeling under-dressed in my long baby blue sundress. "The suit I was going to wear got a stain on it. Kevin said this dress would be fine."

"It's gorgeous. Wear what makes you comfortable Kari, that's what matters. I can promise you the Lord doesn't care, He just wants you here."

I smiled as Jayla squeezed my hand and led me into the sanctuary. Kevin had surely told her how long it had been since

I'd been to church and how uncomfortable I would be.

Everyone was welcoming to us as we made our way to our seats. A few of the older women had even hugged me and complimented my dress. By the time we made it to Kevin, who had saved us seats near the front, I felt much better. He hugged me and gave me a kiss on the cheek. I moved to sit on the other side of Kevin, but Jayla motioned me to sit where I was so that I was sitting in between them.

"You look nice Kari," Kevin said giving me a reassuring smile. We sat and chatted for a minute as the congregation fellowshipped with each other before service began.

The pastor was keeping his congregation entertained with stories and jokes. I felt relaxed and especially enjoyed the choir. There were near sixty people, and they were really good. Gospel music was something else I didn't get into much, but their singing was incredibly hard to dislike as the melodies blended perfectly.

The choir had just finished singing their second selection when a brown skinned woman with long black hair approached the podium. She couldn't have been any older than thirty five and was wearing a stunning purple pants suit. Her big purple hat set the outfit off and she wore silver stilettos.

"Praise the Lord everybody! My name is Sister Helen Leverette and I just want to welcome everyone who came to fellowship with us today. It is such a blessing to enter the house of the Lord and it is even more of a blessing when I enter and see a new face."

Some people in the congregation nodded their heads and I heard a few Amens from the back of the church.

"I am just so excited to share the love of Jesus with you all. I have come such a long way from where I used to be and I know it is only by His grace and mercy."

More people in the crowd shouted Amens of their own. It seemed everyone in the church could understand where she was coming from… except me.

"You can't tell by looking at me today, but I used to be in the streets. I wasn't always saved, ya'll. I was doing everything that the Lord didn't want me to do. And I did it all! Drugs, prostitution, stealing. I did it all."

Sister Leverette was getting more and more into her speech. You could tell she was taking a walk down memory lane and reliving some of the demons of her past.

"I was lost ya'll. I was looking for love in all the wrong places. I didn't want to feel pain anymore, and I was tired of hiding from who I really was. Imma tell everybody right now that all the drugs in the world won't let you escape your problems. No matter how high you get, when you come down, your problems are gonna be right there waiting for you. No matter what you try to hide from yourself or from everyone else, God always knows. And I'm here to tell you that what's done in the dark will always come to light."

When she said that I felt as if everyone in the church was looking at me. Like all of them knew my secret. For the first time since I had arrived at the church I felt uncomfortable, and to make matters worse, I could have sworn I seen Kevin shoot me a look out the corner of his eye.

"You can get out," Sister Leverette continued. "But God is the only way out. Turn to him and I promise He will make it all okay. If you feel lost, turn to God and He will find you. He said it in his word!"

People started to jump to their feet and clap their hands at Sister Leverette's speech. Sister Leverette shouted all the way back to her seat and then some more. Pastor Easton got up and went to his podium.

"Amen Sister Leverette, Amen," he said in his deep raspy voice. "Thank you Lord for her testimony. You know, sometimes God puts you through things to help somebody else. The spirit is telling me she helped somebody in here today, so everybody say amen for that."

It seemed everybody in the church said Amen, except for me. In my mind Sister Leverette had never left the podium. I was still stuck on what she had said. As the words replayed over and over in my head I felt as if I was sitting in the church naked. Was I the person Pastor Easton was talking about? Had the Spirit made her say that just for me to hear?

I couldn't concentrate on the rest of the service. Her words just kept playing in my head. Were my secrets going to come to light too? Would Marvin find out about me and Jonathon? I knew then it was time to make a choice. I couldn't continue to hurt Marvin.

When service was over, everyone began to hug and fellowship with each other, I sat there for a minute still deep in thought.

"Hey Kari, you okay?" Kevin asked snapping his fingers in my face.

"Yeah, I'm fine," I said grabbing my purse and hopping out of my seat. I had to really put on like nothing was bothering me or Kevin would want and sit and play the twenty one question game with me and I wasn't in the mood.

"You sure?"

"I'm positive Kevin, don't start with all that. I enjoyed service today," I said putting a bright smile on my face.

"I'm glad. Jayla really wanted you to enjoy yourself."

"I did. I really did."

Jayla was talking to a woman at the end of the pew. Kevin and I waited for them to finish their conversation and Jayla turned around and smiled.

"Did you enjoy service?" she asked, giving me a big hug.

"Yes I did, thanks for inviting me," I said hugging her back. I appreciated their concern about how I liked service, but all I really wanted to do was get out of there. I needed to get away to sort through my feelings.

"I'm really glad. I hope you'll come back soon and visit again Kari," she said grabbing my arm. We followed Kevin out of the sanctuary and out of the church. As soon as the fresh air hit my face, I started feeling a little better. I felt as if I was suffocating in that church. There was too much coming at me at once.

Kevin and I parted ways with Jayla as he went to walk me to my car.

"I need to talk to you Kari... soon."

"About what?"

"We just really need to sit down and talk. I'm a little worried about you."

"Don't start that worried about you stuff Kevin, I told you I'm fine."

"I know you Kari, and I know something is bothering you. Is it the fire? Because if that's what it is you can talk to me. I understand."

"Why does everything always have to be about the fire? Why

does something always have to be bothering me? Is that why you and Jayla invited me here today, to assess my mood?"

"Kari, you're taking it too far. I just want to talk to you because you been real unstable lately-"

"Okay, I'm done," I said opening the door to my car. I threw my purse in the passenger seat. "And you know what, something is bothering me Kevin, you. You are what is bothering me."

"Oh I'm bothering you?"

"Yes, because you think because of what happened and because I have a history of depression you can use every excuse to try to counsel me. You're always hovering over me and asking me what's wrong, and I'm tired of you. I don't need you harping over me all the time Kevin. Worry about you, and worry about your life."

I got into my car and slammed the door. Kevin just stood there, shocked. I left him standing in the parking lot and headed home.


Marvin was in the living room watching ESPN and eating pizza when I came home.

"Hey baby, how was church?"

"I don't really wanna talk about it. It was okay I guess."

I kicked off my shoes and cuddled up next to Marvin on the couch. He gave me a slice of pizza and I sat there and watched TV with him.

"You watching the game today?"

"I watch the game every Sunday baby, why?"

"I was just wondering. You got anybody coming over today?"

"A few people might stop by, why?"

"Just wondering."

We sat there in silence eating pizza and watching Sports Center. I hoped Jonathon was not one of the people that would be dropping by. After what happened at church, I wasn't in the mood to see him.

"So you just gonna order some more pizza and wings and all that stuff today. I don't need to cook, right?"

"Yeah, that's fine," Marvin answered barely paying any attention to me. He was so wrapped up in Sports Center he was barely listening to me.

I sat there for a few minutes more eating more pizza and spending time with my husband. After the party I was hoping Marvin would want to spend some alone time with me. I was a little tired of always having people around, and it had been awhile since we had gone out and did anything.

I left Marvin sitting on the couch and went into the bedroom to lie down. I had woken up early for church and I was starting to feel a little tired. Besides, if Jonathon was one of the people who might be dropping by my house, I didn't want him to even know I was here.

After changing into something more comfortable I put in a movie, grabbed my throw blanket and reclined in the La-Z boy. I was feeling so guilty and all I wanted to do was forget.

# CHAPTER 27

Jonathon had been blowing my phone up for the past couple of days. I didn't know what the hell he wanted because we hadn't spoken in weeks, but if he kept it up, he was going to give us away. He was calling me at times when Marvin was near me, and since Jonathon had known Marvin for a long time he knew one thing and that was that Marvin was not was a fool.

While Marvin was at work that Monday I spent the day shopping for the baby. I was so excited this was finally happening to me. I was early, but I was already out splurging for the baby. I made sure to buy neutral colors since I didn't know the sex yet.

I was at Babies R Us looking at cribs and bassinets when I got another phone call from Jonathon. He would never stop calling, so I went ahead and picked up the phone.

"So you just gonna ignore all my calls and texts?"

"I'm sorry Jonathon, there's been so much going on I didn't get a chance to call you back. Is everything okay?"

"Does it sound like everything's okay?"

My good mood was starting to fade. I didn't know what the hell his problem was. He was the one who had ruined things between us.

"What's wrong with you?"

"Where are you? We need to talk."

"I'm out, shopping."

"Well you need to take a break and come over to my crib real quick. I need to holla at you about some shit."

"I really can't do that Jonathon. I'm busy."

"Kari I'm not playin' fuckin' games! This is serious, now get ya ass over here before I get pissed."

Jonathon hung up as I rolled my eyes and put my phone back in my purse. All of a sudden he wanted to talk to me. I knew there could only be one reason. I left Babies R Us and headed to Jonathon's house.

When I got to his house, the door was already open so I let myself in. Jonathon was sitting at the dining room table waiting for me. He was wearing a business suit, obviously fresh out of a meeting. He was drinking a beer and had a very stern look on his face. He didn't even smile when he saw me.

"Sit down," he ordered.

I sat across from him and folded my arms.

"You got somethin' you wanna tell me?" he damn near yelled. I was shocked, not by his question, but by his tone. I could guess why he was asking me that, but I wasn't going to tell him. I wasn't going to complicate my life like that.

"No," I said shaking my head. He knew I was lying and that pissed him off more.

"So you not pregnant?"

Trying to avoid eye contact with him, I shook my head. He obviously knew, so I didn't know why I was lying.

"So you just gon sit there and lie?"

I didn't say anything, I just sat there looking at my hands. I never wanted this time to come, but I knew it would. Things had been going so good between Marvin and I.

"Is the baby mine Kari?"

"No."

"How do you know?"

"I just do."

"If that baby is mine, I have a right to know Kari."

"But it's not yours, so it doesn't matter."

"Can you just fuck all the bullshit for a minute Kari? Forget that dumb ass fight! This is us baby. You know what we had and you know it was real so don't sit here and lie, tell me the truth."

I closed my eyes and tried to stop the tears from falling down my face. I had made up in my mind that if I didn't say it aloud, then it wasn't true.

"Kari, tell me what the hell is goin' on," Jonathon said putting his hands on the top of his head.

"I don't know what's goin' on Jonathon. I don't know," I cried.

"You know if there is a possibility that that baby you're carrying is mine. So is it?"

I nodded my head.

"And you just wasn't gonna tell me?"

"I don't know what I was gonna do. Marvin is so excited and everything has been going so good-"

"So you let that man raise a baby that might not be his?"

"But it might be his baby. Then what?"

"But you don't know that Kari," Jonathon said running his hands over his face. We sat there for a moment not speaking, just thinking. We were definitely in a sticky situation.

"If that baby is mine, I'm not gonna lie about it, and I don't want you to either."

"Jonathon why would you wanna do that? It's over between us. Move on, live your life, and have your own kids. Don't take my life away from me."

"Don't take your life away from you?" he repeated. "That's my child you carrying!"

"You don't know that."

"And neither do you."

There was another long pause.

"So basically we're at a standstill until the baby comes. We can talk about it then. Standing here arguing about something we don't know is getting us nowhere."

I got up from the table and grabbed my purse and keys. Jonathon looked like he wanted to say something, but he didn't. I turned to leave.

"Marvin needs to know what's going on."

I turned around.

"Marvin doesn't need to know a damn thing, this is between us."

"He's my friend Kari."

"Now you care about Marvin? All of a sudden he's your friend?"

"He's been my friend Kari."

"Then why did you do this? Why didn't you just leave me alone?"

Jonathon didn't say anything. He just sat there looking pitiful. For the first time I saw the guilt start to set in. He actually looked like he felt bad about what we'd been doing.

"What I did was fucked up, I know that. I never thought it would go this far."

"Me neither."

We sat there both feeling guilty. Marvin had done a complete turnaround since our vacation. He was being so good to me. Although he had done horrible things to me in the past, I knew this was just flat out wrong.

"We don't know nothin' yet so just don't tell him. Let's just wait until we know what's going on."

Jonathon nodded his head and I turned to leave again. This situation brought a dark cloud over my pregnancy. A moment ago, in the store, I was excited, now I was scared. If this was Jonathon's baby I was carrying, when Marvin found out, all hell was going to break loose.

# CHAPTER 28

As my body started to change to accommodate my growing baby, so did my relationship with Jonathon. We weren't talking as much and whenever we did, we ended up arguing about the pregnancy. I could tell that it hurt him that I was carrying on with my pregnancy without coming clean to Marvin. As the months went on, and more people started to take notice, I saw his hurt turn into anger. It had gotten to the point he would leave the room anytime somebody mentioned it. I was starting to get worried. I feared he would explode and tell Marvin everything.

The only word that could describe Marvin's attitude toward the baby was joy. It was a shock how much his attitude toward having children had completely changed. Although he was working hard training with his father and trying to take the company global, he never missed a doctor's appointment or Lamaze class. Anyone could see how excited he was about the baby which was the reason it was hard for me to tell him the truth no matter how much I wanted to.

I had reached four months and it was time to find out what I was having. I was so excited! Marvin and I had been talking about names. He had already decided he didn't want the baby to be named after him if we had a boy. He wanted our son to start his own legacy, not the one his father had already created for him.

On the day of the ultrasound appointment I woke up earlier than Marvin, which was rare. I was too excited to sleep. By the time Marvin got up, I was dressed and had already eaten. Marvin took his time getting dressed and ate a bowl of cereal before we left. I could tell he was just as excited as I was, but he was just trying to be smooth about it.

"I hope it's a girl," I said to him as he drove down the street headed to the doctor's office.

"A girl is cool, a boy is better."

"You always think men are better."

"No, it's just every man's dream is to have a son."

"I didn't know that was your dream."

"My dream is to be with you and make you happy. I didn't realize that until you left."

Marvin put his hand on my belly and looked over at me and smiled.

"You look beautiful pregnant, baby. I love you."

"Thank you baby. I love you too."

I looked out the window so Marvin wouldn't see me frowning. I hated the position I was in. The time I had waited for my entire life wasn't as happy as it should have been.


Marvin and I both watched the screen closely as the doctor rolled the ultrasound instrument over my greased up belly. I got excited as soon as an image came on the screen even though I had no idea what I was looking at. The tech looked at the screen and rolled the wand across my belly some more until she found what she was looking for.

"Okay, this is the head…those are the arms…the legs are right there. It looks like baby has the legs crossed."

Immediately I was disappointed. I had been looking forward to being able to purchase more clothes, paint the baby room, and pick out a name, and I could do none of those things the way I wanted until I knew what I was having.

"Let's see if we can get baby to move."

She began to shake and rub my stomach and I could feel my baby start to move. I said a silent prayer that my baby would uncross his or her legs so I could know what it was.

After a few minutes of playing with my belly, she put the wand back on my stomach.

"Okay…okay baby moved a little bit. Lets see if I can get a better picture."

After a few more minutes of moving the wand over my stomach, she stopped.

"Okay it looks like we have a little man in there. You see that?"

She pointed on the black and white screen to what looked like a mushroom. I couldn't believe what I was seeing and I still couldn't believe I was finally pregnant.

Marvin had a huge smile on his face. He was ecstatic. He grabbed my hand and kissed it.

The technician gave us a printout of pictures from my ultrasound. She even made two copies so Marvin could keep one for himself. When we left the office I was more excited about having our baby.

"So it's a boy. How do you feel about that?" Marvin asked.

"I don't care, I just want a healthy baby. That's all I've ever wanted."

"Well I'm glad I 'm finally giving you what you want."

Marvin kissed me and I smiled. I had nothing to say to follow that. It was times like this when I felt that maybe it was time to tell him the truth. The guilt was killing me. But if I told him the truth about the baby, I would have to tell him the truth about Jonathon, and that's something I knew he would never forgive.


Jamie didn't waste any time coming to my house and talking about her ideas for the baby shower. Since I didn't have many friends, I had asked Jamie to help me plan it.

"You could definitely have the baby shower here, but do you want to?"

"It doesn't really matter. That's up to Marvin because for once I won't be doing any cooking or labor. I can actually just enjoy myself."

"We can have it here," Marvin said taking a drink of his bottled water. He had been hovering around the kitchen since Jamie had gotten there for no other reason except to be nosey. Any other time that would bother me, but we obviously needed his help anyway.

"What kind of food do you want to have Kari?" she asked, writing everything down in our planning book.

"Any food that I don't cook," I joked.

"Do you want finger foods, or real foods?"

"Real food. My Mom would be angry if we had finger food," Marvin answered.

"Okay… and so we have to work on the guest list later."

"Are men supposed to even come to this? It's mostly for women so I can't invite any of my friends?"

"Well sometimes people have diaper and beer parties. It's the same thing as a baby shower, only the men just bring diapers."

"Okay, that's what I'll do. I don't want to be sitting home all day with a bunch of women."

My heart dropped. If Marvin was going to invite his friends, that definitely meant he would be inviting Jonathon. That would be too awkward having both of them there.

"Well why don't you just make a list of all the men you want to invite and me and Kari will add it to the list?"

Marvin left the room, satisfied that he would have men at the baby shower. I could have killed Jamie for suggesting a diaper party, but she didn't know any better. All I knew was I had to tell Jonathon about the diaper party immediately before Marvin had a chance to. He got pissed anytime anybody said anything about the baby. I had a feeling that if Marvin said anything else to him about it, he would come unhinged.

Later that evening I snuck away to talk to Jonathon about the diaper party. He needed to be there, and it would surely raise a red flag if he wasn't. It was important for me to be the one to ask Jonathon because I didn't know how he would react.

I told Marvin I was going to the store and went to Jonathon's house. I couldn't talk to him about the party over the phone, he would only get mad and hang up. I needed to talk to him about this face to face, that way I could try to calm him down and reason with him.

I knocked lightly on Jonathon's door and he answered quickly. I had made sure to call him first in case he had company. He was in the kitchen making himself something to eat. He didn't say anything to me, so I just followed him into the kitchen. Things hadn't been the same between us since he'd found out I was pregnant. He was still mad at me.

"What's up?" he asked, without looking at me. I sat at the

dining room table.

"Look, Marvin wants to throw a diaper party for the baby. That's like a co-ed baby shower. You know he is going to want you to be there."

Jonathon laughed.

"Okay. There's a *Hallmark* store on Corunna road, right? I'll just go in there and find a card that says, 'Congratulations, I might be the father of your wife's baby'."

I could have slapped fire out of him.

"I'm not coming to that fuckin' baby shower Kari. I don't know why you even wasted yo time coming over here to ask."

"Can you please just do this for me? Please. Marvin is already talking about how you don't come around anymore."

"I wonder why."

"If you loved me like you said you did, then you would do this for me."

"And if you loved me like you said you did, you would tell him the truth," he said finally looking directly at me.

"Do you realize what you asking me to do?"

"Yeah, that's why I didn't pressure you about it. I just stayed away. But you can't come over here asking me to go to that party and smile in his face knowing good and well that baby might be mine."

"You had no problem smiling in his face knowing you were fucking me. "

"The rules done changed Kari. We are talking about a child. A human life! Now I said I'm not goin' to that damn party and nothin' you can say is gonna change my mind about that."

I sat there for a minute just looking at my hands. He was not going to budge on the issue. I didn't know why I thought I would convince him.

"Why are you going to tell him you can't come?" I asked softly. He shrugged his shoulders.

"I don't know yet. I'll make up something."

"Please don't tell him," I whispered, unsure if he'd heard me until he came over to me.

"So you just don't care about me no more huh? You really happy? You stayin' with him?" he asked, and for the first time he looked me in my eyes.

"Just please don't tell him about us," I pleaded looking up at him. Jonathon got on his knees and laid his head in my lap. He laid there for what seemed like forever. I didn't know what to do. I was afraid to embrace him or touch him. I didn't want to open the door for anything to happen.

Jonathon finally looked up at me.

"Why are you doing this to me?"

"What?"

Jonathon didn't answer me. He just put his hand on my stomach. I had put on an oversized t-shirt to hide my growing belly from him. Seeing it would only make things worse.

"If this baby is mine, I want to tell Marvin the truth," he told me for the millionth time. But this time he added something else.

"And I want you to divorce him and marry me."

"Okay, get up. I have to go," I said pushing him off of me. I grabbed my purse and headed for the door. Jonathon was right behind me.

"People don't just fall out of love Kari. It's not that easy. So don't act like you don't love me no more, because I know you do."

Jonathon grabbed my arm and turned me around so that I was looking into his eyes.

"I know you do. Tell me you don't love me no more."

"You need to stop this Jonathon. And you gotta stop staying away. Marvin has questioned why you don't come around."

"You know why the fuck I don't come around! Cuz I wanna kill him. You're his wife and I wanna kill him every time he touches you. What do you want me to do about that Kari?"

I pushed Jonathon away from me and left. I could never look him in the eyes and tell him I didn't love him because I would be flat out lying. Maybe the best thing was for Jonathon to stay away, but I couldn't tell him that either. I didn't know what to do. Regardless of who the father was, my life was spinning out of control.

# CHAPTER 29

"Just give it to me straight doc, how much weight have I gained?" I asked when Dr. James came back into the room. I was seven months pregnant and at another doctor's appointment.

"You have only gained six pounds since your last visit," she said easily.

"Only? That's six more pounds to work off."

"You'll be fine. Where is Marvin?"

"He had to be at the office today. You know he was hating that he couldn't be here," I said as Dr. James checked for the heartbeat. It came through, loud and strong and I smiled.

"He's doing good in there, heartbeat is just fine. Anything going on that you want to ask me about?"

"Not really. Am I supposed to go to the bathroom so much? I'm not getting any sleep."

"Yes, bathroom trips will get more frequent the further along you get into your pregnancy. That's nothing you should be worried about. Have you been taking your vitamins?"

"Every day."

"And he's been kicking you pretty good?"

"Absolutely."

"Are you sure you don't have any more questions?" she asked again. I could tell she was surprised because I usually came full of questions. I shook my head.

"Well I will see you next time Kari, tell Marvin I said hello."

"I will."

I got dressed and headed to meet Jamie for lunch to discuss last minute plans for my baby shower. Going home to take a nap would've been better, but we'd already planned to meet. I got in my car and headed east.

I arrived at the restaurant before Jamie and was surprised to see how busy it was. Tara was at the bar, working hard mixing drinks and I waved as the waitress seated me at a booth to wait for Jamie. She arrived less than ten minutes later carrying two tote bags full of stuff.

"Well hello beautiful," she said when she reached the booth.

"Hello, I see you brought goodies."

"I did. I brought the invitations, copies of the games, the food menu choices from that catering company you liked, and the prizes for the games too."

"Okay."

"Yes, we have lots to do. Starting with getting these invitations out. Do you have the registry tickets?"

"The what?"

"Registry tickets. They should have given them to you when you did your gift registry. We have to put them in the invitations."

I didn't answer, but instead sat there with a dumb look on my face.

"Kari, please tell me you did your gift registry."

I shook my head.

"Oh my goodness Kari! These invitations have to go out this week!"

"I know, I'm sorry."

"What have you been doing? You told me you've been shopping, why didn't you do your gift registry then?"

"I forgot."

Jamie took a deep breath

"Well we have to go do them today."

"No, I can't do it today, I'm too tired."

"Well you gotta do it in the next few days Kari. They have to go in the invitations. People need to know what to get you."

I nodded my head to shut her up. She must've forgotten there was a time when gift registry didn't exist.

When I pulled into my driveway, I was confused to see Marvin's car parked inside of the garage. He' told me he had to be at the office today and that there was no way he could get out of it. Now, here he was at the house in the middle of the afternoon.

I got out of my car and went inside the house. It was completely quiet. If Marvin was home, he must have been asleep because I couldn't hear any movement inside.

Maybe he's not feeling well, I thought as I sat my purse and keys on the counter.

When I walked in the living room Marvin was sitting there in silence. He had an unpleasant look on his face, and I could tell something was bothering him.

"Marvin? Why are you just sitting here? What's wrong? I thought you had to go to the office."

He didn't say anything for a minute, he just looked at me.

"I thought I knew you. I thought I trusted you. But you been lying to me."

I didn't know how Marvin had found out about Jonathon, but I knew it was time to start apologizing. There was nothing I could say to make what I'd done okay, or to take away what Marvin was feeling, but I had to try.

Just when I was about to open my mouth to say something to Marvin, he picked up something from off of the floor and threw it on the table. It was my black box I had hidden in the basement under the floorboard.

"We need to talk," he said without looking at me. I opened my mouth to say something but no words would come out. I couldn't move. I just stood there like a deer in headlights as my world came crashing down.

"I kept wondering why you always spent so much time in the basement. Usually around November, the day of the fire, and June 16, your birthday… or what I thought was your birthday."

I stood there with my whole body shaking. Marvin had literally opened Pandora's Box.

"You got something you want to tell me Kari? Because after everything I just seen in this box it looks like you been lying to me since the day I met you."

Unable to speak, I could feel the tears start to sting my eyes. I wasn't ready to face all of my demons. I was seven months pregnant and now was not the time for all of this to come crashing down on me.

"Okay fine, since you wanna be so quiet, I'll start. You told me your parents died in a fire, which is probably the only truth you've told me. Because all of these newspaper clippings say the fire your parents died in was suspected arson."

Marvin looked at the box.

"You never told me all this. I been going over this and over this in my head for a minute Kari, and the only thing I can come up with is that you didn't tell me the fire was suspected arson because you either started the fire, or you know who did."

Marvin looked in my eyes and waited for a response. I didn't give him one. For the first time since we had met I was completely mute. It was as if I had lost my ability to form words. Tears spilled out of my eyes and I bit my lip to stop it.

"Who started the fire Kari? Who? Was it you?"

"I was six," I finally said in a low whisper. Marvin came closer to hear what I had said, but I wasn't repeating myself.

"I think you started the fire Kari and I think somebody helped you."

There was another moment of silence as Marvin looked at the box again.

"You know what else these newspaper clipping said? They said three people died in the fire, not two."

Marvin took a long pause. "Then I found your birth certificate and I found out that you were born a twin."

I lost my breath feeling as if somebody had punched me in the chest. I hadn't talked about her in twenty years and nobody had known about her but Kevin and me.

"Did your twin sister die in the fire Kari?"

Nodding my head, I broke down crying. I missed her so much. Losing my twin was the worst feeling I'd ever felt. I was a twin-less twin. And that made me feel like the loneliest person in the world. I had lost a part of me in that fire and that was the reason I could never get over it.

"I know you started the fire Kari. I know you did. You would've told me about this if you didn't. Who helped you? Did Kevin help you start the fire?"

Without saying a word, I stood there crying my eyes out. Marvin had found out everything. My past had been unleashed and I honestly didn't know what lay ahead of me. I didn't know what would be done if anybody ever found out what we had done. I was having a baby. I couldn't go to prison.

"You gonna tell me what happened Kari?"

When I didn't answer again, it pissed Marvin off.

"Okay you wanna stand there and not say a fucking word, huh? Just stand there and cry? Fine, don't tell me because I don't believe a fucking word you say anyway. You been lying to me since the day I met you. Your birthday isn't even when you told me it was! June 16 is not your birthday," Marvin said taking my birth certificate out the box and looking at it. "You were born September 16th! You have lied to me about everything that has come out of your mouth! How can I raise a child with somebody I don't even know? How can I be married to somebody I don't know?"

I still didn't know what to say. He was right. I had lied to him about everything. He didn't really know me. He never would, nobody ever would.

"Just tell me why you did it Kari. Why would you kill your parents and twin sister?"

"I didn't do anything!"

"You are a fucking liar, Kari! Tell me the truth for once. Don't stand here and tell me you been keeping everything hidden down here in this box because you are completely innocent. You hid all this because you are guilty."

I picked the box up off of the table. I needed to get out of that house. Marvin would never let this go, and I couldn't emotionally handle telling anybody the truth about the fire.

"So you just not gonna say shit? We've been married six years and you won't even tell me the truth? Even after I already found everything?"

"You snuck into my personal belongings! You knew that box didn't belong to you. And I hid it for a reason, which means you went downstairs looking for it. Why couldn't the truth be what I told you?" I cried. "Do you know what the fuck you have just done?"

"What? Kari, what did I do?"

Tears streamed down my face as I grabbed the box and

217

walked around the house unsure of what to do. I didn't know what to tell Marvin. He knew everything! He continued to follow me around the house. The walls started to close in on me. I grabbed my purse and keys off the counter where I had left them.

"You are not going anywhere Kari. You need to tell me something."

Marvin tried to grab the keys from my hand, but I turned away from him. It was hard to maneuver through the house with my huge belly, but I needed to get away from Marvin. He was asking questions he wasn't ready to hear the answers to.

I made it out to the garage and in my car. Marvin stood at my door preventing me from closing it.

"Where the hell do you think you going Kari? Going to burn down some more houses?"

"Get the fuck outta my way Marvin!" I yelled, angry.

"That's what happened. You are a murderer! You burned down a house and killed your entire family?!"

"You have no idea what the fuck you are talking about! You don't know what we had to go through. You weren't there!"

"So tell me then. Tell me what the fuck happened that you would do something like that."

"I WANT YOU TO MOVE THE HELL OUTTA MY FUCKING WAY!" I screamed. My face was completely wet with tears and my heart was pounding out of my chest. My baby started kicking me and that only made me more scared. I wasn't supposed to be under any stress right now. Marvin was going to make me go into pre-term labor if he didn't let me leave.

Marvin took one long look at me and closed my car door. I backed out of the driveway at top speed in case he decided to change his mind. After putting my car in park two blocks away from my house, I broke down. Marvin finding out about Karrie was like he brought her back to life. She was real again. She existed to someone besides Kevin and I. Memories started flooding back into my head. My whole body started to shake. Laying my head on the steering wheel and closing my eyes, I re-lived the events leading up to the fire.

*"I'm telling ya'll, all I have to do is get a cigarette and leave it in the bed. It'll look like one of them fell asleep smoking it. The bed will burn up and*

*that's that."*

*"They don't smoke Kevin," Karrie, always the thinker of the two of us, said. Kevin had snuck into our room after our mom and her boyfriend had gone to sleep.*

*"But if they're dead and we say they did, aint nobody gonna wonder."*

*"I don't wanna talk about this anymore Kevin. It's a bad idea."*

*"Karrie stop being scared. It's the only way."*

*Nobody in the room said a word. I just lay in my bed on the top bunk listening to what they were saying. Kevin might have been taking it too far, but maybe it was the only way.*

*"Look we gotta decide something ya'll. It's gotta happen in the next few days. "*

*Kevin left the room quietly and went back into his. I knew my sister wasn't sleep yet. I could almost feel her tears running down my face.*

*"Kari?" she whispered.*

*"Yeah."*

*"I don't wanna do it. I'm scared. I don't think it's a good idea," she cried.*

*I climbed off the top bunk and lay down next to her in her bed. I wiped the tears running down her face and held her close. I'd almost died when we were born and the nurses in the NICU put us together in the incubator and I immediately started doing better. She was my other half. I felt her pain and she felt mine. Although she was older, I was always the one protecting her. She was born two whole minutes before me and weighed almost two pounds more as well. She was healthy and big, while I was sick and little. That's how they knew us apart. I was the "little one."*

*"I promise it's gonna be okay, Karrie. You don't have to be scared because I'm not gonna let anything go wrong. I promise."*

*Karrie nodded her head and I gave her a kiss on the cheek. "I trust you Kari. And if doing this will keep Avery from hurting you and Kevin, I'll do it."*

*She sat up in the bed and wiped her eyes.*

*"Can you take my necklace off? I wanna see Nana," she asked softly. Our grandmother had given us matching lockets when we were five. Inside was a picture of her with both of us. We were extremely close to our grandmother so the lockets were something we cherished. Our mother wouldn't allow us to have any pictures of our grandmother so those lockets were the only thing we had. I never took mine off, but Karrie liked to look at the picture before she fell asleep.*

*Karrie held the locket open and stared at the picture. She grabbed my hand and laid her head on my shoulder. We fell asleep that night in the bed together.*

*The night we all had planned for came quicker than we expected. I was scared all that day. Karrie was extremely quiet. At one point Kevin had to take her outside and yell at her because he was scared she was going to give us away.*

*I didn't sleep all night. We all planned to meet outside at two in the morning. Kevin would be last since he was the one setting the fire. I looked down at the Ninja Turtle watch he had given me and saw the time was one fifty seven. I got down off the top bunk as quietly as I could. Karrie was still asleep. I shook her lightly and she jumped out of bed.*

*"It's time already? I'm not ready Kari, I don't think we should do it."*

*"It's too late Karrie. It's happening tonight, but I promise it'll be okay."*

*I grabbed my sister's hand and led her quietly out of the room. We were almost to the back door when Karrie let go.*

*"I forgot my necklace Kari. I think I fell asleep with it in my hand," she said, going back towards the room. I grabbed her arm and pulled her back to the door.*

*"It's too late, Karrie. It's already after two. He probably already doing it."*

*"Not this early. I can't leave it behind Kari; you know how much it means to me."*

*I grabbed my necklace that hung around my neck. I knew what she meant. I wouldn't want to leave mine behind either.*

*"I'll go back and get it for you."*

*"No, just wait here, I'll find it quicker than you," she said giving me a brave smile. I watched her until she turned the corner. I hadn't been standing there for ten seconds when Kevin came flying around the corner. He and Karrie must have only missed each other by seconds.*

*"Where is Karrie? We gotta go. We gotta go now!" he said out of breath.*

*"She forgot her necklace, she's coming right back."*

*Kevin looked like he was ready to slap me.*

*"Why would you let her go back? I told you two o clock outside! I gotta go get her."*

*Kevin walked to the end of the hallway and his eyes got as big as saucers. I could see the smoke coming into the kitchen. He started screaming Karrie's name. We tried to listen for her, but we didn't hear her.*

*"We gotta go Kari!"*

*"Go?" I asked confused, "I'm not leaving her."*

*I went to the hallway and could barely believe my eyes. The fire had spread so fast and gotten so big! It was never the plan for the fire to spread so quickly. Kevin said it would take at least fifteen minutes!*

*I looked at him with my mouth wide open.*

*"What did you do Kevin?"*

*"I had to put gasoline on the bed too or the fire wouldn't light."*

*"KARRIE!!! KARRIE!!!" I screamed walking as far as I could down the hallway towards our bedroom. I could faintly hear her and that was when I lost it. I was ready to try to run through the fire to get to her. The smoke was choking me, but I didn't care. I had to get her. I couldn't just leave her behind.*

*Kevin came and grabbed my hand, but I snatched it away from him. I didn't want to leave that house without my sister. I couldn't breathe, but I didn't know if it was from the smoke or if it was because the thought of losing my sister had made my heart almost stop beating. I needed her.*

*"KARI WE GOTTA GO!! WE GOTTA GET OUT OF HERE!" Kevin screamed trying to grab my hand again. I pulled away from him and screamed her name again. I could've sworn I heard her calling mine back.*

*Kevin picked me up and carried me out the house. I kicked and screamed the entire time. I wanted to go back and get her. She was my life. What was I supposed to do without her?*

*Kevin carried me across the street and when he put me down, he just hugged me.*

*"I'm so sorry Kari," he cried holding me tight. "I didn't know she was back there. I swear I didn't know."*

*I just stood there staring at the house. I couldn't believe what Kevin had done. He had gone too far. I started to walk across the street towards my bedroom. That's when I heard her. I heard my sister in our bedroom screaming my name. She was calling me. I had told her everything would be alright. I promised her I wouldn't let anything happen.*

*As the fire got higher, I could hear her less. Kevin was banging on our neighbors door begging them to call 911.*

*I felt the fire ripping through my body. I could feel her pain. I couldn't breathe. I opened mouth to call her name, but the smoke choked me. I could feel it in my lungs. I don't remember anything else. I lost consciousness and passed out in the yard across the street from my burning home.*

DeQuindra Renea

# CHAPTER 30

I lifted my head off of the steering wheel and looked at myself in the mirror. My face was drenched with tears. I tried so hard not to think of that day, and although I could still hear Karrie screaming my name, sometimes I had never truly remembered. Marvin finding out had hurt as if it was the first time. I felt like a six year old again. All I wanted was to lie in bed with my sister. She was my world.

I pulled out my cell phone and called Kevin. I knew I had to tell him and he would not be happy. Getting caught for setting the fire was always Kevin's worst fear. He still had nightmares that the cops would come kicking in his door and arresting him for the murder of his mother, stepfather, and little sister.

The phone rang twice and he picked up. He was in a good mood, I could tell by his upbeat, "Hey sis!" But I knew in the next few seconds, things were going to change tremendously.

"Kevin, he found the box," I said as calmly as I could with tears running down my cheeks. I felt like my throat was closing.

"What?"

"Marvin found the box."

I could hear Kevin gasp for a breath. Aside from that, he was silent.

"Didn't I fuckin' tell you to let me take that damn box? I told you!"

"I need it. It has everything in it!"

"What all do you have in the box Kari?" Kevin asked, trying

to calm himself down.

"Everything! Pictures of me and Karrie, Momma, Avery, Nana, my necklace, newspaper clippings-"

"Well now look what happened. Look what you did!"

"What I did? I didn't do a damn thing! You were never supposed to put gasoline down, that was not a part of the plan!" I cried.

"I had to! I didn't know you let her go back. I told your ass outside at two! That was the plan!"

"Well he found the box Kevin! What am I supposed to do now?"

"You know what you gotta do. Move on. You can't go back to that house Kari. You gotta go...disappear."

"I can't just disappear! I'm seven months pregnant!"

"Well then you should've let me take the fucking box with me like I told you to," he said harshly. "Do you want me to go to prison? You gotta leave town and I do too."

I put my hand on my stomach and took a deep breath. He was right. I did have to leave. If Marvin decided to tell, we could both go away to prison for a long time.

"Kari, did you get the box before you left?"

"Yeah."

"Well then you don't need to go back there again. Just use our account to get what you need. I'll call you in a little bit when I figure something out."

"Okay."

"And Kari, don't waste time. Get the fuck outta town ASAP."

"Okay."

"Love you Kari."

"Love you too Kevin."

Ending the call, I looked around my neighborhood for the last time. This had been my life for seven years. I had been Mrs. Kari Dianne Fairmount and now I had to leave that all behind. I didn't know how to feel. A part of me was happy I was leaving because nobody ever really knew me. Marvin never really knew me. I had spent the last twenty years pretending Karrie had never existed and that made me ashamed. She didn't do anything. As a matter of fact, if we would have listened to her, life may have been different...happier. Any life that included her would have been happier.

She deserved to have a legacy in my heart. I couldn't be afraid to look in the mirror anymore and I couldn't keep lying about her. She deserved much more than that. After taking another deep breath, I wiped my eyes. I could feel Karrie's arms wrap around my body. She was hugging me. Right there in the front seat of my car, she was giving me a big hug. I could feel her. Rubbing my stomach and whispering to me that everything would be okay. I had been to her grave, lay there and talked to her... cried...apologized and I had never felt closer to her than I did now. She was happy. She was happy that I was letting her back into my life. I wasn't keeping her locked in a black box anymore. Now she was free. She could live through me like she was supposed to. Just like we did in that little incubator when we were first born when I was living off of her strength.

I pulled my locket out of the black box, opened it, and looked at it. Me, Karrie, and Nana were smiling like we were the happiest people in the world. Karrie and I were hiding a lot behind those smiles, but the love was still there. We loved each other genuinely. Feeling that love again, I put on my necklace and drove away from my life. Away from Mrs. Kari Dianne Fairmount forever.

I pulled into the parking lot of a nearby grocery store. I had to get out of my neighborhood, but I had to get my thoughts together and make a call. I couldn't just leave town and not say anything to Jonathon. Although we hadn't spoken in months, I still loved him, and I wanted more than anything else to thank him for always treating me special.

Jonathon's phone rang a couple of times before somebody picked up.

"Hello?" a woman answered. My words caught in my throat. I guess I should have expected for a woman to pick up, but it still caught me by surprise.

"Hi, may I speak to Jonathon?"

There was a long pause. I could tell she was debating whether or not she was going to give him the phone. I didn't blame her. A man like Jonathon would make any girl overprotective, hell I was that girl.

"Hello?" Jonathon answered after a few minutes. I was

surprised she hadn't hung up on me.

"Hey, I'm so sorry to just call out the blue like this, I wanted to talk to you for a second."

"Alright hold on."

There was a long pause and I assumed Jonathon was leaving the room. I knew there would be hell to pay for him with his woman, especially if she was anything like me.

"Okay, hello? You okay Kari?" he asked, genuine concern in his voice.

"I am, thanks for asking. I just wanted to call and apologize. I know you think what happened between us meant nothing to me but it did, and I'm sorry things ended the way they did. You always treated me so special and I love you for that."

He didn't say anything. I didn't know what he was thinking so I just continued to talk.

"I want you to be happy Jonathon, and honestly, I'm not the one. I'm not. I know we love each other, but we could never work."

"Why are you saying all this Kari? You called to tell me I'm not the one for you even though we already stopped seeing each other? That doesn't make any sense. What's going on?"

"Nothing is going on Jonathon," I said. "I just want to thank you for being a real man."

There was another long pause. I didn't know what else to say. At this point I felt like a fool for even calling him. This conversation had gone so quick and easy in my head.

"Alright well, I have to go. Take care of yourself Jonathon," I said fighting back tears. This would be the last time I was going to talk to him. I was going to miss him so much.

"Kari?"

"Yeah?"

"Is the baby mine? Is it my baby Kari? Just tell me the truth."

I took a deep breath.

"No, Jonathon, it's not your baby."

He was silent again. I didn't know if that was a good or bad thing.

"Thanks for calling me Kari."

He didn't wait for me to respond before he hung up. That was a hard way for it to end for me, but I knew I had to move on. It would hurt for awhile, but that part of my life was over, too.

I didn't know where to go. Leaving Michigan was going to be hard, but it was something I had to do. For the sake of my baby, I had to make sure it was somewhere I wanted to give birth to a child.

After buying a ticket to California, I made my way to the airport bathroom. My bladder was full and I felt as if I would pee on myself at any moment. The baby was sitting directly on my bladder. I hated it when he did that.

I sat in the waiting area at my gate. Kevin had been calling me, but I hadn't answered the phone yet. I had a lot on my mind. I couldn't stop thinking about the night of the fire. I loved my brother a lot, but deep down inside I blamed him for everything, especially for the death of Karrie. He had never said anything about using gasoline in the fire. He had promised me that if I got Karrie on board, he would make sure everything went right. She was always hesitant and I should've listened to her. Instead I listened to my big brother who was only manipulating my young mind to get me to go along with his plan. He didn't try hard enough to save Karrie from the fire. That was the reason I shut him out so much. He would never understand what I lost in that fire. I died in that fire, not him. He would never understand that.

They called my flight and I grabbed my purse and headed toward my gate. My phone rang again. I looked down at the phone, down at my brother's picture. Him, smiling at me. He was handsome. He had always been the most handsome man in the world to me. I loved my brother, but I hated him for killing Karrie. I hated him for taking her away from me.

After taking the battery out, I threw my cell phone in the trash. I stared at the trashcan for a long time before I tossed my purse over my shoulder and headed through my gate.

DeQuindra Renea

# CHAPTER 31
## Kevin

"Ya'll know Nana love ya'll, right?" my Nana asked all three of us after she'd made us sit down at her feet. She sat in her rocking chair looking down at us, her light brown eyes squinted and chubby face serious. She had smooth caramel skin and long brown hair which she had pulled back into a French roll. Her usual soft face was filled with stress and even at the tender age of 8, I could see that.

"All three of ya'll mean the world to me, you know that."

She didn't say anything for a minute. I was afraid to look her in the eyes. The twins must've been too because they sat, their legs folded Indian style and both sets of their eyes glued to the navy blue carpet.

"Kevin, Kari and Karrie," she called looking at each one of us. "Whatever is going on you can tell me. I will protect ya'll, I promise."

We didn't say anything. Kari looked over at me, but I gave her a look that told her to keep quiet.

"Karrie," Nana said looking her directly in the eyes. "Don't be scared baby. Is there something you wanna tell Nana?"

Karrie shook her head and lowered her eyes, a dead giveaway that she was lying. Nana was smart, she knew which one of us to ask.

"Kari?" she asked, raising her eyebrows.

Kari didn't even look at her, she just shook her head.

229

"Okay, ya'll can get up and go. Kevin, you stay."

The twins got up and scurried away. Once alone with me, Nana narrowed her eyes at me, her face twisted in a way I had never saw before.

"Kevin, you are the oldest. It is your responsibility to protect your sisters. Now tell me the truth baby, what's going on?"

"Nothing Nana," I said, my voice cracking. I wanted to tell her, but I was scared. Even if Nana did know the truth, could she protect us?

"I love you Kevin and your sisters. I would never let anything happen to ya'll. Never. I promise I will put an end to whatever is going on. You can trust me baby."

"I know Nana."

She gave me a long hug and held me close for a long time.

"I won't ever let anybody hurt ya'll. I promise I will find out what's going on and put an end to it. Nana aint no fool. I know what a rat smell like."

And after all those promises, she died, and me, Kari, and Karrie were all alone. I can't say she aint try, she did. But after she confronted my Momma about Avery molesting the twins, Momma said she couldn't see us no more. Sometimes I think that's what killed her. We did mean the world to her. Either way she was gone, and I hatato do what I hadta do to protect us. Like Nana said, it was my responsibility to take care of my sisters. What else was I 'sposed to do?

My suitcase was sloppily packed on the bed and I sat next to it with tears in my eyes. Rocking back and forth, I tried my best to get myself together so I could leave. Kari's call had fucked me up.

I stood up and paced the room, taking deep breaths to calm myself down. I didn't hear Jayla come in, she just appeared at my bedroom door.

"Hey sweetie, you gotta go out of town?" she asked, referring to my suitcase on the bed. I would have answered her had I realized she was talking to me, but my mind was stuck in time warp, back in my Nana's living room as an 8 year old boy.

"She made all these promises, then she died," I said aloud.

"What? Kevin? Who died?"

"What was I supposed to do?" I asked more to myself than her. I thought a lot about what would have happened had I just told Nana the truth, but there was no way I could change the past.

"Kevin?"

I could hear Jayla's voice getting closer to me, but I wasn't listening to her.

"I didn't know what else to do. I had to..."

"Kevin, baby you are scaring me so bad. What's wrong? Who died?"

I cried. I broke down and cried like a baby. It hadta happen, it was long overdue. I didn't care that I wasn't alone or that I was in front of a woman. I was hurting and I was scared. Hell, sometimes men hadta break.

Jayla came and wrapped her arms around me, but I wasn't in the mood to be hugged.

"I can't Jayla, I gotta go," I said pushing her away.

"I'm not letting you leave Kevin. Look at your condition, look how you're acting! You can't drive like this."

Jayla pushed me on the bed as best as she could and stood over me.

"What is wrong with you? You're sweating, and your heart is beating so fast," she said putting her hand on my chest. "Just calm down and tell me what the hell is going on."

"I can't stay here, they might be comin'."

"Who is coming? Kevin, what is going on? Are you is some kind of trouble?"

"I don't know."

"Then why are you leaving?"

"Because I have to."

"Why?" Jayla asked, getting annoyed.

"I gotta go," I said getting off the couch. Jayla grabbed my arm trying to stop me.

"Kevin tell me what the hell is going on right now because I swear if you don't the only way you will leave this apartment is by dragging me at your feet."

I looked at her and saw the concern in her eyes.

"Kevin whatever it is, you can tell me."

Jayla pulled me into a hug and held me there. She rubbed my back softly.

"Whatever it is its going to be okay. I love you and I'm here. You can trust me baby."

Jayla kissed me softly and led me back to the couch. Tears started to sting my eyes and I closed them tight. I had never told anybody the truth, I had buried it deep inside, kept it to myself and dealt with it on my own. I didn't want to, but I loved Jayla and she deserved the truth.

"Jayla I don't know if you're ready to hear what I'm about to tell you. I really think it's best that you let me leave."

Jayla shook her head.

"I can't do that. Just tell me what's going on and we can figure it out."

I took a deep breath.

"Do you remember how I told you my mother and her boyfriend died in a house fire?"

Jayla nodded her head.

"Well there's more to the story than that."

Jayla waited for me to continue.

"I... I started the fire that killed them."

"Well I'm sure it was an accident Kevin. Kids play with fire all the time. I don't think that's a reason to leave."

"It's not like that Jayla, I did it on purpose."

"What do you mean? What are you saying?"

"I'm saying I purposely started the fire. I killed them."

I could tell by the expression on Jayla's face that she couldn't believe what she was hearing.

"So you're telling me that you killed your mother and her boyfriend?"

I nodded my head.

"And that's not it."

Jayla looked shocked all over again. I could tell she had no idea what else there could possibly be."

"Kari... she was... she had a twin. Karrie. She was my sister and she..."

I tried to fight the tears, but the thought of Karrie broke me down. Jayla grabbed my face and wiped my eyes.

"Your sister died in the fire too?" she asked softly.

I nodded my head with tears still falling.

"Kevin, why did you do that?"

"When I was about 7 my Momma got a new boyfriend, and he changed her. She stopped givin' a damn about us and all she cared about was him. Then... He started..."

I took a deep breath.

"At night after my Momma went to sleep he started comin' in my room. I was a little boy and I knew it wasn't right, but I was ashamed to tell anybody. I finally confided in the twins, but I made them promise not to tell anybody. Kari told anyway and my Momma beat her. That's when I knew she wasn't interested in protecting us."

"What about your Dad?"

"We didn't really know him. I mean, I remember seeing him when I was really little, but he wasn't in our lives. The only family we had was my Nana, my maternal grandmother. She was the only one that cared. She knew something was up, but we were too scared to tell her."

"What happened to her?"

"She died, then we had nobody. Then, on Karrie and Kari's 6th birthday, Avery slapped Kari in the face in front of my Mother and she didn't say anything. That's when I knew I hadta do something. I loved my sisters. And if my Mother wasn't going to protect them, I hadta. I couldn't let him hurt them."

Jayla just sat there with a blank look on her face. I waited for her to say something but she just looked at me. I knew this was a lot to take in, I just hoped I hadn't made a mistake in telling her.

We sat there for a minute just looking at each other until I spoke.

"I never meant for Karrie to die," I said fighting back tears. "I hated Avery and I hated my mother, and I wanted to kill them. I just didn't mean for that to happen to her! Every time I look at Kari, I see Karrie. And that emptiness... Kari has emptiness in her eyes. I see it every time I look at her and I know it's my fault."

"Kevin, you just said you never meant for Karrie to die."

"I know, but I...I put gasoline down...I didn't tell them... and Kari let her go back. The fire spread so fast ...And she... Kari tried to go back and get her-"

I broke down crying again. I cried every time I thought of Karrie. The guilt I carried on my chest every day was becoming unbearable. I needed to tell somebody.

Jayla wrapped her arms around me and rubbed my back.

"It's okay baby, shh...it's okay."

I cried for awhile, then pulled myself together. Jayla grabbed my face and made me look into her eyes again. I spoke before she could say anything.

"I was scared Jayla. I was so scared. I knew it wouldn't stop. And I thought after awhile he would get tired of me and try to hurt my sisters. I couldn't let him hurt them too, I was supposed to protect them."

Jayla nodded her head like she understood.

"I didn't wanna tell you this Jayla. It's not your cross to bear, but I couldn't just leave you without telling the truth. I love you and you are the only person I have ever told."

"So if I wouldn't have showed up you would have just left me?"

I nodded my head.

"I was going to write you a letter. I wasn't going to just leave."

"But you would still leave?"

"I have to Jayla. Marvin found out everything. If he goes to the police, I can go to prison for the rest of my life."

"He can't prove anything Kevin."

"He doesn't have to! The fire was already suspected arson."

"But it's been twenty years since the fire. I'm sure that case is dead and buried."

I shook my head.

I don't know Jayla. I can't. I already sent Kari ahead. She's gonna call me and tell me where to go."

"So what about me?"

I looked down at Jayla and ran my fingers through her hair. I didn't want to leave her, but if I did get caught, I didn't want her to get in trouble. I kissed her gently.

"Don't ever forget about me. And no matter who you love or who you marry remember they'll never love you like I do."

Jayla shook her head as tears ran down her face. I wiped them away quickly.

"So that's it? No more us, no more marriage?"

"I'm sorry Jayla. You know I don't wanna do this."

"Then why are you?"

"Did you just hear what the fuck I just said? I could go to prison. I could get in a whole lot of fuckin' trouble if this gets out."

"So you just leave me? That's the solution?"

"You don't wanna be with me Jayla. Look what I did. I killed three people!"

"That's not your choice to make."

"I'm not lettin' you get in trouble I have to leave."

"If it's that easy for you to leave you never loved me anyway."

"Does it look like this shit is easy for me?"

"Then why are you leaving?"

"I have to."

"I want to go with you."

"I can't let you do that Jayla."

"You know what Kevin, it sounds like you're making a bunch of excuses," Jayla said getting off of the couch. "You don't want to be with me, you want to leave, and this is your excuse."

"Jayla are you fucking crazy? Can't you see that I am trying to protect you?"

"By breaking my heart? By leaving me to pick up the pieces and tell everybody what Kevin? That you just up and left because that's exactly what you're doing."

"WHAT DO YOU WANT ME TO DO JAYLA? YOU WANNA GO TO PRISON WITH ME? THAT'S WHAT YOU WANT?"

"YES! If that's what I have to do to be with you, yes."

"I'm not gonna let that happen Jayla. I'm not gonna let you throw your life away for me."

"Then don't. Don't let me. When I met you, you made me feel so special. You made me feel like you could do anything and you can. So I don't care if we stay here or move away, I just don't want you to leave me."

I grabbed Jayla's hand and kissed it. I pulled her close to me and passionately kissed her face. This woman loves me more than anything.

"There was nobody in the world I loved more than my sisters and Nana until I met you. Every day I walk around with that guilt of killing Karrie on my chest. So if something happens and the police find a reason to put you away, I wouldn't be able to live with that."

"There has to be a way Kevin."


My phone didn't ring until almost three in the morning. I had fallen asleep with it in my hand. Jumping up and, I answered without even checking the caller ID.

"Kevin, it's me."

"Kari where are you? I been tryna call you all day. I was worried, I almost went to your house."

"Kevin I'm fine."

"Where are you?"

"Kevin that's why I called. I think you should stay in Michigan."

"What? What the hell are you talking about Kari? Where are you?" I said getting out of the bed and leaving the room so I wouldn't wake Jayla.

"Kevin I need some time alone. I need to sort things out in my mind and I can't do that with you always breathing down my neck."

"I'm not breathing down your neck Kari, I'm your big brother. All I wanna do is look out for you. You can't function on your own."

"The thing is I can Kevin, and you won't let me! Ever since you found me after we got separated you have smothered me. I need to deal with things on my own sometime."

"But we went through the fire together Kari."

"No we didn't. You lied to me. You told me if I got Karrie on board you would make sure you stuck to the plan. Kevin the reason Karrie died is because you used gas on that fire. We had no idea it would spread that fast."

"I always knew you blamed me."

"Kevin," Kari said sounding like she had said something she regretted. "I love you so much. We were kids and we made a huge mistake. I blame both of us."

"I blame me and only me."

"Kevin stop. It happened and it's over. Marry Jayla and be happy. Just give me time to myself."

"And what are you gonna do with that time Kari?"

"Raise my son and stop hiding from my past."

"And what, we just don't talk no more. I'm supposed to just act like I buried you with Karrie?"

"No Kevin, just give me time please. I'm not doing this to hurt you I just need to take care of myself and depend on me. Not you, Marvin, or anybody else."

"Kari I don't wanna be away from you. I need to know that you're okay and you're safe."

"I am. Just trust that I can take care of myself. That's all I need from you Kevin."

"And you'll call me if you need anything or anything happens?"

"Yes Kevin. I just need to be by myself for awhile."

"I love you so much Kari, you know that. And I'm so sorry I took Karrie from you."

"I know Kevin... I know. And I love you more. I'll be fine, I promise."

DeQuindra Renea

# CHAPTER 32
## Jonathon

I drove in silence on the way to Kari's house. I needed to talk to her. I didn't like the way she had sounded on the phone when she'd called and deep down inside I felt like she was lying about the baby not being mine. She was scared. That's why I wanted to talk to her. I needed to tell her that I would take care of her and the baby. She didn't have to worry about anything.

I pulled up to the house and rang the doorbell. It was almost noon, so I was surprised when Marvin opened the door. I had come early on purpose so I could talk to Kari while Marvin was at work. Her phone had been going straight to voicemail and she hadn't returned any of my text messages. I didn't know what was going on, so I was hesitant when Marvin opened the door and let me in.

"Hey man," he said leading the way into the living room. "Excuse the house, my maid's on vacation," he said laughing.

I had noticed the house wasn't immaculate like it usually was. It wasn't bad, but for a house that stayed clean at all times like Kari and Marvin's, one would call it junky.

I sat with Marvin in the living room and Marvin turned off the TV. He was dressed in dress pants and a white t-shirt. I also noticed Marvin had poured himself a glass of whiskey although it was still morning, but he was a grown man so I kept my mouth shut. I was trying to find out where Kari was. That was the whole reason for my visit.

"What's up man, what brings you by?" Marvin said with a strange look on his face.

"I was just in the neighborhood and decided to stop by and see how ya'll was doin'. Everything alright man, I haven't heard from you in awhile."

"Yeah it's been pretty crazy over here," Marvin said still with a strange look on his face.

"Oh yeah?" I asked, not really caring to hear what he had to say. I was there for something, and it wasn't to have small talk with Marvin.

"Yeah. A lot of things are starting to come into perspective. A lot of secrets and lies."

Marvin took another drink. I didn't know what the hell was going on. Had Kari told Marvin about the affair? What the hell was going on?

"Kari's gone, in case you haven't noticed. But I'm sure you have."

I didn't say anything, I just waited for Marvin to say what was on his mind. At this point I was ready for whatever. I was never scared of anybody or anything. And I loved Kari, and I was prepared to fight for her.

"How long she been gone?" I asked, growing concerned.

Marvin shrugged his shoulders.

"Bout two weeks. Maybe three."

"Have you looked for her?"

"She's a grown woman. If she wants to leave, it's her prerogative."

I couldn't understand how Marvin could be so nonchalant about Kari being gone. She was seven months pregnant and she was his wife!

"Why you so quiet man?" Marvin asked, watching my every move. He was trying to read me and I could tell he was clueless as to what was going on.

"My damn phone got cut off man. You know I'm used to Kari taking care of all the bills. So I paid my phone bill, and you know since she been gone and hasn't called and isn't answering her phone I got the phone records to see who she had been talking to. Your number came up... repeatedly."

There was a moment of silence as Marvin took another drink.

"I went into her past records and your number kept showing

up. I haven't gotten the phone records for the house, but I can bet your number is all over it too. Mostly when I'm at work."

"So you got somethin' you wanna ask me man?" I said, getting annoyed at the way Marvin was beating around the bush. This wasn't a fucking movie, he needed to get straight to the point.

"Have you been fucking my wife?"

"No, I haven't been fucking your wife. I'm in love with your wife."

Marvin nodded his head. I could tell he was beyond pissed, but he was trying to keep his cool.

"How long has this been going on?"

"Long enough for me to know that I love her."

Marvin was getting more pissed the more I talked. I'm sure he must have thought I was some cocky muthafucka to sit there and talk to him like Kari wasn't his wife, but I loved her. I meant what I said when I said I didn't care what anybody thought. I sure as hell didn't care what Marvin thought.

"So what were you planning? For her to divorce me? That's what was supposed to be happening?"

"What happened between me and her is none of your fuckin' business."

"I can make it my business real quick motherfucker. I don't give a damn where you're from."

"Never asked you to nigga," I answered unfazed by his threat.

"You've been fucking my wife and you think you're about to just sit there and talk to me like there won't be repercussions?"

"I been sittin' here waitin' on you to throw some hands, but you been sippin' yo drink and runnin' yo mouth like a little bitch."

Marvin stood up and so did I. We were looking each other dead in the eyes. Marvin, standing in the living room of the home he built with his wife... a wife he obviously wasn't willing to let go. I was standing in the home of my ex-good friend ready to fight for the woman I loved... a woman that wasn't mine. I knew what I had done to Marvin was fucked up and he had every right to want to beat my ass, but I had fallen for Kari. It was never supposed to go that far. From the moment I laid eyes on Kari, I wanted to fuck her. It was nothing against Marvin, but Kari was bad as hell and Marvin should've kept a bad bitch like her locked away from all his homeboys, especially if he was going to treat her like he did. But he didn't, and that left the door wide open for me to come in for the kill. And that I did. But somewhere along the line I had fallen in love with her. And that was when things got real complicated.

Marvin kicked over the end table and sent its contents flying all over the floor. He got closer to me as we stared each other down.

"I should kill you motherfuker. I should KILL you!" Marvin yelled.

"Then stop talking and do it."

Marvin punched me and it landed right in my mouth, but I was quick. I gave Marvin a right hook to the jaw that sent him stumbling. Seizing the opportunity, I gave him a jab to the ribs.

Marvin was in pain, but it didn't matter. He was so angry it was like he could barely feel anything. He needed answers, answers that I was never going to give him and that enraged him.

Marvin caught his balance and pushed me away. Taking that time to prepare himself, he caught me with a punch to the stomach, then a hard punch to the jaw.

I was no match for the rage Marvin had built up inside of him. The way he saw it, we had both betrayed him and we were two people he thought he could trust.

"You gonna come in my house and disrespect me? Huh?"

Marvin went to punch me again, but I dodged the hit. Before Marvin knew it, I had given him a jab to the back, putting my high school boxing skills to work. Marvin dropped to his knees in pain, the hit taking all the strength in his legs.

"You don't want it with me Marvin, you don't want it with this nigga. I don't play games muthafucka."

Marvin slowly got up on his feet. I stood there with my fits up waiting for Marvin to make another move. I didn't really want to fight him, but I would if it was necessary. I hadn't come over to talk to Marvin about Kari, but since he wanted to, he could talk about how he was going to sign those divorce papers and tell me where Kari was so I could go be with my family.

"You're crazy if you really think Kari was going to marry you."

"What the fuck is all this was shit? Where is she? What did you do to her?"

Marvin laughed.

"You're so concerned about her Jonathon," he said mockingly. "But you don't really know her. You don't really know who she is. She lied to you just like she lied to me!"

"What are you talkin' about?" I asked, completely confused.

"You and her is none of my business remember? So I guess it would be up to you to find out on your own."

"What did you do to her?" I asked, even more concerned. I was starting to fear the worse about Kari's disappearance.

Marvin didn't answer me. He just walked to the bar and poured himself another drink.

"What the fuck did you do to her muthafucka?!"

"I didn't do anything to her. Think about it. Do you think I would ruin my life and everything I've worked for for a woman that lied to me our whole marriage? That would kill my father."

I believed Marvin didn't hurt Kari, but I didn't believe he didn't know her whereabouts.

"If I find out you knew something and you didn't tell me, I will kill you," I said. It wasn't a threat, it was a promise.

"Kill me? Please. How dare you stand in my face threatening me when you were fucking my wife? You were coming over here pretending you were my friend when all along you were fucking my wife!"

I just stood there and stared at Marvin. It was fucked up, but I didn't give a damn anymore. The way I saw it, Marvin didn't have anybody to blame for the affair, but him. It was his own fault that he mistreated a good woman. Kari had been good to him, faithful. She blew me off for a long time before anything happened, and as much as I hated to admit it, it was her unhappiness that drove her to the affair, not my game.

"You heard what I said. If I find out you know anything about Kari I will fucking kill you."

"Get the hell outta my house, man," Marvin said motioning toward the door. I left the house slowly, never letting Marvin out of my sight.

DeQuindra Renea

# CHAPTER 33

Loneliness was something I was unfamiliar with. I had never truly been alone. I wasn't alone in the womb, and I wasn't alone in the incubator because I had Karrie. Until I was six I never had to be alone, and even when Karrie wasn't near me, I always had her. She felt my pain and I felt hers. But then the fire happened and she was taken away from me. For the first time, I was alone.

The next six years of my life, I was by myself. As I bounced from foster home to foster home and I had no one by my side or no one to trust. I thought Kevin had gotten a new family and left me behind. I was abused, molested, hurt, stolen from, and no one was by my side. No one cared. That's why when Kevin found me when I was twelve years old, it took me awhile to trust him again. In my eyes he killed Karrie, got adopted, and left me behind.

Leaving Kevin for California wasn't easy and being alone was harder. I missed Jonathon, his touch, his kiss... I missed his love. But I knew he had moved on and he had every right to. Marvin finding the box had forced me to leave, but I was relieved. Honestly, I had no idea whose child I was carrying and it was my punishment to myself to do this mothering thing alone. Neither of them deserved the disappointment of knowing the truth, because both of them wanted the baby to be theirs. I hadn't called either of them, and didn't plan on ever seeing them again.

As I lay there in the hospital bed, pain ripping through my body like I had never felt before, there were no familiar faces or family members. I was alone holding the hand of a tall, blonde-haired nurse named Miranda. I could tell she felt bad that I was by myself. Her shift had ended over two hours ago, but she wanted to see my baby. It was nice to have someone supportive by my side.

I tried my best to breathe through the contractions like Miranda was telling me to, but it was hard. All I wanted to do was hold my breath and tense up. Suddenly the monitors started going off like crazy. Nurses and even the doctor ran in to check on me and the baby.

"His heartbeat is dropping. He's in fetal distress. We need to do a C-section immediately," Dr. Kilmen ordered. She looked at me and gave me a comforting smile.

"Don't worry about anything honey. Your son will be fine."

The nurses prepared to take me into an operating room and Miranda changed into scrubs to go in with me. I frowned when I noticed.

"You can go home Miranda, I'll be fine from here. Go get some rest."

Miranda shook her head.

"I've stayed this long, it's almost over now. Besides you need someone here. Nobody should have to go through labor alone."

I didn't know why Miranda cared so much, but I would be lying if I said I wasn't relieved. It was depressing experiencing this alone. I'd done some messed up things, but I didn't feel I deserved it, and I knew my baby didn't.


Hours later my son, Elijah Douglas Alexander, was born at eleven- seventeen p.m. after putting me through twenty six hours of labor. As soon as Miranda laid him in my arms, I fell in love. He was so warm and sweet and as he looked up at me with his beautiful light brown eyes, I knew immediately who had fathered him. His black, silky, curly hair and the structure of his nose was a dead giveaway. He looked just like Jonathon. There was no way Marvin could have looked at him and not seen it.

At this point though, I didn't care who his father was. They were both miles away and in the past. I was his mother, and that was all that mattered.

"Hi, Elijah, I'm your Mommy. Happy Birthday!" I said kissing him on the cheek. I couldn't believe I was finally holding him in my arms.

I spent enough time with him to shower him with a million kisses before I finally let Miranda have a chance to hold him. She definitely deserved it after she had stuck by my side.

"He is adorable," she said rocking him gently.

"Thank you."

"He might be a model one day with those eyes. Just wait, he's going to be a ladies' man."

We both laughed, and after a few minutes she handed him back. Before she left, she gave me her cell phone number so I could call if I needed anything. I thanked her, but knew I'd never see her again.

Adjusting to life as a new single mother was a difficult job. There was no one there in the middle of the night to take turns feeding Elijah, or change his diaper. I did it all. I never called anybody and I never needed anybody. The only person I needed was Elijah and as long as I made him happy, and kept him safe, then my life was complete.

I sat in my bed and rocked Elijah back and forth humming Jesus Loves Me to him, but he wasn't going to sleep. He was looking up at me with those big beautiful light brown eyes and a wide toothless grin. This was pure happiness. Holding my child in my arms and having him smile at me gave me a feeling in my heart I had never felt before. For the first time without Karrie, I felt complete and at peace. I finally had a child, my child, and no one could take him away from me.

# CHAPTER 34
## Kevin

"I thought this was something you were supposed to do without me," I said, as Jayla dragged me to yet another bridal shop. She was obsessed with finding the perfect dress, but I didn't know what she needed me for. I didn't know a damn thing about picking out dresses. She needed one of her girlfriends for this shit.

"Can you just not argue with me today Kevin? I wanna know what you think about this dress I tried on the other day while you were at work."

I dragged my feet into the store and sat in one of the chairs in the waiting area. I watched as Jayla chatted excitedly with the receptionist as they looked through the racks of white dresses. I waited impatiently playing a couple of games on my phone. An incoming call interrupted an intense game of Tetris.

"Hello?" I said, grateful for the call, although I wasn't sure who it was.

The person on the other end didn't answer. They just cried. And it wasn't just a regular cry, it was a cry from the soul, like something was wrong. I didn't even have to hear the voice, I knew who the person on the other end was.

"Kari what's wrong? You okay?"

She didn't answer, she cried for a long time and that worried me more.

"Kari, come on answer me. Tell me what's going on."

She took some deep breaths and tried to get herself together before she finally spoke.

"Kevin they took... they took my baby. They took Elijah."

I immediately stood up.

"Who took Elijah? Where are you?"

"I'm in Michigan now. I got arrested in LA."

My heart melted and dissolved in my stomach. My worst fear was coming true. Just a few minutes ago my fiancé was dragging me into a bridal shop and now the wedding probably wasn't going to happen.

"What do you mean you got arrested? How?"

"It had to be Marvin, Kevin. Who else knows?"

"I'll straighten it out Kari. I'll come up there and tell them the truth-

"Just come see me this weekend Kevin."

"I'm not waiting until this weekend, I'm coming now. You are not about to sit in that prison one more second and be away from your baby. I'm gonna make it right."

"Don't do anything, just do what I said Kevin. We'll talk about it when I see you."

"Okay Kari," I said reluctantly. "I'll come Saturday."

"Okay, I love you. Kevin?"

"Yeah?"

"No matter what happens, take care of Elijah."

"You know I will Little One, you don't even have to worry about that."


I was sweating bullets as I waited for Kari. The last place I wanted to be was anywhere near the police, especially since I knew they were holding Kari for something I was responsible for.

The guard escorted Kari out of the cell and she came over to me. She was wearing a jail jumpsuit, and her hair was pulled back making it easier for me to see her face. She was scared. She had a look in her eyes I hadn't seen since we were kids.

"Kari what's going on? Are you okay?" I asked, before she had a chance to say anything.

"Yeah I'm fine. Do you have Elijah?"

"Yeah. He's with Jayla right now."

Kari nodded her head.

"Kevin, I'm so sorry about what I said to you the last time we talked-"

"I understand Kari. You don't have to apologize. You have every right to feel the way you feel."

"You were just trying to protect us. I let Karrie go back, that was my fault. You were right."

"Kari, I don't want you thinking about that right now. I'm gonna get you out of here," I whispered. "I'm gonna tell the truth."

"I don't want you to do that."

I looked at her like she was crazy.

"I have a plan. I just need you to take care of Elijah for a while."

"What plan? What are you talking about?"

"Just do what I say Kevin. Take care of my baby."

"You know I will Kari, but after awhile the law is gonna get involved and they gonna give him back to Marvin. He is his father."

Kari looked down at her hands.

"Look I'm gonna make sure I do all I can to keep that from happening. Kari don't worry. Just tell me what the plan is. Tell me what you're gonna do."

"I can't. Kevin I love you so much, but I've been keeping something from you."

"What? What are you talking about?"

Kari took a deep breath.

"Kevin, Marvin is not Elijah's father."

My mouth dropped open.

"What are you talking about? Marvin is your husband! If he isn't the father, who is?"

Kari didn't say anything for a minute. She had a faraway look in her eyes.

"I want him to be with his father. I know he will love him. I just have to handle some things first. Just take care of Elijah for awhile and then I promise you will find out what the plan is."

I had no choice but to trust Kari. She had trusted me once and I had failed her. This time she was in control and I knew she wouldn't fail me.

"Okay."

Kari grabbed my hands.

"Kevin, I am going to make sure neither one of us stays in prison. I promise you."

She gave me the brightest smile I had seen in awhile and that was the only thing I needed to see.

"I love you Kari."

"I love you too, Kevin. Don't come back here until the next time I call."

I told Kari all about what Elijah had been doing lately. I knew it killed her to be away from her son, but hopefully whatever plan she had she would make sure they were reunited soon.

# CHAPTER 35
## Jonathon

I never thought I would be the type to chase a woman. Never. Women usually chased me. And it was nothing I did on purpose. Just blessed enough to be good looking with some charm added on. Some people tried to hate and say it was only because I was mixed. Maybe it was. But I wasn't going to waste my time arguing with them about the fact that I was also respectful, sexy, successful and sweet. Anybody who didn't see that wasn't even worth the argument.

There was something about Kari that drove me crazy. I didn't know what it was, but it had me chasing her. I mean searching. For almost a year I looked for her everywhere and hit a dead end every time. For some reason I knew she wasn't dead. There was somethin' real funny about true love, you could feel it from miles and miles away. I knew she was far, but I had no idea where to look.

I had almost given up on finding her, letting myself believe that she had gotten lost in the world and fallen in love with someone else. I had almost convinced myself that was true, until I saw her on the news.

I had just gotten in the house and turned on my TV. Flipping through the channels, I stopped when I saw her. At first I thought my eyes were deceiving me, but when I flipped back, I saw her face. It was the same as I remembered it, except this time she had fear written all over it. The words Woman Charged for Triple Homicide were plastered on the bottom of the screen. I shook my head in disbelief. Kari would never hurt anybody, and she definitely wouldn't kill anyone.

My eyes stayed glued to the screen as the police escorted her down the sidewalk in handcuffs and shoved her in the back of a police car. There were cameras everywhere and I could tell Kari was fighting back tears. I didn't know what was going on, I had tuned the audio out on my TV. Whenever I saw her face, nothing else mattered. I had to get her out of whatever bullshit she had gotten herself into.

After I saw the news, I spent all of my time trying to find where she was being held. I called around, but no one would release any information to me. Kari would never call Marvin and even if she did, he wouldn't give me any information. The only other person who would know her whereabouts was her brother and although we had chilled a lot over the years at Kari and Marvin's' house, I had no clue how to get in contact with him. After almost two weeks of the same runaround, I gave up. She would get in touch with me soon, I had to believe that.

Weeks went by and I still heard nothing. She wasn't even in the news anymore. I was beginning to think it was time for me to give up. Maybe she had moved on and forgotten about me. Maybe our love wasn't as real to her as it was to me.

After a month, I knew there was no more that I could do. I had to get over Kari. My heart hurt every time I thought about her, every time I pictured her sitting in a jail cell alone and scared. I knew she needed me, I just didn't know why she wasn't calling.

I tried to get over Kari the only way I knew how: seeing other women. I dated as much as I could because staying home alone only made me think about her. It didn't matter who I brought home or how many different girls I fucked. One thing was not going away: I was in love with Kari Fairmount.

Just when I thought there was no more hope for me ever talking to Kari again, I finally got a call from her. It was early on a Tuesday morning and I was in bed with Camille, an old friend from college. She was a dark skinned beauty with short jet black hair, big brown eyes, and an even bigger bra size. Childbirth had given her thickness in all the right places and I admired her as she lay tangled in my gray cotton sheets. Her hair had sweated out from the sex session we'd had the night before. She ran her manicured fingers through it.

"I told you not to mess up my hair," she mumbled with her eyes still closed.

"I aint touch your hair."

"You didn't have to."

Camille rolled over to me and threw her leg around my body. I could feel my manhood jump under the sheets.

"What time is it?" she asked.

"Seven ten."

"I gotta go. I'm gonna be late for work."

"I told you to set an alarm."

"I thought I did."

Camille sat up and stretched. Her breasts bounced with each movement. She got out of my bed and gathered her clothes from where I'd thrown them.

"I'm gonna take a shower," she informed me. She didn't wait for a response before she left the room.

I lay in bed with my eyes closed trying to decide whether or not I was going to follow Camille into the bathroom. Watching her ass jiggle as she walked out of my bedroom had made all of the blood rush to my little head. I was just about to go into the bathroom and bend Camille over the sink when my phone rang. I thought about ignoring it, but I didn't want to miss a business call.

"Hello?"

"You have a collect call from an inmate in the Michigan Department of Corrections. If you accept the charges, say yes."

The woman couldn't finish her sentence, I was already damn near screaming yes. There was a long pause.

"Hello? Kari? You there?"

"Hi Jonathon," she said softly. Those words alone made me forget about fine ass Camille in the shower. Kari made my world go round. All these other women were just stunt doubles.

"Kari, what's up baby?"

"Jonathon I need to see you. We have to talk. Can you come visit me Saturday?"

"You know I will Kari. I miss you. I been lookin' everywhere for you."

"Oh yeah?" she said dryly. I couldn't understand how she could be so unfazed. I loved her, I missed her. This call would never be enough to tell her how much.

"You know I do. You shouldn't have left me."

"I did what I had to do."

"I love you Kari. I miss you. Don't you miss me?"

She didn't respond. I could still hear her breathing so I knew she was there.

"Jonathon where are your clean face towels?" Camille asked coming into the bedroom. She was still naked, but this time it didn't affect me. I put my finger to my lips to signal her to be quiet, but it was already too late.

"I gotta go Jonathon, just come on Saturday, okay?"

"I will, but Kari-"

"I gotta go."

Kari hung up and I sat there with the phone in my hands. It happened so fast it felt like a dream. Saturday was four days away and that was four days too long to be away from the love of my life.



"Thank you for coming to see me," Kari said without making eye contact with me. She was as beautiful as I remembered, even in the orange jumpsuit and with all the stress lines on her face. She looked sad. Her sparkle was gone, and that broke my heart.

"I told you I was comin'. How you doin' in there?"

"I'm locked in a cage so I can't be doing that well." She still wouldn't look at me.

"Kari, I love you. I missed you. I been looking for you everywhere."

Kari just sat there. Her eyes were looking in my direction, but she wasn't looking at me. She was looking through me as if I wasn't there.

"You find somebody else to love Jonathon," she finally said with no emotion. There used to be a time when she would kiss me, slide her tongue in my mouth. Whisper she loved me too. Open her pretty legs wide for me and let me make love to her until she was afraid to go home. Now here we were, separated by a huge piece of glass and she wouldn't even really look at me.

"I don't want anybody else Kari and you know that already. Just look at me baby, just for a second."

She closed her eyes like she was fighting back tears. She still wouldn't look at me.

"Find somebody else to love," she said slowly. "Just forget about me. I'm getting charged with three counts of murder Jonathon, I'm never getting out."

"That's not true. I'm gonna get you the fuck outta there Kari. You don't belong in there."

She sat there looking at her hands. She didn't respond to me.

"You trust me don't you? You know I got you right?"

I sat there and looked at her, waiting for her to respond. She looked like the same Kari, but she wasn't. She had no spirit. I was gonna work to get her out of there before that place sucked out her soul, but it looked like it was too late. She didn't have the heart for prison, she wasn't built for it. You would find somebody like her hanging in her cell in three months at the most.

She covered her face with her hands like she was hiding from me. It seemed like forever passed before she finally spoke.

"I asked you to come see me today because I wanted you to know…"

She hesitated for a minute then continued.

"My son Elijah, he's your son."

"What?" I said, leaning in closer. I knew I couldn't be hearing her right.

"The baby I was carrying was yours."

My mouth dropped open.

"No, he can't be Kari, because I asked you… I asked you if the child you were carrying was mine and you told me no. We never lie to each other."

She nodded her head with a look on her face like she was in extreme pain.

"I know. I lied and I'm sorry. I should've told you the truth. He's with my brother. You can go see him whenever you want. I told him you'd be coming."

I sat there for a minute trying to absorb what I'd just heard. I couldn't believe what she was telling me.

"Okay, I'm gonna go see him today. But I'm gonna get you

out of here too baby. I'm gonna take you home and marry you."

Kari shook her head.

"Don't worry about me, just get our son. Don't let him hear all those lies about me. Tell him I was a good person that made a lot of mistakes."

"Stop talking like that Kari."

"Two Minutes!" the guard yelled. I looked at her and she was still looking down at her hands.

"Can you please look at me before I go baby. I came all this way to see you, I just want to look into the eyes of the woman I love."

"I don't deserve to be loved by you, trust me. You don't know anything about me. If you knew the real me, you would let me rot."

"Kari I do know the real you, that's why I'm here. I don't give a fuck what the media is saying. I know you and I know you didn't set that fire. You don't deserve to be in here. You need to be home with me. I'm gonna get you out baby. I love you and I'm gonna get you out."

Kari finally looked at me. It was only for a brief second, but that was all I needed.

"I love you," I repeated.

"Then get our son and don't come back here again."

She didn't wait for me to respond. She got up and left me sitting there. She had just dropped a bomb in my lap and I had to go handle our business.

After I left the prison from visiting Kari, my mind was in a million different places. I was confused. I didn't know whether to be happy or pissed. Why had she lied to me and told me the baby wasn't mine when she knew there was a chance it was? Why didn't she call me when the baby was born? I had so many questions only she could answer, but she was on a different kind of lockdown now. I couldn't just call her and get her to sneak over.

I drove straight to the address she slipped me, her brother's apartment. I wanted to believe her, but I needed to see him for myself. If he was mine he was coming home with me. Kari's brother would be welcome to have him anytime of course, but a little boy needed to be with his father, especially if he couldn't be with his mother.

I tried not to get my hopes up as I went and knocked on the door. After a couple of minutes, Kevin came and opened the door. Today though, he didn't know how to feel about me. It was obvious he had no clue about me and Kari until recently and that made the situation awkward.

"What's up Kevin, how you doin' man?" I asked, holding out my hand for him to shake. He did reluctantly, then stepped outside and closed the door.

"I gotta be honest with you Jonathon, I didn't know about any of this. I knew things between her and Marvin wasn't the best, but I had no clue she was having an affair."

I nodded my head.

"It wasn't something we planned at all. I know how much you love her and it's not my place to tell you all about us, but I do want you to know it's not just sex. I am in love with your sister and I'm gonna take care of her and that baby no matter what. I'm never turning my back and I'm never walking away."

Kevin nodded his head and shook my hand again before he let me into the apartment. I was nervous. But when I went into the living room and saw my son in Kevin's fiancée's arms, my heart melted. I walked over to where she was sitting and looked down at him. His eyes were closed slightly, so I couldn't see the color. He had silky, curly black hair just like mine, and my nose. He looked a lot like my baby pictures, but he looked more like his mother.

"Hi," Kevin's fiancée said softly. She gave me a warm smile. "You wanna hold him?"

I nodded my head and she stood up and gave him to me. His eyes opened long enough for me to see their light brown color. I almost cried, but I couldn't bring myself to do it in front of them. I was angry. For a few minutes I was pissed at Kari for lying to me and making me miss the beginning of his life. I loved him already and I had only known him for all of five minutes. He was mine. He had to be. Only the love that Kari and I shared could create someone so beautiful.

"I wanna take him home," I finally said.

"I know. Kari said you would. She wants you to," Kevin said.

"I don't have everything ready right now. I just need a couple of weeks."

"It's cool man. Take as long as you need. I know this all happened so fast."

Looking down at my son again, I was unable to believe I was holding him and he was mine. I had to figure out how to get Kari out of jail. We both needed her.

"Have you heard from Marvin?" I asked Kevin. I wanted to know if he had been concerned at all about Kari and the baby. After all, he didn't know it wasn't his.

Kevin shook his head.

"Not since before she left. I think he's the one that told the cops on Kari."

"What makes you think that?"

"He's only person that knew. He found out everything, that's why she left."

"Why did she do it?"

Jayla and Kevin looked at each other and I could tell I had stumbled upon a sensitive topic. The look on his face told me Kevin knew something, but I didn't want to believe he had his sister sitting in jail when he knew the truth that would set her free.

I visited with Elijah for a few hours, then I got ready to leave. I dreaded leaving, but my house wasn't ready for a baby. Now that was my number one mission, the rest of my life would have to take a backseat.

# CHAPTER 36

"Kari, if you are found guilty for setting that fire you will spend the rest of your life in jail. That's a guarantee. You will be charged with the first degree murders of Avery Chapman, Helena Alexander, and Karrie Alexander. If you know the truth, you better speak up immediately."

My lawyer's words rang in my head over and over again. I couldn't close my eyes because I couldn't stop thinking about what he'd said.

"You will spend the rest of your life in jail. That's a guarantee."

I was confused. What my lawyer was asking me to do was impossible. If I told the truth, Kevin would spend the rest of his life in jail, or possibly both of us. He had been the one to set the fire, but I'd helped him plan it. That meant I was just as guilty as he was.

The rest of my life without Elijah, the thought alone, made me sick to my stomach. It tore me in two. I had already missed so much of his life, and I was going to miss everything. I would miss every day of his life, every birthday, every Christmas, his first word, his first step… I couldn't do it.

"I have a plan," I said aloud, trying to convince myself what I was about to do was the right thing. It was the only way. I almost wished my cellmate was there to tell me to shut the fuck up and go to sleep, but she was in the hole for cutting somebody in a fight the day before. Now was the only time I would be able to

261

carry out my plan. I couldn't let Kevin down, and I had to do what was right. Being in this cell was killing me. There was no way I would be able to do it. I was lonely. And the funny thing about loneliness was that it could either be the best thing that ever happened to you, or it could eat you alive.

I sat up in my bed and pulled off my sheet. Tearing the fabric into thick strips, I cried silently. There was no use in trying to live when I was already dead. I had died the night Karrie died. As soon as I felt complete again, Elijah was taken from me. That was pain, and living in a world where I couldn't be his mother wasn't a world worth living in.

Not telling Kevin my plan was for the best. Everybody would understand when they found the letters I had tucked into my pillowcase. They would know I was only trying to protect the ones I loved. I didn't deserve to live in a world without Karrie, Kevin, or Jonathon, and I didn't deserve to have to be a prison mother to my son. I was broken from the start and it was better for everybody if things went my way for once.

I tied the homemade rope tightly around my neck and to the top of my bunk. For once I was grateful for being short. My face was wet with all my tears and I used my covers to wipe them. My heart was beating fast and hard. Maybe this was how it felt when you knew you were about to die. After taking one last breath, I jumped before I had a chance to change my mind.

My feet were close to the floor, but not close enough. I tried to open my mouth to breathe, but I couldn't get any air. My feet jerked as I tried to balance them on something, my body naturally fighting for me to live.

Things are better this way, I thought. Now you can be with Karrie.

My eyes started to bulge out of my head. I wasn't getting any oxygen to my brain. My vision blurring and my body getting weak, I didn't feel any pain. I hung there, no longer able to move. The room started to fade from my vision and the world seemed more out of my reach. My last image was holding Elijah the day he was born. After a few minutes, everything was pitch back and I was deaf. I had no more emotions, no more feelings about anyone, or anything. At that moment I tried to think of my son, the most important person in my life, and then I felt and remembered nothing. I knew then that I no longer existed and the horrible ways of the world were far behind me.

DeQuindra Renea

# CHAPTER 37
## Kevin

Dear Kevin,

I am so sorry I had to leave you. Please don't be mad. I couldn't tell you about the plan because I knew you would only talk me out of it. Things are better this way. The reality is one of us was gonna have to take the fall for the fire. I made it so that never happens. I don't care if people think I did it as long as they don't think you did.

My decision to end my life had nothing to do with you. I never ever want you to think I did it out of any type of anger for you. I love you more than I love myself and I know you only tried to protect me and Karrie. Thank you. Thank you for all the times I cussed you out instead of saying it. I should've told you I love you enough times to last forever... and I do. Always remember that. Regardless of the fire and everything else, I love you, and I thank you for always loving me unconditionally.

Even though I left you, I want you to always remember one thing: I didn't leave you alone. I left behind my most prized possession, and I expect you to love him with the same unconditional love you always gave me. Tell him how much I love him and never let him forget it. Tell him all about me and Karrie and don't leave him in the dark about the fire. When he is old enough to understand, I want you to tell him the truth. He deserves to know the truth from you and not from what people

265

tell him. You are the only one that knows the truth.

Stop blaming yourself for the fire, it happened and it's over. Live your life and stay away from the darkness. Never stop smiling and don't hurt Jayla. She loves you so much. I wish I could be there in person on that special day when you marry her, but I will be. I will be standing right beside you the whole time. I'm so proud of you and I love you so much. I'll always be with you. Every time you look into Elijah's eyes, every time you feel his heartbeat, and every time you hug him, that's me telling you I love you. And I do. Always and forever.

Love always,
Kari Alexander
"Little One"

I sat in the room with tears in my eyes. I didn't want to believe it. It was already hard enough to believe that Kari was in prison, and I had gotten the call in the middle of the night that a guard had found Kari hanging in her cell by a sheet from her bed. All I could do was scream. Jayla jumped out of bed and grabbed the phone. She finished the conversation and hung up. She told me to get dressed so she could drive me to the hospital.

"The guard found her just in time, but she's not out of the woods yet. She needs to stay here for awhile."

"Is she gonna be okay?"

"It's hard to say right now. She's really lucky. It's amazing she was able to live without oxygen for that long. I don't know how she did it. She's a fighter, so I don't think you should worry."

The short blonde haired doctor smiled and put her hand on my shoulder.

"I hate to see this. She's so beautiful."

I couldn't even open my mouth to thank her. I was just staring at Kari lying in that hospital bed. She looked sick and weak. She looked like she hadn't been taking care of herself. How had I let her talk me into not visiting?

The doctor gave my shoulder a light squeeze before she left the room leaving me alone with Kari and the letters they had found in her pillowcase. There were three of them: one for me, one for Elijah, and one for Jonathon. I had only read mine, but I could guess what the other two said. All of them were letters of her saying goodbye to us… suicide notes.

Pulling my chair up beside Kari, I grabbed her hand. I hadn't been right since she gotten locked up, but I thought she had a plan. Had I known her plan was to kill herself, I would have carried mine out sooner.

"Kari, I love you too. And when you get out of this coma you gonna be a free woman. You gonna go home to Elijah and you don't ever have to worry about feeling like this again."

Kissing her hand, I lay my head on the bed and prayed just like Nana had taught me to do. Prayed she would pull through this. And I prayed she wasn't angry at me for finally doing the right thing.

DeQuindra Renea

# CHAPTER 38

Slowly I opened my eyes. The bright lights were blinding me. I thought I had made it and that I was looking into the light I had heard older people talk about, the one you saw right before you got into heaven. When my eyes adjusted, I saw Jayla sitting in a chair next to my bed. She was almost asleep, her eyes only tiny slits. She was wearing a jogging suit and it was the first time I had ever seen her dressed down. She didn't have on any makeup, and her hair was wild all over her head.

"Why am I here?" I asked, but my voice came out low and raspy. My voice was extremely dry and I tried to swallow a mouth full of spit to give it some moisture.

Jayla's eyes opened and she jumped up to get me a drink of water. After taking a few swallows from the straw, I opened my mouth to speak again.

"Why am I here?" I repeated.

"Because you're supposed to be here Kari."

"No, I'm supposed to be in heaven. I'm supposed to be with... I don't wanna be here."

"A guard found you in time Kari. You're in the hospital," Jayla said softly, holding my hand.

"Where's Kevin?"

Jayla gave me a warm smile and I could tell it was something she didn't want to tell me.

"Why are you here and not Kevin? He would be here, where is he?" I asked, my eyes scanning the room for my brother.

269

"Kari, I don't think you should worry about that right now-"

"Jayla please, I'm scared. Where is my brother?"

"Kari, Kevin really thought you had a plan. He never thought it was to kill yourself."

"That's what I wanted. Now where is he?"

I was getting annoyed. I loved Jayla, and I really didn't want to slap the shit out of her, but I needed my brother. I had to know where he was. I needed to talk to him.

"Kari, Kevin turned himself into the police. He's in jail."

My breath caught into my throat. Kevin's worst fear had come true and it was all my fault. It was my fault we had gotten caught. If I had given him the box, our secret would have remained safe. Tears rolled down my face.

"Why did he do that? I need to talk to him. I know he's mad at me."

Jayla shook her head.

"Kevin is not mad at you. Kevin loves you so much. He feels responsible for all of this. He did what was best... what was right."

This time I shook my head.

"He should have talked to me about it first, we could have figured something else out."

"Kevin followed your lead. He waited until he knew you would be okay, and then he turned himself in. He knew you would only talk him out of it."

The room was silent for a minute.

"Kari, Kevin believes he is where he should be. We are gonna hire him a damn good lawyer and fight this. He is finally gonna tell everybody what that animal Avery did to him. Ya'll were kids. Not a person in this world would convict him."

Jayla got up from her seat.

"Wait here while I get the doctor."

Jayla left the room and returned a few minutes later with a short blonde haired nurse. She smiled as soon as she saw me.

"Mrs. Fairmount, it's so good to see your beautiful eyes."

"Call me Kari," I said dryly. Being called Mrs. Fairmount made me uncomfortable. She was a little too chipper to be dealing with a suicide patient anyway.

After taking my vitals, the doctor explained how lucky I was to still be alive. I knew it wasn't luck at all. She also told me I would have to spend some time in the psychiatric unit before they released me. She left the room and Jayla and I were alone again.

"So Kevin told you everything?"

"Pretty much."

"He told you about Karrie?"

Jayla nodded her head.

"He told me how close the two of you were. He said you needed her."

"I do need her. That's why I was trying to go be with her."

"That's not the way Kari. Your sister wouldn't want you to do that. Your son wouldn't want you to do that."

"What kind of mother was I going to be to him in prison? What kind of life would that have been for him?"

"Well Kevin made it so you never have to find out. He said he is giving your most prized possession back to you. He said Elijah was what you needed to save your life."

Jayla pulled out a picture and held it up to my face. It was my son. He had grown so much. His black curly hair looked just as soft as I remembered it. He was sleeping in the picture so I couldn't see his eyes, but I saw his smooth, brown skin. I missed his sweet baby smell. He was the one thing in this world I knew would complete me and now I got to have him back. I had a chance to be his mother again and that brought the sun instead of the darkness.

After almost three long weeks in the hospital, it was finally time for me to be released. I didn't know how to feel. Going back to Marvin's would never be an option and I couldn't go back to California. Now that Jonathon was in his sons' life, I could never take him away.

I sat in my room waiting to sign my release papers when Jonathon walked in. He looked as sexy as he always did and I got a feeling in between my legs I hadn't felt in a long time. There was a time I thought I would never see him again. Then there was a time I thought he wouldn't love me anymore. Then there was a time I thought he was better off without me. As he stood in front of me that day, I didn't know how I felt.

We didn't say anything for a long time. He just stared at me.

The way he was staring made me uncomfortable so I looked at my hands to avoid eye contact with him.

"You still won't look at me huh?"

I didn't want to look at him and let him see the real me. He was used to Kari Fairmount, the woman I had made up. The woman somebody else wanted me to be. He didn't know Kari Alexander. He didn't know me. He didn't know the Kari that had a past. The Kari that had helped plan a fire that killed three people. He didn't know my story and if he looked in my eyes now, he would see it all.

"It don't matter if you look at me or not. I'm not leaving without you."

"How did you know I was in the hospital?"

"Jayla told me. She been helping me out with Elijah. He misses you though."

"I miss him too."

Jonathon walked over to me and put his hands on my face.

"What about me? You miss me too?"

I didn't answer, but the feeling I got in my legs when he touched me told me I did. Of course I missed him, I loved him. I just didn't know if he could ever accept the real me if I couldn't even do it.

"I miss you Kari, and I wanna take you home to our son."

"You don't love me Jonathon. I meant what I said. You need to find somebody else to love. I'm too fucked up-"

"I wish you would stop all that shit. I wish you would stop acting like I don't know you. You know I love you, you know what we had. I don't give a fuck what you did when you were a kid. You made a big mistake, I know you did. But I also know you live with that mistake every day. I would never stop loving you because of that fire. I wouldn't put you through that. You already don't love yourself because of it."

As much as I wanted to, I could not look this man in the eyes. I was afraid to start a life with him. I was afraid of what people would say and think. He was one of Marvin's very close friends. How was I just supposed to carry on life with him?

Jonathon didn't say anything to me for awhile. He just looked at me. I could feel him just staring at me. I didn't deserve a man like him, somebody to love me unconditionally. I was damaged beyond repair.

"I'm not who you think I am. Being with me won't be easy-"
"When has being with you ever been easy, Kari? Stop making excuses about why I shouldn't love you and just let me love you." I didn't know what the future held or what people would think. But for once I didn't care. For once I did what was best for me and what I wanted and after I signed those release papers, I let Jonathon take me home to our son.

# CHAPTER 39

Going to visit my brother for the first time in prison was awkward. I hadn't felt so uncomfortable talking to him since he found me when I was twelve after we got separated. When he sat across from me in his orange jumpsuit, I didn't know what to say. I just looked at him, fighting back tears.

"Hey little one," he said smiling as if he was the free one.

"Hi Kevin."

"You look good. You look so much happier."

"I am."

Kevin nodded his head.

"You know that's all I ever wanted for you."

He paused and took a deep breath.

"That's all I ever wanted for you and Karrie. I'm the big brother, I was just tryna protect ya'll."

"I know Kevin. I'm so sorry. I'm sorry things ended up this way," I said unable to hold back my tears any longer.

"Stop, don't do that to me Kari. Don't cry. It's my fault, I did wrong. I'm in here because of what I did, so don't you ever blame yourself. You didn't do anything wrong."

I didn't know if he was saying that because he meant it or if he was just trying to make me feel better. It didn't matter because I knew I was to blame for my brother being in prison and I told him so.

"I should have let you have the box. I should have never let

Marvin find it."

Kevin shook his head again.

"That box was all you had left of Karrie. You were dealing with your grief the best way you knew how."

I tried to wipe my tears away, but they kept coming.

"I didn't want you to have to be in here. I don't want to be free without you. I need you. I never wanted you to be in here. That's why I tried to..."

I couldn't even bring myself to say it to Kevin. Killing myself would have never been an option for him.

"I already lost one sister Kari. I would rather spend the rest of my life in prison than have to bury you."

Speechless, I gave him my brightest smile. I couldn't understand why my life meant so much to everyone but me.

"You're so strong Kevin. I wish I could be strong like you."

Kevin shook his head.

"You always have given me too much credit. I'm no stronger than you are. Don't ever think I live my life carefree after what happened. I know losing Karrie changed you, and every day I wish I could take that back. But don't forget she was my sister, too. You have your own issues to deal with, so I never burden you with mine, but I have problems. I have to face my own demons for what I did. That's my cross to bear."

We sat there in silence for a minute.

"I'm glad you came to see me," he said smiling again. It was amazing how he could be facing life in prison and still look as if nothing was wrong.

"How's my nephew? Did you bring me any pictures?" he asked.

"Not this time. I'll mail you some. I'll take a bunch when I get home. He is getting so big."

"I know. He grew in just the little bit of time I had him. I miss him."

"I'll bring him to see you."

"Not yet. We'll figure it out, but I don't want him to see me like this. But tell him I love him so much and I will always be his uncle."

"I will, I promise. Have you talked to Jayla?"

"She writes me every day. Says she's gonna wait for me. We'll get married when I get home."

"Jayla is such a good woman. I always liked her."

"I don't want her to wait for me," Kevin said, and for the first time since he sat down, he looked sad.

"I love her and I wanna marry her, I do. But I have to face the possibility that I might not be getting out."

"You are gonna get out. Jayla and I are working to get you the best lawyer there is-"

"And that still might not be enough. They're making us out to be some type of little child killers. We ran for twenty years without telling the truth. I gotta be real with myself Kari. There is always a possibility."

"Well I'm gonna make sure that doesn't happen. But in the meantime, what do you need from me?"

"I need you to live your life and be happy. And send me lots of pictures so I can live it with you."


When the time came for us to say goodbye, I didn't want to leave. I knew I wouldn't be able to pick up the phone and call him when I wanted to. I even missed all of his annoying check-up calls. Living life without one sibling was hard enough, now I had to live without them both.

DeQuindra Renea

# CHAPTER 40
## Marvin

"Can you explain to me why my business is going to hell?"

That was the question my father asked right before he pushed his way into my house at seven in the morning. I was hungover and not in the mood to deal with his bullshit.

"I know you are not in here sleeping. Up before sunrise, I taught you better. Fairmounts start to work while the world is still asleep."

If his loud voice wasn't enough to wake me up, his turning on every light in the house definitely did. I hadn't been active at work in months. I couldn't focus on anything.

"What have you been doing? Lounging? Relaxing? Must be nice."

My father moved my decorative pillows out of the way and lay back on the couch. He put his hands behind his hands and closed his eyes. He looked like he was asleep.

"It is nice," he finally said with his eyes still closed. "I wish I had time to do this when I was your age. I was too busy working my ass off to start a business."

I sat in the loveseat and waited for him to say what he had to say. He hadn't come over for nothing.

"Your mother is worried sick. I'm getting calls from the office. You're walking out of meetings and not answering your phone. What the hell has gotten into you?"

"I don't know Dad. It's hard living in this house. I dread

coming home every day. Everything reminds me of Kari."

My father rolled his eyes and sat up.

"Then pack up and move! Get over that tramp!"

"She's my wife-"

"She fucked your best friend," he said harshly. "And not only that, she got pregnant! I raised you better than this Marvin. I told you from the beginning a woman that pretty would bring you nothing but trouble, didn't I?"

"Yes sir."

"And you just had to fall in love," he said sitting back and shaking his head.

"I shouldn't have called the police," I said as low as I could. I didn't really want him to hear me, but I needed to tell someone. "I took it too far. I ruined somebody's life."

"That bitch deserves whatever she gets. Your loyalty is to this family and this business. Forget about her!"

"But Dad-"

"This little fuck up your dumb ass caused is gonna cost our company thousands of dollars! Walking out on meetings isn't free! Missing appointments and canceling doesn't bring the company any money."

"I'll fix it, Dad."

"I don't want you to fix anything, you've done enough. You never fail to disappoint me Marvin. You're the eldest and the dumbest. Sometimes I worry about letting you run my business."

I sat there staring at the TV although there was nothing on it. I didn't want to look at my father and see the disappointment on his face. No matter how hard I tried, I could never please him. Giving up my whole life and ruining my marriage to run his business still wasn't enough. All he ever told me was how much of a disappointment I was.

"I want you to take another week off. Then shower, shave, get a damn haircut, and go back to my office like a Fairmount. I don't want to hear another word about you missing any more meetings. Do I make myself clear?"

"Yes sir, crystal clear. I'll be back in the office in a week."

"Call your mother, let her know you're okay. Then I expect to see you at dinner this Sunday so she can get off my back."

"Yes sir."

My father gave me a few more commands and requests, all of

which I had no choice but to oblige. He was not the one to talk to about Kari. He didn't believe in emotions and guilt, he believed in karma. In his eyes I had given Kari exactly what she deserved and the case was closed. My father stayed long enough to scold me about the condition of my house and check my mail, and then he left without saying goodbye. His visit was scary because the way he treated me reminded me of the way I treated Kari. As pissed off as I was about her having an affair with Jonathon, I couldn't blame her for being unhappy. I knew I was one hundred percent responsible.

After my father left I cleaned my house and started searching for a good realtor. My father was right about one thing, I did need to pack up and move on. I still loved Kari, but I knew she was never coming back. Our relationship was damaged beyond repair. She would never forgive me for turning her in to the police, and I would never forgive her for the affair. The only choice I had now was to move on, learn from my mistakes, and get it right the next time.

# EPILOGUE

"I don't want you to go away Karrie," I said squeezing her hand tightly. "Stay with me."

Karrie shook her head and smiled showing all of her pretty white teeth. She let go of my hand and hugged me tightly. "I'll always be with you Kari. And I promise everything is gonna be okay."

Before I had a chance to say anything else, she let me go and turned to go into the house. It looked the same as it did before the fire. I watched her the whole time, her pretty pink dress bouncing with each little step. The wind blew causing her long brown hair to wave lightly through the night air.

I could feel that horrible feeling of dread enter my body as soon as she turned the doorknob to go inside. I tried to scream for her, but my mouth wouldn't open. I couldn't run after her because my legs were stuck. All I could do was stand there and watch as my six-year-old twin sister closed the door on her life.

As soon as the door slammed, the house vanished before my eyes and I stood there alone. Although there was no fire and she never once screamed my name, I knew that she was gone...

Two months after I was released from the hospital, I had my final dream about the fire. When I woke up, I was a different person. I had survived a suicide attempt and that was nothing compared to what I felt at that moment. It was like I had been reborn.

I never told anybody the truth about my suicide attempt, not even Kevin. Nobody would believe me if I told them I died that night. I stood outside of my body and watched myself die. I was more than ready to walk through the pearly gates Nana used to talk about all the time, until I felt someone grab my hand. I didn't know if it was God or the Devil because I was ready to spend eternity in whichever place God wanted to put me until I heard her voice.

"It's not your time Kari," she whispered softly.

Tears spilled out of my eyes as I started crying uncontrollably because I was so close to her, but I still couldn't be with her. I was half a person without her and I no longer wanted to live in a world where she didn't exist.

But I had to. That was what she told me. There was so much more I had to see. Karrie made sure I didn't cross over from the living to the dead. Sure, the guard had found me, but Karrie saved me. She made sure I held on long enough to survive. But that was something personal. Nobody needed to know how deep our connection ran. That was something I could keep to myself.

Life can be funny though, because anything good always travels with some bad. I was thankful for my rebirth, but it came at the expense of Kevin's freedom. That was one thing I still felt badly about. I knew his story more than anybody else and I knew he didn't deserve to be in prison.

For most of my life, I was living a lie. I lied to everyone about who I was, how I grew up, and who I loved. I had loved Marvin at one time, I'd been crazy about him. But people change and grow apart and I couldn't be who he wanted me to be anymore. I truly felt bad about what I'd done to him and how things played out, but he had to know he wasn't innocent.

Our divorce was final almost a year ago. For awhile I had mixed feelings about it. Marvin was a good guy, but he didn't know how to handle his life. He couldn't be a good husband and please his father at the same time. I was never his number one priority and when he started trying to put me first, it was too late. I had already fallen in love with someone else.

What goes around definitely comes around. Marvin made that clear in more ways than one. Because of him, my brother was in prison and for me that was punishment enough for what I'd done. But maybe Marvin thought it was important for me to feel exactly what he'd felt. And maybe moving in with Jamie and her kids into a four bedroom home in Ann Arbor would be payback enough for him, but who was I to judge? They are engaged to be married and she is pregnant with his first child. If that wasn't karma's mean ass slapping me in my damn face, I didn't know what was. I couldn't waste my energy being angry at small stuff anymore. For the first time in my whole life, I was truly happy and I wasn't going to let anybody ruin that.


The sun and I were twins and it was shining down on me as I sat on our outdoor swing in my yellow sundress. I smiled watching my son run around the yard. He was throwing a football and pretending to be the players he watched on TV with his Dad.

I almost never held him again. How could I have been so stupid to almost walk away from this?

I said a silent prayer giving thanks to God. I knew He was the reason for my happiness. I didn't know why He hadn't given up on me, because I had given up on him for so long. I thought somebody like me couldn't be forgiven, but Jayla had told me to ask God for forgiveness and I did that every day.

When I opened my eyes and saw Jonathon at the grill cooking our dinner, I knew I was blessed. I was blessed to have a son by such a good man, someone who had always loved me. The way we'd gone about it was wrong, but us being together was nothing but right. He loved me unconditionally and I deserved him as much as he deserved me.

At the end of the day people are going to have something to say about the decisions I made in my life. I couldn't worry about that. I had to live for myself. I was busy being a mother, a fiancée, a sister… I didn't have time to concern myself with the opinions of people who knew nothing about me. Because for the first time in my life I knew me, and I was living for myself.

28060269R00167

Made in the USA
Charleston, SC
30 March 2014